Other Avon Books by
Antonya Nelson

THE EXPENDABLES

In the LAND of MEN

ANTONYA NELSON

AVON BOOKS  NEW YORK

AVON BOOKS
A division of
The Hearst Corporation
1350 Avenue of the Americas
New York, New York 10019

Published in hardcover by William Morrow and Company, Inc.; for information address Permissions Department, William Morrow and Company, Inc., 1350 Avenue of the Americas, New York, New York 10019.

First Avon Books Trade Printing: February 1993

AVON TRADEMARK REG. U.S. PAT. OFF. AND IN OTHER COUNTRIES, MARCA REGISTRADA, HECHO EN U.S.A.

Printed in the U.S.A.

OPM   10 9 8 7 6 5 4 3 2 1

TO ROBERT,

TO JADE

AND NOAH

ACKNOWLEDGMENTS

With profound gratitude for their faith in me, I would like to
thank the following: the National Endowment for the Arts,
Bonnie Nadell, Maria Guarnaschelli, The Jerry's Writing Group,
and Robert Boswell.

Grateful acknowledgment is made to the editors of the following
publications in which some of these stories first appeared:
Northwestern's *TriQuarterly* and *Redbook:* "In the Land of
Men"; *Kenyon Review:* "The Happy Day"; *Antioch Review:*
"Human Habits"; *Story:* "The Control Group"; *Epoch:* "Fire
Season"; *Southern Review:* "Fair Hunt"; *Soundings East:* "How
Much We Could See"; *Sonora Review:* "Bare Knees"; *North
American Review* and *Louder Than Words II:* "The Facts of Air";
Massachusetts Review: "Fort Despair"; PEN Syndicated Fiction
Project and National Public Radio: "Inertia." "The Control
Group" will appear in the anthology *Prize Stories: The O. Henry
Awards* in April 1992.

CONTENTS

IN THE LAND OF MEN

SINCE my attack last year, when I get off work at night one of my brothers is always waiting for me in our family car, the rusted boat, engine idling, double-parked on Halsted right outside Mizzi's, where I wait tables. No one asked them to do this and we don't talk about it, but when I emerge from the steamy restaurant into the biting, steel cold of Chicago, my heart offers up a grateful sigh at the presence of one or the other of my brothers' placid, safe faces.

Tonight they all three show. Sam, nineteen, the oldest boy but four years younger than me, sits on the hood with his pointed black ankle boots wedged between bumper and car. An inch of bare skin is exposed where the boots and pants cuffs don't quite meet, which is Sam's style. It is zero degrees out, according to the radio, factoring in wind chill, but Sam doesn't wear a coat.

"Too cool to feel cold?" I say.

He shells out a pittance of a smile. "Let's go." He hops off the hood to hold open the front door and presses my back with his palm. Sensing his eyes casting about protectively behind me, I catch my first whiff of something gone awry.

"I love a warm car," I say, settling in the passenger seat with my hands in front of the blowing heat vents. My other two brothers sit in the back the way the youngest always do. I say to them, "Hey."

Sam slams the driver's door and jerks us out of Park. He drives as if our transmission is not automatic, shifting into low or neutral frequently, keeping one hand active on the thin metal stick. Even as his older sister, I stay a certain nervous distance from Sam. Beneath his meticulously maintained smooth surface is a rage that can erupt and break windows or punch walls.

For a time I just ride along in the warmth, quietly losing my waitress aches. Lately I've found real comfort in these pocketlike moments of heat and peace, which can be as refreshing as deep, unconscious sleep. I breathe out, at last, hating to end it, but knowing I must. "So, what's the occasion?"

Sam grimly says nothing, flicking his eyes to the rearview. I turn, catty-corner, to Donald. Seventeen, the worrier, he looks alarmingly pale in the passing streetlights. His hand is in a fist under his nose as he bites a fingernail, staring desperately at the sidewalk and storefronts like a trapped dog. Donald has ulcers, migraines, all the ailments symptomatic of early adulthood. Beside him, Les, the family baby, seems more rosy-cheeked than usual, as if he's siphoned off Donald's color to top his own. But even happy Les has an uncertain smile on his face and watches Sam for cues. His teeth chatter, despite the car's abundant warmth.

Without taking his eyes off the panel van in front of him, Sam says tightly, "You got any plans tonight?"

I point at my chest. "Me? You're talking to me?"

"That's right. Anything you were going to do?"

"Is something wrong?" I ask, simultaneously anxious and annoyed that they are protecting me by withholding. "Is it Dad? Has something happened to Dad?"

"No," Donald says, looking at his watch. "Time for *WBN News at Nine*. Pistachios and beer."

From behind me, Les pats my arm soothingly. "Dad's cool," he assures me.

Sam catches my eye and we share an older siblings' smile, as if over Les's head. "He's fine," Sam says.

"And here you guys are. So what could it be?" I sit back,

relieved: My family is alive. Lesser scenarios occur to me. A surprise party. An unexpected friend waiting at the airport. A trip to the police to clear up some minor infraction before my father discovers the offense. But here we are, enclosed and fine and balanced. I enjoy, for a second, suspense's tantalizing luxury. "So when do you tell me, guys?"

Sam stops uncharacteristically at a yellow light. We rock forward with inertia, rock back. Pedestrians, loaded down with afterwork, early Christmas shopping, plunge into the crosswalks, heads ducked in irritation against the cold. Telltale forest-green Marshall Field's sacks swing from their gloved fingers. It's late and they're homeward bound. A man carries a paper funnel of flowers, shielding it with his chest, turning his back to protect this gift for some woman. Ashy snow blows up in the six-way intersection, sings along the cracks in our car doors, and the taxi in front of us decides to turn left; a signal begins flashing. Generally, this draws a heavy lean on Sam's horn, but tonight he simply waits.

"You have a decision to make," he says.

Les adds excitedly, "A very *important* decision. Mega-important. Man, it's big, really big. Life and death, you could say."

Sam frowns into the rearview mirror at Les, his profile so sharp and grown-up I have a sudden moment of wonder: My brother's a man. I quickly look at Donald—has he, too, crossed the line? But no, Donald has no beard, no jutting jaw, no buried rage. He shakes his young head pessimistically, eyes still glued in appeal to the passing world.

The light changes.

"We got your perp," Sam says to me as we take off again and slide around the taxi. He shifts his eyes momentarily from the road to my face. He's a dangerously handsome man, the family heartbreaker, and his direct gaze has a life—volition, power—of its own.

"My perp?"

"Perpetrator!" Les shouts gleefully. "We got your perpetrator! That guy! He's in our trunk."

* * *

LAST YEAR on a night not unlike tonight—that is, a night in which one instant knifed the odds of my otherwise fair life—a man looped his bright red wool scarf over my head lasso-style and pulled me to his chest. Fast and easy. He was right behind me and I could feel the serious metal cylinder of gun at my back.

"Let's walk," he suggested, "and not make too much racket."

We'd been the only two people waiting for the bus and I hadn't looked closely at him. His red scarf had been woven around his neck, and his hair stood up comically in the back as a result. A cane hooked over his forearm. That's all I remembered. Innocuous. Maybe he wore a long camel's hair coat. Behind me, he matched his footsteps to mine so exactly that if I looked down I could see his right galoshes toe coming forward just behind my own. There weren't many people on Fullerton Avenue that night and those who were seemed to misread my frantic blinking eyes. What could our peculiar closeness have appeared to be? He took me as quickly as possible to an alley. I heard our bus pass without stopping, its upward-shifting gears, feeling furious with the driver, who knew my name, who knew I always rode home with him. . . .

"Got any money, baby?" the man asked as we hastened down the alley, leaning near enough to my ear for me to feel his eyelashes kiss it. I stumbled, but he led me through my clumsiness like an expert dancer. We were approaching the back of Mizzi's, and I prayed for one of the busboys, Danbo or Rudy, to be outside smoking a j. But it was too cold; they would be up above the walk-in refrigerator, in the airspace between floors. There wasn't a soul in the alley. I heard the muffled clatter of dishes and the motor of the Hobart, could easily imagine that lively, hot kitchen only a few crucial feet of space away from me.

"Money, babe?" he reminded me.

I nodded in my scarf sling. "I do. Take it, please, in my

bag." I lifted my right shoulder carefully to draw attention to my purse hanging there.

He said, "Good girl. You a good girl? It would be in your interest to be a very good girl, you know." He had a precise British accent, cheerful and civilized-sounding. Could I have felt relief? We'd stopped and he positioned me face first against the rear wall of the empty storefront down the block from Mizzi's. It would be open in a month, its front windows claimed. A comedy club. I'd passed the sign a hundred times. Open mike on Wednesdays, no cover, two-drink minimum. He pushed me gently to the wall, nose to brick, and told me to grab on to the black window bars on either side.

"You hang on for dear life, do you hear me?"

I certainly did.

His gun, that metal erection, pressed into my lower spine, sending its insinuations to every part of me. Without lowering the gun, he dropped his cane to the ground and told me to put a foot on either end of it. I concentrated on the rubber tip and the curve of its worn handle. The worst thing that *could* happen, I told myself, was not going to. Then he drew my head back by the hair and slammed my forehead against the bricks. I tasted red wool.

DONALD SAYS, "He can probably hear us, you know. The trunk is right here." He pats the seat behind him, leaning away from it. Les looks startled and also tips forward.

Even the remotest possibility of this man's presence has made me queasy and I clutch the door handle, as if waiting for the right moment to escape. "You can't be serious," I say hopefully.

"Serious as a heart attack, sweetheart," Sam says.

We're heading west on the Eisenhower. Magnificent, colorful Michigan Avenue has given way to gloomy industrial warehouses. Traffic is light and, for the second time in my city life, I wish it otherwise. Cars, humanity, witnesses—but to what?

I say, "How can you be positive it's him? I mean, did you ask him?"

"We didn't *talk* to him," Les says. "God, it was hard enough to find him. We've been watching him for a long time. We knew it was him. He had that England accent. Plus the cane."

My feet arch reflexively at the mention of the cane, the dry texture of scarf once more in my mouth. "What do you mean, you've been watching him? What are you talking about?"

Donald says, "*They.* These two have been staking out this guy since last winter. Not me. I was ready to let the police do it."

"The police," Sam scoffs. He shakes his head once.

"That's right!" Donald says. "The cops. You can't just go around being above the law."

Sam says, "Says who?"

"I thought about dressing up like a girl," Les tells me, and new images unreel before my eyes at a dizzying speed. "A decoy. But I would have looked like Bride of Frankenstein, and I kept thinking, what would Mom have thought?"

"Mom," Donald says, "would have wondered where you guys were all those nights. Mothers know where their kids are. With Dad, it's like, 'Oh, Sam and Les? Huh. Studying in their rooms, I guess.' Mom would never have let you out the door."

I say, "What are you saying?"

"They chased the guy," Donald explains.

"We *tailed* him," Les corrects. "There was no chasing. Chasing means running."

"Whatever. They *tailed* him. They—"

"We waited until he was alone," Les says. "We saw him at that same bus stop, you know. . . ." He clears his throat to indicate discretion in alluding to my rape.

"And?" I say.

"And we followed him home."

"On foot," Sam says pointedly. Since he's had his driver's license he's hardly walked anywhere.

Les bounces on the seat as he talks. "We know where he lives!"

"Pricey," Sam adds. "Yuppie."

"After we found out, we watched his walk-up, we saw him through the curtains. He's got those see-through kind, the ones Mom always said were a bad idea on the first floor. But we couldn't get him alone. He would walk out the door, and we'd start to get out of the car—here comes some people. Man, it was frustrating. I don't see how you could make a living doing it."

Sam says to me, "It *is* weird how hard it was to find him by himself."

The car is silent for a moment, all of us meditating on my rapist's extended good fortune. Then Donald says, "These two have been out asking for it, just asking for—"

"We had a gun," Les protests. "*He* didn't have a gun—"

"Luckily for you," Donald interrupts.

"—but we *did*, see, that's the whole point. We were in charge. Once we got some privacy, the rest was so easy you couldn't believe it. He comes out to get the paper, nobody around, and bang, Sam's there with the gun."

"Bang?" I ask. "Bang? Oh guys, you didn't shoot him?"

"Not bang like that, just bang, like, get in the car, bud, let's go for a cruise. We didn't even have to tie him up."

"But he had a gun," I say. "Last year, he had a gun."

Sam turns to me. "Nuh-uh. Piece of pipe. We've been watching, like Les said. We saw asswipe's weapon. Carries it in his coat. Jesus. Little six-inch pipe."

Donald, relinquishing his role as the voice of reason for a moment, giggles and says, "Saturday night plumber's special." They all three laugh, a frightening expulsion of breath.

"Please tell me you don't have a man in the trunk of this car."

"Sorry," Sam says. "No can do." His coldness, his assuredness—the way the thrust of his strong, righteous jaw seems to drive the very car—these things let me know they not only have a man in the trunk, but the right man. I now feel his weight, as if the back end of the automobile were notably lower to the road.

"Please," I say weakly, "could we think for a minute about going to the cops with this?"

"They'll turn him free," Sam says. "Right now we have him, he's ours, but they'll set him free."

"You know what the problem is?" Donald says speculatively. "The problem is overcrowding in jails. I've been thinking that they should just stick the smaller-crime guys in the army. You know how the army always needs recruits? Two birds with one—"

"Dumb," Sam says. "Put *that* guy in the army?"

"Not him. He's in prison for life. I said, *small*-crime guys get in the army."

"Dumb," Sam repeats.

"Why? It could work," Donald says, then adds, "But now it's too late to go to the cops. Now we'd be in trouble, even me, accessory after the fact. This is a no-win situation."

"We followed him on a date." Les leans against my seat, elbows on either side of me. "Movie at the Biograph, coffee at the French place. We could see him through one window, and you waiting tables right across the street through another window. Was that bizarre, or what?"

"We thought about getting him *and* his date," Sam says. "See how he'd feel about that."

"I can't believe we finally got him!" Les says in awe. "We waxed his ass. We showed him!"

Donald shakes his head at the sorriness of Les's logic. "Right. Let's talk counting chickens before they're hatched. He's still here." He indicates the trunk with his thumb. "We haven't shown him thing one."

FOR TWO weeks after the rape, I didn't go back to work. I didn't often leave the house, and, if I did, I was escorted to and from like a politician or criminal. I read the *Trib* every morning looking for other attacks. They seemed to be epidemic, but what doesn't, once it's happened to you? The cops told me my assailant sounded like one they'd been after for months. They liked to name their rapists; this one was Big Ben. He *did* have a British accent. He *did* speak in complete sentences. I saw a counselor. She'd been raped before, too. It was like a club. I prepared myself for nightmares, as instructed, but never had any directly related to that night. The signs in my dreams were more oblique. I would be pursuing a seemingly safe course on a road, then suddenly I would look around—where were the landmarks of civilization? Billboards, buildings, traffic lights? Surrounding me would be blank, cool air. High as an airplane, I would suddenly realize even my vehicle was gone. Nothing kept me from plummeting. The road, my world—all of it snatched out from under me, and it was then that horror would return.

I took sedatives. I slept like something dead.

And then two weeks later I was back at work. I'd been emptied but other things began inevitably to fill my life again, so that the attack was, soon enough, supplanted. Or, at least, shuffled into the deck. Still, it was the marked card, the one dividing before and after.

"**I** could kill him," Sam admits calmly, and I realize he's speaking the truth. He could. "If it was me, I'd kill him, but you decide." He turns to his brothers. "We'll do what she decides." We're parked a few yards from an off ramp, in front of the boarded windows of the Five Cents Germ-Free Cleaners. Inland from Lake Michigan, the snow falls more heavily and soon the car is its own late-model Ford igloo of isolation.

"I thought we were going to definitely kill him," Les whines. "I thought we had a plan. We had a lot of plans. Tell her about the Dumpster plan, Sam."

"Shut up," Donald says. "Really, just shut up. The right thing to do is turn around and go back to his house. We have to let him go. Otherwise we're all in trouble. Doesn't that make sense, Sam? He doesn't know us."

"We pull up, dump him, say, 'Hey, sorry, pal, just a joyride'?" Sam says this snidely, whirling in his seat to face Donald, behind him. "Who do you think is going to press charges at that point? We kidnapped him, basically."

Donald puts his finger to his lips. "He might be listening," he whispers. "You're giving him ideas."

"What about the drive-the-car-into-the-lake plan?" Les goes on. "That was good. We get a new car out of it, too, so it's a double good plan." His teeth, crooked and spotted with minuscule notches from his braces, chatter loud enough for us to hear over the sound of the wind. "Or castrating him. We talked about that."

"Jesus," Donald says.

"What if he's dead?" Les says suddenly, his teeth still. "What if he suffocated back there?"

Sam nods solemnly. "Back to the Dumpster plan. Dead, we don't have a problem."

"Man, if he's dead we have about ten million problems," Donald says, forgetting to whisper.

"But alive," Sam continues, "alive, I'm not sure what to do with him." He turns to me. "Like I said, it should be up to you. What do *you* want?"

"Shoot him," Les pleads. "Choose shooting."

"Shut *up!*" Donald orders. They all three look at me. The car has grown so cold I can see their breath. It would be colder still in the trunk. I review my options: Turn him loose, maim him, kill him, variations thereof. The moment I say the word, we all move into the future. For now, however, we're in one of those pockets.

Of course I have wanted this man punished, but I never went further than hoping he would *get what he deserved*, a concrete wish with only abstract underpinnings, one I would have been happy to let someone else make real. I never saw the man's face—maybe if I had I could have declared the correct retribution, hollowed the perfect scar—but as it was, he might have been any man, and any man might have been him.

"Maybe I should look at him," I say, stalling.

"Yeah?" Sam takes the keys from the ignition and spins them on his forefinger. "Yeah?"

"I want to see him," I decide.

Sam reaches across me and pokes the glove compartment open. A gun spills into his waiting hand. "Okey-doke," he says. "You want it, you got it."

"He's ugly," Les warns me as he clambers out.

From the outside, our car looks like one abandoned, the four swung-open doors leaving gaping holes in the storm. Feeling a curious and appealing sense of déjà vu, I imagine our walking away, four children on a long winter trek. But, of course, passive as it is, even walking away is *doing* something.

Les whisks the snow off the trunk with his bare hand and raps on the metal. "Anyone home?"

"Listen," Donald says. "Okay, we don't let him go, that won't work. But . . ." He ticks off steps on his fingers. "We drive to the police station, we say Les and I got the guy— we're under eighteen, so it's a juvenile crime—we know he's the one, the cane, et cetera, and she"—he nods at me—"she identifies his voice. She makes him say what he said to her last year, he sounds like Prince Charles, they book him. It can happen. Okay?" He moves his head up and down as if he can coach us into agreement.

"Finished?" Sam asks.

Donald sighs. "You all are crazy, I swear."

Sam tries to hand me the gun.

"I don't want that."

"Yes," he says, "you do." He nudges my fingertips with the cold handle.

"I'll hold it," Les volunteers. "Let me hold it. I haven't gotten to hold it yet." This from my fourteen-year-old brother, the one who, until he was at least twelve, cried when he saw dead animals in the road.

"Give me that," I tell Sam. I use both hands and find myself with my knees bent like a TV cop.

"Ready?" he says, key to the trunk lock.

I shake my head no. It's funny, but even with a gun in my hands and the lid locked I don't feel at all invulnerable. Donald turns and begins walking away from us.

Sam yells to his back, "Keep a look out for cars."

Donald stops at the street, his shoulders drawn, as if trying to decide whether to step off the curb and keep on going.

"You watching?" Sam calls to him. A horn blows in the distance.

When Donald turns our way, I admire his loyalty to his brothers' bad cause. He nods to Sam. I aim the gun at the back of our car, quaking.

Then I say, "Now." Without taking my eyes off the bumper, I blink rapidly so I won't have to when the lid flies up.

The man lies fetuslike, filling our trunk, back to us. Expensive camel's hair coat. A cane thrown on top of him like an afterthought. The little light inside shows half his face, one closed eye, which, while I stare, opens.

"Shut it!" I yell at Sam. "Shut it! Shut it!"

OUR MOTHER died three years ago. We worried all along about the wrong things. We fretted about her recovery from cancer, chemotherapy, and the fluctuating number of months her doctors had thrown around as her life expectancy. But those things never turned out to be relevant. Some percentage of people slip away under anesthesia. It's a risk of every operation, a posted figure, like car accidents, like crimes. After my mother was gone, with only my brothers and my father and me, I thought, *Here you are in the land of men.* I never missed her more, I never felt more outnumbered, than when I came home from the police station last year. I told myself growing up meant losing things, but then it didn't feel so much like loss as it did theft.

"What do you want us to do?" my brother Sam asks me patiently. He must know that patience, or its illusion, is a grown-up virtue. Back in the driver's seat, he is tired, his duties in this territory of his own kind so mercilessly never-ending.

"We can't just leave him there," Donald says. "For one thing, this is our *car*. What if we want to go somewhere? For another, it's cruel and unusual punishment."

Les, brave and savagely young, proclaims, "He could rot in there, for what he did to our sister!"

"That's true," Sam agrees. "He could rot . . . and he could not. You want him to rot?" he asks me.

I look out at the blanketed and beautified ugly buildings around us. Is there any wish made more often than the one for time to stop? But the snowdrift forming around our car has gotten deeper, and soon, if we let it, it will trap us, all five of us. What I want is for him to disappear, but I consider my real choices and also the misnomer *justice* in an unjust world. Soon I will insist on driving the car back into the city, back to the lights and signs and authorities created by mankind to keep us civilized.

Meanwhile, my brothers wait.

"I'm thinking," I tell them.

THE HAPPY DAY

THE BRIDE wants children in the ceremony: ring bearers, flower girls, a choir of pure bell-like voices. They stand soldierly in their deep-green velvet vests and tunics, lined up rank and file, their parents off to the side tilting heads and smiling to see the artistry, Marty shaping them like clay—pinching a boy closer, wetting a finger to flatten a cowlick, raising a girl straighter by her chin, coercing them together by suggesting they are afraid—until their grouping pleases him. Beth thinks Marty has acquired a kind of permanent commercial Vaseline blur to his vision. The white gazebo backdrop looks like the plastic top of a wedding cake, greenery and baby's breath poked into its latticework like that phony, inedible icing. "Whiskey," he tells them on an intake of breath.

"Whiskey," they shout. His shutter snaps and he drops his hand, releasing his breath.

"Father of the bride?" Marty says flatly.

"Dead!" the kids shout back.

"Oh."

From shooting weddings, Marty says he has learned that he will never marry. Beth is frightened to think she has discovered the same thing. She is too young, twenty-four. She lifts her Pentax, the color load, and catches a boy wiping his hand angrily beneath his nose. The abrupt way he does it reminds her of a fighter, someone knocked but not yet down. As Marty's assistant, her job is to shoot the less conventional moments, what they call in this business the candids. Things gone tender or real or wrong, the off-center parts that lend the standard event its idiosyncratic patent. Back at the shop, they'll go through the negs making two piles, keep or toss. Beth steals those shots the family would never purchase, those that cross the line. She's papering her apartment walls with them: the bloated cheeks puffing up to contain an unseemly belch, the willful hand during its misplaced fondle, the thigh or shoulder giving an accidental tease of binding underwear, and the inevitable closed eyes—whole groups of people in their finery, tux and tails and slips and mottled plastic pearls, eyes shut, not one of them seeming able to bear what's before them.

Today's wedding is the second for both sides. Bride and groom are in their thirties, and share between them three children of those first mistaken vows. Beth cannot recall which of the little cadets had been pointed out to her as the sons of the bride and daughter of the groom. She's heard there are optimal times in a child's life for divorce and so assumes there must also be converse, disastrous times. Did such considerations enter into the plans? She watches for pettiness, jealousy, sulking. But maybe the children have given their blessings. Maybe this new snap-together family is just the thing.

Marty rounds up the bride and her grown-up entourage, grimaces at their varied heights and weights, the gap-toothed way their green gown hems meet. Their dresses are skimpy and they have goosebumps, noticeable nipples. June wedding, though in Chicago it is not safe to assume June weather. The party keeps looking hopefully at the clouds as the fickle sun surfaces and retreats. Marty doesn't care; he uses a flash with everything, indoor or out, unilateral unnatural light. It will be up to Beth to capture the real atmosphere of the day, which is part of that long, damp Midwestern transitional season neither spring nor summer.

"Suck in," Marty prods the women. "Say honeymoon."

"Honeymoon," they say through locked smiling teeth.

"Oh, ladies!" Marty swoons. "Like you *mean* it!"

"*Honey*moon."

Beth catches them just after Marty, their faces fallen,

mouths open as they step away, complain of the wind, the loud children, the way this peculiar leafy green is not only not their color but not anyone's, narrowing their eyes at Marty, wondering if he's a homosexual.

Marty nudges as if by accident into the pipe-smoking, smiling Jimmy Stewart–like friend of the family who's been trailing around with a video recorder.

"Oh, pardon me, brother," Marty says rudely.

Taking Marty's professional poses and using them for his home movie. Marty hates an amateur. Beth lifts the Nikon from around her neck, black-and-white load, and snaps a shot of her boss with his fist on his hip, pouty lip, pudgy fag. He's a redhead and even his eyes are freckled.

But the video camera annoys everyone. And the man is not really respecting the wedding dress code, certainly not the bride's evident preference for green. White Mexican shirt, khaki bermudas, those ubiquitous brown ribbed nylon old-man socks worn with rubber-soled hiking boots. His pipe makes him appear benign, avuncular, though no one seems to claim him. He turns sharply when Beth targets him, as if by focusing her lens she had created a vortex he felt on his back. He points *his* video machine at *her*, dueling photographers. Beth has an urge to cover herself; it's as if she could see what he's seeing, a boyish young woman also not dressed for a wedding, three heavy cameras slung around her neck like anchors. She doesn't take the shot, with a blushing face discreetly focuses on the suburban house behind him, takes a picture of the bridesmaids' wide green bottoms—huge spring buds—as the women step up through the sliding glass doors.

Beth could never make it as a professional photographer, the type that has to nose in and confront; she imagines a thousand hostile faces as seen through her lens, fingers and hands raised in anger. . . . Her inclination is toward the covert. Marty hired her because she didn't know the first thing about photography. He got to fashion her, adjust her like any other subject. Beth eased into his direction as into warm water, following like a shadow on the periphery of his center-ring antics, grateful for a job with possibilities. When he looked at her work now, Beth saw his growing impatience, could almost hear him mutter about his hard times in finding good help. Her parents used to get fed up in the same way, asking why she couldn't just finish what she started, find a direction—*any* direction, they finally allowed—and pursue it. They worried that she had no place in the world to link herself. "Skip art," Marty has told her. "There's a million artists out there. This is a paying job. I've seen art; you've seen art. Art is depressing. I mean, be honest, all the customer wants is to make a bunch of regular people look like royalty, like they got a divine right. Can't be done with a Polaroid, so they call in yours truly."

The longer she took pictures, however, the more obscure Beth's work became: She was trying to keep track of something but she never knew quite what. Some exciting little logic would present itself and after it she would go. Last week she shot two rolls of nothing but the backs of heads, a ludicrous processional plastered chronologically, movie-footage style, along her kitchen wall. If you looked long enough, with sufficient abstraction and irony, the wedding party appeared an odd breed of human having no eyes or nose or mouth, featureless heads of shrub-coiffed hair.

"Get the bride at her vanity," Marty tells Beth. He mimics the application of mascara while batting his white lashes. Marty's popularity as a wedding photographer has to do with his policy of insidiousness. He permeates a party like an oil slick. Where most will leave after a couple of hours, he stays until the end. The limo drives off at two in the morning— Marty catches its taillights, the dancing Coke cans. The father of the bride falls asleep at a table, head resting on his meaty, responsible arms, surrounded by ribbon and champagne corks and melted wax—Beth shoots his peaceful expression. But she's also shot the best man, on his knees in a reception hallway, puking into a Styrofoam ice chest. She showed up half an hour early today and caught the arrival of the bride's paralyzed brother, wheeled prone into the house like a dead man and rolled like a log onto a living room couch. His stretcher disappeared down a hallway and he was draped to his neck with an afghan whose many shades of green made it appear, oddly, purple.

Beth couldn't decide whether to use black and white or color: Go for the hard-edged or the garish conflicting greens? Photojournalism or kitsch? Either way, it wouldn't have been the candid Marty has in mind when he sends her prematurely to wedding shoots; this would have been one for Beth's wall at home.

"No pictures," the man had said.

Beth looked around the room, as if he couldn't have been speaking to her, her color load at her eye. The room was empty but for them.

He said something else, something Beth caught the meaning of just as she'd smiled and said, "Beg your pardon?" trying then to swallow back the phrase.

"Fuck away. That camera," he'd told her, inaudible linking words sitting between his lips.

She recalls with shame the way his body tried to move under the cover, the burrowing slow-motion turn of his face toward the couch seat.

"You don't shoot crips," Marty scolded her later. "Man, you gotta know you don't shoot crips." He thumped her knuckles with his broad freckled index finger.

She feels he will have to fire her soon.

A restrained rain has begun. Beth stands at a window thinking how equitably it falls, neither harder nor softer on those folks in rich Winnetka and those low down on the South Side, down the el routes that are discussed, by everyone, as descents into hell; those driving expressways to the zoo or mall or hospital; those working weekend hours in the unnaturally quiet Merchandise Mart who, like Beth, might be distracted by the simple gray striation outside the window, watching briefly as it lifted like a sheet in the wind and then blanketed infinite Lake Michigan. Her thoughts are only variations of what she often thinks in Chicago: too many humans, dense as molecules, and as endlessly and pointlessly busy, marrying, conceiving, divorcing; bumping into each other and spinning away, scarred or not. She has come from an Indiana town where people often exclaim at the smallness of the world, but in her new city, wedding guests arrive and she knows not one of them. Small water spots mark their clothing and Beth knows this to be an invitation, of sorts, to intimacy. She could say, "Nice day for a wedding, huh?" but doesn't.

Wherever there is a mirror a guest stands before it primping. The bride has belted her train around her waist with a knotted yellow bungee cord. Two bobbypins hold her bangs in pincurls, the day's humidity ruining her hairdo. Beth follows her from the study she's using as a dressing room to the front hall. They pass her brother on the couch each way, still in the room by himself. Smaller chambers surrounding him are full but no one joins him. For this fact Beth feels an ungenerous glee. The bride says "Shit" when she sees the rain, and then stomps her foot for emphasis. "Chicago never once gave me a break," she says.

"Should do it private," her brother tells her with effort. His voice cuts like a machine's, batteries low.

"Yes," she agrees, "that's the kind of thing I always think of too late. But, you know, there's no percentage in doing it privately."

He smiles briefly, then warns Beth, "No pictures."

The bride stops. "Of course we'll get a picture," she says. "Come here." She motions for Beth to follow.

She sits squarely on the couch near her brother's shoulder, pushing him back as she does so. "This is my day to be boss."

"Every day."

She tells him, "You know, the world was *wondering* when the next bitter war vet would show up." As soon as she hears the word *war* Beth realizes the afghan is precisely the colors of military camouflage. The chill of irony passes over her.

"This the. Real thing?" he asks his sister.

She leans down slowly and lays her cheek on his. "I hope so," she says softly.

"Don't take. My mug. Until real thing."

His sister sits back up and pats her bobbypins, looking down at her dress bunched on her lap, shaking her head. "Not a pretty sight," she says, motioning Beth to shoot nonetheless.

"Ugly face," the brother warns.

"You *are* an ugly face. Or maybe you mean my face?"

He says, "No," painfully, conceding.

Beth looks through the viewfinder as the bride lifts her brother's head awkwardly onto her thigh and kisses his brow. His mouth moves just slightly when his sister makes contact, as if her lips were hot.

"Not in. The album," he says. "Bet anything."

"If you had anything to bet," the bride says, leaving him.

"You. Looking at?" he demands of Beth, all compliance gone.

Startled, she says, "I don't know."

W H E N the bride and groom are in the room together, they make an obligatory show of shielding their eyes, of not seeing one another. Along these same lines, the bride wears not white white but jade-tinted white. There seems to Beth a kind of unintentional comment in every piece of the day, thrown in like comic relief for those canny enough to catch it. The event obviously needs a chain of command, someone to give orders, subordinates to carry them out, but the flustered widow, the bride's mother and owner of the house, makes a feeble general at best, herding people from the front entrance straight through to the back as if her job were merely to keep open a fire lane. Once outside people stand under a few umbrellas, waiting for the caterers to finish setting up chairs.

"You can't leave these in no rainstorm," one of the hired men says, rolling his eyes and tucking his lips primly. "These seats is padded. It's in the contract, foul weather clause."

"Yo, woman," another adds, when the widow glides by without a glance.

Beth sits in a chair that sits on an incline and braces herself. She shoots the backyard, the oddly placed gazebo and the early guests seated by themselves across the makeshift aisle. She contemplates shooting the black umbrellas that remind her of funerals. The children chase in and out of the gazebo, rocking it because it has no foundation. A tiara flies off a girl's head and lands on the grass. When the children have disappeared back into the house, a squirrel moves in dashes across the lawn to the tiara, sniffs it, lifts it, considers it, drops it. The guests turn at the sound of Beth's motor drive.

Marty sits heavily next to her.

"See that squirrel?" she asks him, laughing at her luck. This is a picture the widow will buy.

He says, "Been consulting with the matron of honor. Groom's parents won't show."

"Why?"

" 'Breach,' she said, 'of etiquette.' "

"Huh?"

"Irrelevant," sighs Marty. "Weirdo Martians with their green wedding. Did I mention I wasn't ever getting married?"

"It's come up a time or two."

"And that crip. Man, I definitely don't like that guy. Asked me if I'd bring him something to spit in, got allergies or some such. 'Just . . . a . . . drool . . . cup,' he says to me. Too much. Makes me want to go back to natural disasters." Before Marty shot weddings he shot hurricanes, floods, fires. He fell into it by witnessing an act of God on his father's farm in Medicine Lodge, Kansas, a tornado touching down like an inquisitive finger in a wheat field. After that, he chased upheaval, recorded its effects, sold photos to homeowners, insurance companies, wire services, rubberneckers. "Back when I wanted to die, anyway," he'd explained to Beth. "What'd I have to lose? Figured I might as well come face to face. One step and I was in lava at Mount Saint Helen's."

"But now you want to live?" Beth had asked, getting to what she thought was the heart.

He shrugged, indifferent. "I guess." He calls weddings unnatural disasters. Today he confides what has just recently been confided to him, that the bride used to be married to the groom's brother.

"That's why his parents won't come," Beth deduces, immediately wondering if she'll catch both brothers and their shared wife in a photo together. "How ironic."

"Yeah," Marty says, sighing unhappily, "and I hate irony. It's so common."

"Common?"

"Like dirt. Think how much rarer the life is that doesn't have it. And here's the matron of honor, dying to tell me how weird her family is. Mr. Crip on the couch? He wasn't blown apart in Nam, he was blown apart the year after he got back, being a camp counselor at YMCA Winnehaha. The widow's husband drowned in a hot tub two weeks after a triple bypass. Of *course* the woman's marrying her brother-in-law. Who else? Dime a dozen irony. There's so much of it here you'd need two magnets to pull it apart."

"I like it," Beth admits, looking again at the umbrellas.

"It's a stage," Marty tells her, "not unlike puberty."

From inside comes first electronic distortion, then organ music, the bride's aunt warming up.

"Recess is over, sweetie." Marty pats her knee.

Beth shoots the woman's chunky pink hands, skin as smooth as plastic. She adds accompanying options, oboes and violins and timpani. Soon a thickly layered canned orchestra rhumba-rhythms through the house. The woman smiles clownishly in her makeup, her hair a sprayed helmet upon her head, pumping her bare feet on the pedals. Beth grins, shooting those yellow feet, rough as rhino hide, bunions on each like sixth digits, the toenails opaque as tusks.

"Ten minutes," the widow says to them as she swoops through.

Beth wanders upstairs, peeking in doorways. The house is messy in the way hired help cannot fix. Paper clutter, personal matter that can't be wiped clean and done with, things over which decisions must be made. Beth prefers home weddings. Her private interest in those things discarded—shoes, smeary-lipped drinking glasses, wadded tissue—guides her. She shoots the artful disarray on the bathroom sink, the forgotten Baggie of marijauna beside the open Colgate tube. Snaps the hallway shrine of school photos, births, previous weddings.

There's today's bride ten years ago, on her father's arm, her first marriage still before her like the red runway she walks on. Her father's death, too, waiting ahead. Beth steps away from the wall, including in the composition the surrounding frames. Diplomas, baby announcements, vacation poses with everyone holding up the Leaning Tower, a spray-painted child's handprint in plaster of Paris. She wonders if today's wedding picture will supplant the old one or complement it? It would be Beth's temptation to slip the new bride and groom right over this photo, like changing the month on a calendar or inserting a new name on an apartment mailbox, but she's certain the family wouldn't embrace such callousness.

From down the hall she hears something, a scuffle like unwatched pets. In a far bedroom where the silver-wrapped wedding gifts sit reflecting light, two toddler girls, too young to be by themselves, stand holding up their green skirts. Surrounded by palatial opulence, they crunch their heels into plastic mail-package bubble-wrap. Perfectly dedicated, listening as each pocket of air pops. Through the window comes the surfish murmur of the crowd on the lawn, the wafting organ music.

Crouching to catch their knees, the excess pocket of dirty white hose that sags beneath each, Beth asks them what they're doing.

One hesitates, looks to the other, who looks right back, wrinkles her baby brow. Annoyed by having to think about it, she finally says, "We don't know."

"I see."

Beth tries to decide how to present the room's essence, the U-shaped arrangement of surfaces covered with the excessiveness of wealthy bad taste. The grotesque rococo ornamental quality. She thinks of gold-capped teeth, flashy pimp Cadillacs, Liberace from long ago. This room nudges itself toward that class of spectacle and, further, the real photograph would have to make you feel as if you'd eaten a pound of cheap candy.

Suddenly she realizes one little girl has wrapped the other's face in the plastic wrap. The backdrop is a silver platter like a mirror, like armor, the bride and groom's last name etched on the rim, the same name, Beth thinks vaguely, as the first marriage. In the foreground, for an astonishing second, the child in front of her is suffocating, eyes and mouth open behind the seal. When she takes the photo before thinking to save the child, Beth wonders if this shouldn't be her last wedding shoot.

"I was just teasing!" the bigger girls wails as Beth yanks her hands away. The smaller child stands still, breathing, tasting injustice.

"Let me get your picture," Beth suggests, breathing a bit shallowly herself. It occurs to her that she may have just saved what could now go on to be the happy day.

The children clasp hands, instantly recovered, squeeze their cheeks up against their eyes as if smiling for the camera was the act of diminishing their vision.

B E T H has not one photo of herself in her apartment, not of anyone she knows, not of those events she tags as milestones in her life. They would be images so close up as to be unrecognizable: the crucified form of her boyfriend lying face-down on a bed, crying; his curled—pubic? chest?—hairs like question marks on her own belly after making love for the last time; when he slept, the sweaty cave composed of his neck and hair and ear against the pillow. He is gone, home to that same Indiana town, so who now would understand? She imagines bringing one of these guests to her Wrigleyville apartment, leading up the stairs, explaining her neighbors as their noises give them away, the salsa music, the parakeets, the man who reads aloud to himself, the endless succession of el trains that shake the building. She imagines taking the bride's brother up the freight elevator and through her door, imagines asking him in the reciprocated shorthand of his language, "Warm? Hungry? Happy?"

Marty would argue there is substance to color and flash and posturing. Having climbed back from the brink of a deadly fall, he finds the institution of life, as a member of its audience, engaging. He likes to dress it up and show it off. Beth can appreciate his point of view and still disagree: Even untouched (unretouched, in this biz), she finds life daunting. For now she watches it in black and white, in natural light, in candids, in irony. She looks forward to the stop bath, to standing alone in the darkroom tonight waiting for her own confusing and peculiar truth, that awkward unphotogenic creature, to show itself beneath her fingers.

IN A MOVE Beth admires, the bride has requested no photos during the actual wedding. Marty chooses to smoke and read coffee table books in the living room but Beth sits like a guest to watch the ceremony, wishing she had worn at least a dress.

The procession begins, organ beat dictating the cadenced step of the grown-ups but having no effect on the children, who hurry, then slow, look to one another for instruction. The flower girls clasp hands and so cannot drop their petals on the walkway. When they reach the end and discover their baskets still full, they squat and begin scooping great handfuls, making a pile. The guests chuckle warmly. When the rest of the wedding party has joined the girls and the organ ceases, all the children except one clump together and run to the gazebo, where they are to wait quietly until after, when they will sing. They leave the boy who bears the rings, who looks longingly after them. Their shiny black shoes sound like taps, their strained whispers like hissing steam. The judge clears his throat and reads.

A strong wet wind blows up and water shakes down from tree limbs. The canopy over the catered food sways treacherously; the caterers wag their disapproving heads. An umbrella snaps inside-out and an unoccupied chair blows over. Beth imagines this all taking place on a large screen right in front of her, happening in slow motion. She's always employed slow motion when things bordered on going astray, casting grace and intention where there is otherwise nothing but clumsiness and accident. It is this, she realizes, that has made photography easy for her.

Smiling, intrepid, the judge pauses, his thin hair blown vertically from his head. He looks serenely out as if sharing a familiar anecdote, one whose ending his children, this crowd, all know to be secure.

When the gust dies, he says, "Now, Todd, do you promise to be her sweetheart?" The word, so secular and dear, hangs in the air like a thin-skinned pink balloon. Generally Beth likes the kiss best, the open eroticism not only tolerated but encouraged, yet this appeals, this notion of a sweetheart, as innocent and alluring as childhood.

Perhaps because he's rehearsed, Todd is not thrown by this clause and agrees, he will be hers. The judge asks the bride, "Eileen, do you promise to be his sweetheart?" Beth searches the woman's face for the real answer. After all, Todd is her first sweetheart's brother. When Eileen whispers "Yes," Beth feels every consciousness in the yard lift, for an instant transcendent, above any mere piece of weather. Beth wonders if she will faint, disoriented as she is by the palpable faith of the group. She puts her head between her knees. Unbidden, she thinks of the way her boyfriend used to kiss her by licking her lips, the way her lips were always chapped. When she straightens she finds one hundred people facing forward, the power of their concentrated gaze propelling a man and a woman toward a more standard kiss. Those two, and the rest, despite whatever evidence to the contrary, must believe their love will sustain them.

Then an amateur, shooting illicitly, runs out of film. His automatic camera begins rewinding itself, whirring like white noise, grounding the ceremony once more as he turns red. Beth catches for posterity his futile attempt to muffle the mechanism in his jacket.

"CHEAP CHAMPAGNE," Marty complains. "Spend a thousand bucks on film footage—fucking *hemorrhage* money on egg rolls and fondue and buffalo wings— and skimp where it counts. Tell me how to make sense of it all. Plus, what good are we with Joe Video on the job?"

Beth's wondered herself. The video man lurks just behind Marty and Beth, appearing to be documenting the documenting of the day. As a matter of fact, he has just filmed this exchange about himself, standing in the doorway watching through his screen, giving not the slightest indication of having taken offense.

"The man's amazing," Marty says. "Someone should cut him in."

Beth goes to catch the bride distributing gifts to the children. After the kiss they had sung three touchingly unmelodic songs and as a reward receive water toys that make Beth snort: for the boys, pistols, and for the girls, huge circular wands that create long tubelike bubbles. They are relegated to the outdoors while the grown-ups all escape the murky elements. Beth, intuitively, sticks with the kids.

They play well for a time, boys shooting boys, girls dipping their wands into a tub of soapsuds, then running, leaving great blimps of logy bubbles lumping behind them. But the suds sink and the boys chase the girls and the girls cry out and a boy dumps the suds onto the lawn and another slips, soaking his official green suit and pink face. A girl, the young one whose cousin wrapped her in plastic earlier, laughs. She laughs so genuinely she must quit everything else, consumed by it. She has forgotten the bubble wrap incident and Beth smiles, though sadly aware of the adage that says true humor always comes at somebody else's expense. She takes the girl's picture.

But the boy, pride wounded, retaliates, fills his gun with the last of the soapy, now-brown water, approaches, and fires into the little girl's face. She screams and the children stop, freeze dramatically in place, like a startled forest. When she doesn't quit screeching, they look toward the house, toward Beth, forming a tentative ring around the pair as if to contain them until authority arrives. Beth steps closer as other adults emerge from the house and run to the children, suddenly aware that she once more could have interceded earlier.

Water drips from the boy's face, slides along the plump contours of cheek and chin. He is furious, volatile, gun still in hand; the girl continues to scream, clawing her eyes. The hose is retrieved, her eyes bathed. The boy stands clenching whatever of himself he is able—forehead, thighs, fists—rigid, a frightening childish parody of the man he might become. Beth imagines the time-lapse pictures that could chronicle it, like that superhero who turns from man to monster, bursting his suit seams. Where the boy's anguish rivets him, vibrating, the girl's makes her limp as rags, rich velvet dress circling her like a sofa cushion, the dark streaks down her bodice like blood from a tender wound. Her dimpled fingers cover her features; the tiara sits sparkly and askew in her damp hair. Beth shoots the shiny black patent-leather shoe that lies unbuckled beside her.

When she looks up, the video man is next to Beth, watching her. He says, "Huh," as if he's made a discovery. His pipe has gone out—or maybe it was never lit—and he has finally stopped filming. "Outta tape," he explains, stretching. His machine rests on his shoulder and he blinks his eyes, still watching her. "Smile," he orders Beth, showing his own weathered teeth to illustrate. "Like this."

Now that it's superfluous, the sun has emerged and attached long shadows to everything. Beth moves away from the video man before he can quote the fact that it takes fewer muscles to smile than frown. She keeps shooting, black and whites, the ones that will last. Sunny ugly snapshots at the end of a Saturday afternoon, one that is ending all over town, up in Lake Forest, over at the Brookfield Zoo. Everywhere in Chicago people are clashing, dying, making love, injecting insulin, selling shoes, stepping into steaming tubs of water, rearranging once again the idle components of a million interchangeable lives. It is too much. She watches her sector of the planet from the future—images coming to fruition in the wrist-temperature developing bath, the adult faces straining forward like boxing match fans, hostile boy and pouting girl—while in the present the responsible parties prod their offspring to action. The ring-bearer must apologize. The flower girl must forgive. But she won't get up, he won't come forward; she is limp and unforgiving, knees grass-stained and face sticky with soap and cake. And he is angry, glistening as if with sweat, unrepentant.

She is lifted beneath the arms, a parent on either side; similarly, the boy is brought.

"Say you're sorry."

"I'm sorry."

"Tell him it's okay."

"It's okay."

At the insistence of his parents the boy tilts his dripping face toward the girl's; her burning eyes say she flinches. Beth chooses this moment: He is not sorry; it is not okay. One of the grown-ups says, "Go on now, kiss her."

HUMAN HABITS

RORY ELDER was the kind of man who needed two homes: the one in which he lived, and the one to which he escaped. He was just now in the latter, trying to discover why its thick walls seemed suddenly transparent, newly inadequate to the old task of protecting him.

After all, he'd come here and been rescued before.

The first time he returned to his bachelor house was after he and Marta had been married only three months. Marta's son, Beau, then thirteen years old, had decided he wanted to live with his mother again. Beau was failing in New Jersey, where he lived with his father, stealing money and drinking beer. Marta bit her cuticles, looking anxiously at Rory as he decided: Could her son come? Rory, though he'd never met the boy, felt a familiar kindred flame. In his chest cocky pride blossomed: He would succeed where the first husband had not. Marta's face was fretful and vulnerable before him, inviting him to supply the complements: strength, certainty.

The boy, large and soft and pale-skinned, moved in. Rory could find nothing to inspire affection, the reality of Beau so much bleaker than the fantasy. It was clear he would not fit easily anywhere, his face locked into an outsider's sneer. He stood in the room Marta had cleaned for him and dwarfed the second-hand single bed, the boy's chest of drawers, the desk and chair. He would not study, Rory saw, he would not hang baseball posters or maps of the world. Rory resigned himself to a tougher job. He would approach Beau by circumnavigation, reach him when he least expected it.

Marta worked hard those first weeks, trying much too blunt a method with the boy, laying options before him like a smorgasbord and waiting hopefully for his decision. Beau was sullen with her and ignored Rory altogether, a condition for which Rory was often grateful. Beau went to the junior high down the street, a long brick building surrounded by an eight-foot chain-link fence, reassuringly prisonlike. His disappearance each morning infused the house with air. Rory, who was between jobs, made appointments for the late afternoon so that he could take advantage of Beau's absence. He and Marta would return to bed in the morning, making love frequently, enjoying leisurely breakfasts afterward. With Beau safely gone, Rory believed he could master the difficult problems of marriage and stepfatherhood.

Rory had stayed single well into his thirties, finally marrying a woman three years older than he. Marta had a kind of lively optimism Rory envied, his own vision having grown cynical; most women would not tolerate it. On just their second date Marta told him, "You lack innocence. I feel sorry for you." She'd held his hand maternally. She contained an enormous emotional repertoire that intrigued and baffled Rory, laughing out loud daily, able to weep in a heartbeat. Completely alien. Rory envisioned their relationship as a symbiotic one in which he supplied the cloud and she the silver lining.

He had known she would not stay single for long; there was no end to the men who wanted her, who confided in her, who were gratified in pleasing her. Yet she chose Rory. His friends, cynics like himself, came from everywhere for the wedding, convinced he would not go through with it.

But here he was. Rory sometimes saw his life as a whirling tornado, a gradually narrowing event that had left him, at last, with all other options and possibilities thrown from its central eye, the clear space where he now stood.

All options, that is, except his small house.

The desert tract-housing development he and Marta had bought into wound over and through a dry wash, newer models appearing every few months. From their window, Rory could watch as the borderless areas of cholla and palo verde and saguaro fell to the regular checkerboard squares of suburban planning, green rolls of grass, the burlap-wrapped roots of nonsucculent vegetation. The construction would have outraged him if he hadn't owned his other place, the little urban adobe hovel dead center in Tucson's barrio. As long as it was there, development in the suburbs did not reach him in any meaningful way. In fact, he took a sort of pleasure in man's stubborn, insistent dominance over something as ornery as a rocky patch of mesquite and prickly pear.

When he and Marta argued, the other house he'd kept would invariably creep in. Rory pictured it as something eccentric and animate, a favorite uncle or old dog. He'd brought dozens of women to it before he was married, undressing them in the cool dark living room, leading them through the open doorway to his mattress on the floor, where, on their backs afterward, they could look up and see ancient vigas dutifully supporting the mud roof, the hearty vines that grew through cracks in the wall, their leaves like animal tracks across the ceiling. Rory imagined the house's earthy smell to be that of sex.

"You can't have it both ways," Marta would say. "You can't be married *and* live by yourself. Not with me, anyway."

"I'm not trying to get away with something," Rory told her. "You make it sound as if I have a lover. It's just a house."

"But the sensible thing would be to sell it," Marta countered. "We could use the money—"

"It's an investment as it is."

"—and you could commit yourself to this house."

"I do commit myself here," Rory said, pulling her near, knowing his commitment ended just beyond his hand on Marta's shoulder. He looked at the cheap sparkly walls, low ceilings, and shag carpet of their home, which smelled not of sex but of cooking grease, and wondered how anyone could invest his loyalty in such a structure. He felt fortunate that he had another life, an escape, and did not want to let go of it or of Marta. Fortunately, the argument continued to fizzle and

Marta would soften, her anger diffuse, her body and character become pliant.

After Beau's first few weeks with Rory and Marta he began talking more, coming out of whatever shell he'd crawled into in New Jersey, greeting them in the morning with celebrity news gleaned from the television, which he moved to his bedroom. He watched incessantly. Rory's dreams began including the drone of a newscaster or burst of a laugh track. Beau had an amazing memory for foolish banter and could recount whole scenes from sitcoms. He memorized commercials, dropping his jaw and rolling his eyes as he sold household products, held label forward at his cheek, always followed by a face-breaking huckster's smile. Marta applauded, her sense of humor a wide and various commodity. Even though nearly forty years old, her personality and tastes were easily swayed. She seemed to Rory as impressionable as a child, as eager to get along. Beau's talkativeness, though irritating to Rory, cheered Marta enormously. Rory made an effort to at least lift his lips in what passed as a smile.

But he and Beau did not take to one another. The boy brought out the worst in Rory; he worried that Beau reminded him too much of himself with his teenage pessimism and donkeylike laugh. To Marta, who had grown up with six siblings in small quarters, her son's self-absorption and obnoxiousness were mere stages, phases to live through and laugh about later. To Rory they were straws on the camel's back, nails in some coffin. The bathroom was always occupied, food never stayed put in the refrigerator, doors were left unlocked, keys were lost, mail accidentally thrown away, liquor watered down, phone bills ballooning, bad influences gathering on the back porch.

Rory woke one night to hear a girl's laughter, the hisses of people shushing her. Beau's TV voice selling something. Rory flung the covers over snoring Marta and stomped, naked, to the sliding glass door of the porch, *his* porch, goddammit. Three teenagers sat on the glider, cigarettes in their hands, Beau leaning on the screened sill, speaking. "Are you sponging

off your wife? Unemployed? Pussy-whipped?" His friends
laughed, swinging languidly. Rory's rage nearly drove him to
opening the door, hurling his fists in Beau's fleshy face. But
his nudity prevented him. He returned to the bedroom and
dressed, then slipped quietly out the front door and walked all
eight miles to his house in the barrio.

FOR A WHILE he cooled off. He thought about
everything he did not know about Marta, the vast expanse of
her past, the numerous pieces of it he had nothing to do with.
It dawned on him for the first time that Beau was not going to
go away. He'd understood these things intellectually when he
married, but now there was the boy at his other home, his wife
who loved that boy, who'd given birth to him, who'd once
made love with his father. What had seemed morally correct
in allowing Beau to come stay with them now was obviously a
naive man's mistake.

Marta phoned him but Rory let the machine take her calls.
Though he knew it was unfair, he let himself blame her for
Beau. He decided to accept a job at a print shop and worked
seventy hours his first week, sending his paycheck to Marta
without explanation. A few days later she was waiting on his
front step when he got off work, her feet drawn up under her
Indian skirt, a worried frown on her sweet face as she pulled
a prickly pear spine from her thumb. Rory was immediately
sorry for what he'd put her through, his anger gone that fast.
He loved her; he would overcome his hostility toward Beau,
he told her.

"I'm so glad you said that," Marta said later, as they lay on
Rory's mattress on the floor. Their sex had been wonderful.
Rory remembered—the way one remembers in the middle of
the day last night's dreams—how tough times inspired better
lovemaking. Marta ran her finger along the inside of her thigh,
absently wiping away semen. She said, "Beau's promised to
get along, too. He's had a hard life, you know, I wasn't much
of a mother when he was young."

"I can't believe that," Rory said. He could conceive of nothing bad about her tonight. He took her hand, touched the wet finger and felt a thrill of connectedness link them.

"No, it's true. I always wanted to please his father and I just kind of ignored Beau. I put him second. He's paying me back by being nasty to you."

"You think?"

"Oh, I'm sure of it. He and I have had some really good talks since you've been gone. We're really communicating."

"Huh." Rory was content to discuss Beau from this distance and in simplified terms, naked in bed with his wife, peacefully watching the orange light of sunset enshrine the room. The idea of rehabilitating the boy again interested him, gave him the energy of virtuous intentions. They would go hiking, he decided. He could tell Beau about cacti and snakes and rock formations.

And so Rory left his little house and went back to the one where Marta and Beau had been living without him. It took him a long time, but eventually he persuaded Beau to come hiking. They took off on a cool, clear February morning, driving to the parking lot at Sabino Canyon. Rory had decided an easy walk was the best way to initiate the boy to the wilderness. They followed the paved trail for a few miles, Beau already huffing and puffing, then took a side path toward a spring Rory knew. Beau stopped a few yards down the dirt trail and pulled his canvas loafers off, one at a time, shaking stones from them. "Sorry-ass nature," he muttered.

"You could have borrowed my other boots," Rory said, fighting to keep annoyance from his voice. *Pansy*, he thought.

"Wouldn't fit."

"What size shoe do you wear?"

"Eleven. Lot bigger than you." He squinted. "Double E," he added.

"Well. I'm average, I guess. Nine and a half."

Beau dropped heavily on a rock and wiped his sweating face with both hands. "What are we doing out here?" he asked then. "I mean, what is the point?"

Rory squatted, wishing a covey of quail would appear, a mule deer or rattler. He would have liked a more striking illustration of The Point. Apparently the mountain and silence were not sufficient. He tried honesty. "Your mother wants us to be friends."

"Uh huh." Beau sighed. Rory tried to remember when he was thirteen. He and his mother had always lived together in Tucson, just the two of them, companions. He'd been agile, physically and mentally, the student good teachers liked and bad teachers hated. He was quick and sensitive, hadn't caused his mother problems, but then she'd never remarried, so he hadn't had to share her love. He tried to put himself in Beau's place, but found little to latch on to. The boy's large lumpy presence prevented it.

Beau said, "I really don't want to hike up this hill."

"I appreciate your frankness. What would you like to do instead?"

"Nothing. Go home and watch TV."

Rory stretched his hands above his head to keep from throttling him. "Fine."

Thereafter, Rory arranged to spend two nights a week at his little house in the barrio. It was a compromise, a way for Beau to continue living with them without driving Rory crazy. When Marta and Beau began their idiotic conversations—wheedling and relenting, whining and acceding—Rory had only to recall that he would be at his own house, by himself, soon.

Curiously, Beau became interested in bodybuilding, probably from having watched so much late-night cable television. He persuaded Marta to buy him a membership at a health club and began working out seven days a week. At first, Rory was simply grateful to have Beau gone. Plus, the boy's enthusiasm for something, however insidiously dull to Rory, lifted his spirits. Marta would drive him to the club and then he would jog home. His friends changed; now muscular, older, non-smoking boys would come home with him. Beau pleaded with his mother until Marta agreed to buy him vitamins, which overran the kitchen windowsill and refrigerator shelf. Every meal, Beau would shake out a dozen or more and swallow them with a viscous bran drink he whipped up in the blender.

Muscles began taking shape. His face found angles. He now

lay out in the sun when he came home from school and soon had a fine tan to go with his biceps and deltoids. He lost weight in his jowls and belly and gained inches in his chest and arms. Though he was no more pleasant to live with, he *was* easier on the eyes. He lived and breathed physical fitness, criticizing dancers on MTV for lazy muscle tone, complaining about the school cafeteria's high-fat food, remarking on which peers he could most certainly pulverize. As he watched Rory critically one morning, he asked, "What can you press?"

"A trigger," Rory answered.

To distract them all, however, came the announcement that Marta was pregnant. They had been trying, then not trying, for the whole first year of their marriage. Rory's reaction to the news was just as ambivalent; he'd been more taken with the idea before he met Beau. But Marta's age had pushed them into a corner: now or never.

Pregnancy was good to her. Her hair thickened, her complexion shone. Rory was fascinated to watch the brown line at her pubis make its way up her body, dividing her. Their sex improved because of the necessary inventiveness. On her knees, off the side of the bed, in the tub. She was a willing partner. The baby's revolutions in her womb were sometimes so violent Rory could feel them while he and Marta were coupled, and that too elevated his passion.

Tests were administered. She lay on a gurney and they and the midwife watched the baby perform on screen. In a freeze-frame his budding penis was pointed out to them. He became David then, named *in utero* for Rory's father, and when he was delivered Rory took him in his arms and welcomed him, teary-eyed, to the new world.

Beau, for the first few months of David's life, was a model older brother. So overwhelmed had they been with baby preparations, Beau's fifteenth birthday had passed unnoticed, remembered by Marta in the recovery room, at which point she called him to apologize.

"No sweat," he'd said calmly. And now he held his brother in his meaty arms. Rory could not get over the stunning fact that both these dissimilar creatures had emerged from Marta.

When the baby could hold his head up, they went as a family to the mall and had a portrait made, Beau cradling David, Rory with his hands protectively on Marta's shoulders, all four of them looking at the same stuffed toucan on the photographer's tripod.

Marta and Rory had read aloud to each other the dangers of expecting too much from a baby, of postpartum depression, of difficult babies, so Rory was not worried when he did not feel, initially, what he would have called love for David. He found it hard to kiss the baby; he was such a light parcel that Rory always lifted him with too much force, upsetting the child. And it was clear already that he would prefer Marta, who had infinite reserves of patience.

David did not thrive. His measurements and weight put him in the tenth percentile for his age group, a figure that gradually dropped to the single digits. "Beau was little, too," Marta would tell Rory desperately, as if he might blame her. "It's genetic." Nonetheless, the pediatrician began cautioning them about possible diseases. David had to gain a full pound in the next month or be put in the hospital for tests.

Marta, who had taken maternity leave, quit her job altogether. Her swollen breasts leaked milk; she had enough for two or three babies. David ate frequently, but only for a few minutes each time. Marta began looking nocturnal, her eyes circled by dark rings, her skin jaundiced. Most often Rory found her on their bed, shirt raised, anxiously coaxing David to latch on and suck.

"Maybe we should try that high-cal formula," Rory suggested.

Marta's eyes were wet. "I didn't get to breastfeed Beau when he was a baby. I listened to the doctor and my mother and my husband and just about everyone except myself. I want this baby to be different."

"He can be different in every other way."

"Oh, Rory, I'm so scared." She looked down at the baby and her shoulders shook, causing her nipple to escape his lips. Milk dribbled on her loose belly and the baby cried, a sound from which Rory reflexively retreated. He knew he should go

to his wife, hold her, and assure her she was an exemplary
mother. All day long she had no escape here at home from the
immediacy of their tiny child, whose unhappy piercing voice
filled the house. In his whole life, no one had as clearly needed
Rory as Marta did now. He knew the right thing but he did
not seem able to do it—the movement to the bed would have
embarrassed him unbearably, he was perplexed and annoyed
to discover. Instead, he turned without saying a word and went
to the refrigerator for a beer.

Beau stood at the sink running water absently over his
hands. When Rory slammed the refrigerator door, the boy
barked a laugh. "Steady," he said, mocking Rory by using an
expression Rory often used himself.

"Shut your fucking mouth, I'm not kidding."

Beau turned off the water and faced Rory. He gripped the
counter so that his muscles flexed, then squinted menacingly
as if sizing up an opponent. He was no longer the weakling
he'd once been and Rory felt in a flash the monstrous foe
Beau had become. Suddenly the boy feinted toward him, arms
positioned like a wrestler's. Rory raised his beer bottle as a
weapon, his opposite elbow as a shield. But Beau stopped
short, relaxed, and grinned at Rory as he reached past him for
the tea towel hanging on the refrigerator handle.

"Chill," he said, drying his big hands.

AT WORK a woman named Lily flirted with Rory.
Where Marta was compact and voluptuous, this woman was
rangy and angular. Her seduction lacked any of Marta's shy
smiles and wide innocent eyes. Instead, she bumped into him
every opportunity she got, as if she could not control those
long-reaching appendages of hers. Her hip would slide across
his butt as they passed in a narrow hallway, her chin brush his
shoulder when she watched him proof copy. Rory sometimes
fantasized about her, the way she bent at the waist when she
fed the press, the way her hair always covered a fraction of her
face and made her that percentage unknown.

Fortunately, baby David's health improved. When he was

eight months old he had a sudden growth spurt and no longer had to be wakened at night to eat. He loved the starchy solids the doctor had put him on, trying to feed himself much earlier than was normal. It was as if he'd suddenly realized he could not escape this world and might as well embrace it, feast on its offerings. His baby milestones began coming quickly, moments that Marta alerted Rory to when he returned home at night.

"Watch this," she'd say, setting David in his crib. The boy would look around puzzled for a second, then reach for the bars and pull himself to standing. Marta and Rory clapped and David crowed at their pleasure. The baby's feats fascinated Rory; human habits he had taken for granted all his adult life now came to David fresh and forced Rory to reevaluate them. When the baby focused on his own hand, rotating it and crossing his eyes in concentration, Rory made a fist and looked at *his* hand, wondering for the first time in years at its complex dexterity. When David squealed in fear as the military jets flew over and shook the house, Rory was newly awakened to their deafening noise. It seemed you could forget to respond to the world; David was reminding him how.

Rory discovered one day that he'd been ignoring Lily's overtures, that he hadn't noticed her clothes or hair lately, and was happy in his unconscious fidelity. At home, the phone company sent a warning that he hadn't paid the bill for his barrio house and Rory realized he hadn't actually visited the place in over a month. He thought he had left his bachelorhood behind him for good and was glad, taking his new roles on with renewed enthusiasm.

Because Marta had quit working they no longer could afford Nautilus or megavitamins, things she felt terribly guilty about denying Beau. "I'll buy you a once-a-day vitamin," she explained to him. "All the rest are superfluous, anyway. And you can keep in shape doing yardwork or running at the school track."

Beau sputtered at her ignorance of such things. Rory felt both sympathy and amusement, perversely glad that the boy's extravagant lifestyle would now halt. Beau phoned his father in New Jersey for the first time since he'd moved in nearly three years ago. Apparently there was no help coming from that quarter, either.

Beau's body lost its tone fairly fast. He ate all the junky food he'd abstained from as if making up for lost time. His fat was differently arranged now, puffing up in his neck and chin, cushioning what had been his chest and shoulder muscles. Marta felt terrible that he had given up.

Rory said, and believed, "He'll snap out of it."

And for David's first birthday party, Beau brought a girl. She, too, was marble-white–skinned and overweight, but amiable enough, Rory thought. Beau spent the afternoon keeping his eyes downcast, awkward and gruff at having introduced a girl at home. Marta was thrilled. Her elder son had a girlfriend, her younger son was already walking and saying a few words. Rory enjoyed her pride in them.

A few weeks later Beau babysat David while Rory and Marta celebrated their third anniversary. Home early, they discovered Beau's door shut and locked, and David standing in his crib yelling. After calming the baby, Marta rapped on Beau's door. Eventually, both Beau and his girlfriend emerged, the girl terrified and Beau pissed off, both disheveled, blinking in the bright lights. The next day while Beau was at school, Marta pulled back his covers and discovered semen spots on the sheets. She greeted Rory with this find when he got home from work.

"Talk to him," she requested.

But Beau began spending less and less of his time at home, something Rory wished to encourage, and so he never spoke with him about his presumed sexual activity. Instead, Rory looked into selling his little house. Though the market was not particularly a seller's, he owned the place free and clear, and they could use the money. Rory contacted a real estate agent without telling Marta, wishing to surprise her with a check in the not-so-distant future. He and Mr. Blylock met at the barrio alley that backed the house.

They shook hands and Blylock cleared his throat. "I believe you said the structure was uninhabited?"

"Right." Rory fished in his pocket for his hefty key ring.
"My old bachelor pad."

"I believe there's someone there now," Blylock said, not
following Rory to the door. "I believe I heard some activity
inside." He cleared his throat again, politely, and scuffed his
wingtip in the dirt.

"What the—" Rory flipped through his keys looking for the
square-headed one that fit the lock, flipped through again,
faster. When he could not find it, he realized what had happened and rage filled him like poison. "You fucking punk!"
he screamed at the back door, fists rapid-fire on the wood.
"Open this fucking door!"

Blylock had returned to his sedan, parked in the alley. Rory
whirled when he heard the engine turn over.

"Where the hell are you going?" he yelled. Blylock
reached with one hand to press his doorlock down and the
other to shift into reverse. He drove away without a glance
at Rory.

Rory picked up a rock and smashed the back-door glass out
of the small window. He reached through and released the
latch. He stormed into his bedroom still holding the rock,
intending to use it on Beau's head. No one was there. Rory
thought for an instant he'd lost his mind. But then he saw the
sheets and comforter, tangled in a gray knot on the floor,
and a litter of soda cans and cigarette butts which were still,
respectively, cool and warm. A ventilating breeze sifted
through from the open front door.

Rory lifted the phone receiver and was greeted with silence.
He walked to the Circle K on the corner and made three calls:
to a locksmith, to the phone company, and to Marta. "I'm
staying in town for a while," he told her.

THIS TIME Marta brought David with her when she
came to the barrio. The two of them were sitting in the side-
yard dirt when Rory arrived home from the print shop. He'd
had lunch with Lily that afternoon and felt her bare foot on
his calf under the table. The memory pulsed through him like

electricity all day. He had to shift gears when he saw his wife and son.

Marta looked older to him, partially because of Lily, who was only twenty-five, and partially because the contrast between Marta and David was so dramatic. She could have been his grandmother.

"He said *other house*," Marta told Rory, blinking up at him expectantly. "You're such a big boy," she congratulated David. She wore her glasses, which shrank the size of her eyes, hair in a stumpy ponytail, and her bell-bottom jeans from fifteen years ago. Again, the image of Lily superimposed itself, her sleek business clothing and clean blond hair.

Rory knelt to hug David. David grunted until Rory extended his arm to include Marta, telling himself she was the real thing, knowing it was true.

"I can't live with Beau," Rory said.

"I called his father. He's leaving Saturday."

Stunned, Rory dropped from kneeling to sitting, David on his thigh. "Just like that?"

"Yep."

"Did he tell you what happened?"

"Mostly lies. It was Donna who told me."

"The fat girl?"

Marta laughed, wiping her mouth with her hand and leaving a streak of dirt like a mustache above her lip. Once, Rory would have cleaned her face but today he let her go on with it dirty.

She said, "He's made no effort to be civil to you, I realize that, and I told him I couldn't have that in my house."

Rory, in getting what he wanted, began offering compromises. "He could at least finish the school year. It'd be hard to switch this late."

Marta nodded. "He has reservations Saturday, though, and his father expects him. But it's up to you. Whatever you think."

Rory, empowered, decided to be reasonable. "He can stay until summer."

★　★　★

A calendar hung on the barrio kitchen wall, days until the end of the public school year. Rory marked through them with great pleasure, seven days at a time, as he now spent only one night a week in his little house.

He'd decided to plant a wall of prickly pear around his tiny property to hide the cyclone fencing his neighbors had recently installed. Prickly pear was cheap and easy and reproduced its comical ears in a matter of weeks. He envisioned a low-maintenance, living moat of isolation. Scavenging the neighborhood he and Marta lived in, he found huge piles of the cactus where the newest part of the development was going up. As he loaded the prickly pear into his car, Rory realized that planting it meant he was not going to sell his other house. In town, he poked the ears into the dry ground.

When he looked up from his work, just after dusk, he saw Lily standing at his gate clutching her purse, which gave her a prayerful look. "I wasn't anywhere near the neighborhood," she called out. "I drove halfway from hell to get here so I thought I'd drop in."

Rory stood, leaving his work gloves on, as if they might protect him. "I'm really busy and I don't have anything to offer you to drink," he said. She smiled, her white teeth luminous in the darkening air. He added, "Come in."

Not counting Beau's fat girl and Marta, Lily was the first woman in more than four years who'd slept on Rory's mattress.

As if in punishment, the next morning Marta called to tell Rory the baby had a fever and blood in his stool.

THEIR little boy had started to lose weight again. He had never had the baby chubbiness of other American children but now he looked Third World. The pediatrician arranged for tests, which meant an overnight stay at the hospital. David's combined symptoms did not add up to any easily diagnosed disease. It was possible he had several, possible he had none.

Marta settled herself in for the night, pulling two chairs together beside the sterile crib, speaking in her normal cheerful voice to David so as not to alarm him, naming all the surrounding medical paraphernalia the way she might animals at the zoo, and David would earnestly repeat the words in his singsong voice.

"My other son was very small, too," Marta had told the doctor, over and over, had told anyone willing to listen, her voice just on the edge of shrill. Rory looked at David now and wondered how much of the boy was Marta, how much himself, how much the baby's failure to thrive had to do with the mix.

"Rory," Marta said, "Rory, will you do me a favor?"

He joined her at David's crib, that tiny bed in the bowels of monstrous St. Mary's. Air-conditioning sucked at the atmosphere, muffling the ordinary sounds of living. Rory thought of death, circulating in the cooling system. Their son was coaxed onto his side, where he lay blinking as he fought sleep—another human habit, resisting that abundant lapse— his long lashes slowing their fluttering until finally pressed together, at ease. David's small mouth was slack and Rory could see his son's lips lose their wet sheen as his steady breathing dried them.

Because here, in the hospital, it seemed it could happen, he was going to say, "What if he stops?" but Marta was already speaking.

"Rory, will you do me a favor and stay with Beau tonight?"

DRIVING HOME ALONE, Rory finally had time to think of what he'd done the night before. There was no thrill in the memory of Lily's skin and breasts, of her scent on his fingers. She meant nothing to him, less now than before. She'd been a temptation, a forbidden novelty, and now she was not even that. Marta would not find out, but if she did, she would forgive him, Rory knew, so that Lily had as little leverage in his life as she did in his desire.

Somehow this conclusion did not cheer Rory. When he

pulled into the driveway, he sat in the car for a few minutes collecting himself, trying to catch hold of the scattered energy he felt flicking through him.

The house was dark and Rory hoped he would catch Beau fucking Donna in there. He wanted to have a genuine reason for a scene. The front door would not open when he unlocked it; apparently Beau had thrown the deadbolt from inside. Rory stormed to the back, to the sliding glass door, and was gleeful to discover that it, too, had been fortified from inside, a broomstick in its track. He pounded on the glass.

"Here we go again, you fucking moron! Open the goddamned door!" His voice filled the quiet neighborhood. Nothing stirred inside. Rory then tore through the ugly chokeberry beneath the windows, wrenching at each metal frame, waiting for one to give. He rounded the house, clanging the gate behind him, his fury growing. At David's room, the glass slid so easily Rory nearly broke it. He clambered through, dropping onto a toybox, kicking Legos from his path.

At the bedroom door he stopped, sniffed the air. David's room smelled of fried chicken, french fries, other food. Dog shit. He flipped the switch and saw that the baby's crib was filled with trash, fast-food wrappers, chicken bones, crumbs, oily stains, and spilled drinks. Picking through it, Rory discovered a pile of shit centered on the baby's pillow.

Rory's body carried him before he could see where. The next thing he knew, his thumbs were deep in Beau's flesh and he was presenting him with the choices of getting killed or getting the hell out.

DAVID came home having gained a few ounces. Marta and Rory took turns feeding him meals, spooning the high-fat milkshakes into his mouth, praising his every swallow.

"It's so ironic," Marta said as David shook his head *no* to an offered bite. "We got upset when Beau ate too much, and this one, this little David—" She waved the spoon tantalizingly at David's pursed lips and sighed. "Isn't it ironic?" The test results from St. Mary's were so far inconclusive and Rory felt the passage of each day as a stay from doom. He had cleaned the baby's bed the night he returned home and had told Marta only about the food remains. Beau had left and there seemed no point in mentioning the shit, which Rory had decided was not a dog's but Beau's.

At work, Rory ignored Lily. She took every opportunity she could to bad-mouth him to the other women, which he thought was probably a good thing, all in all, simplifying his life, cutting down in advance other opportunities of transgression. He rarely visited his barrio house, though one night, drunk from after-work happy hour, he'd driven to it without thinking, out of a kind of homing instinct. He realized his mistake only a block or two away from the house and corrected himself, wheeled a wide U-turn and drove to the suburbs and his family, to the triangle he was a part of, to the life he had chosen.

Later, when David was out of the woods, well and normal, when Marta had returned to her job, when Lily had been transferred, when another woman had narrowly failed to tempt Rory, Beau's father called one Sunday morning to tell them Beau had tried to kill himself. Marta and Rory had just finished making love, an unsatisfactory session in which Rory had been chafed raw before coming.

"He cleaned out the medicine chest," Marta's other husband said. Beau was sedated now, in a hospital in New Jersey.

Rory listened to Marta talk to Beau's father while he got dressed, idly picturing the boy—the bulk of him beneath a white sheet—as he pulled a T-shirt over his head, laced his boots, combed his thinning hair. He heard Marta crying as he closed the front door behind him.

He could hear her now as he went from room to room in his other house. The sound penetrated his heavy walls and the dusty air. With his fist, he killed a line of ants working obliviously in his kitchen, furiously moving food from one place to another, marching over the bodies of their dead comrades. Rory trailed them outside and to their mounded little home. He got a can of STP from the car and poured it over the crawling line, into the hole itself. Still they worked on, side-stepping, creating new paths, wasting no time. Rory saw they were invincible and gave up. He sat down in defeat on his back stoop. In the yard, as if in further testament to the fate of his old home, trash and tumbleweeds had blown here and stayed, a wall of garbage and refuse, held tenaciously by the spines of the prickly pear shrub Rory had not so long ago planted.

THE CONTROL GROUP

T V MITCHELL fell in love with his fourth-grade teacher. An odd and uncomfortable prospect, his love was a secret he confessed to nobody, not that there was anybody he could have confessed to, and not that he quite understood his feelings as, in fact, ones of love. He knew simply an unbearable ache like illness, the knot in his gut Mrs. Dugas could tie and twist with such torque he thought he might, quite literally, die.

And TV, alone among his nine-year-old peers at Hamilton Elementary, *did* comprehend death. Unlike his baffling love for his fifty-two-year-old teacher, he spoke freely about that which he understood. His mother had murdered her father, TV's grandfather. TV's tale did not differ substantially from the other gruesome stories heard over lunch from the boys' corner of the playground, but his had the unbeatable edge of truth. The others might escalate their stakes, recount babysitters finding dripping blood in the bath or vampires under the bed, phone calls from hatchet-bearing mental escapees, timely electrical blackouts, hairy hands sprouting from the seeming innocence of wing chairs or garden spigots.

But they couldn't outdo TV's penetrating simplicity. "She pounded him with a hammer," he told the boys. They stood scuffing dirt, hands balled in front pockets. "She stuffed a handkerchief in his mouth," TV went on, "to keep him quiet." He carried the handkerchief with him for further drama, its pure whiteness and ancient embroidered monogram somehow proof enough. TVM, his grandfather's and his own initials, the navy threads worn nearly away under TV's worrying fingertips. A single blow to the forehead, a round blue contusion meant to resemble a bruise from an accidental fall.

MRS. DUGAS'S classroom was a portable annex set off from the rest of the school. Her students studied, primarily, animals. There were tanks of fish and gerbils and mice and miniature frogs and little chicks who'd been hatched from plain eggs under a heat lamp. Those eggs that did not result in chicks were buried outside the annex, cracked open and poured into a hole deep enough to discourage roaming dogs. Embryonic beaks and feet could be identified floating in the bloody yolk. A snapping turtle had once escaped from Mrs. Dugas's room and now lived beneath the annex. When the class read, they read about the migration of loons, or about panda bears whose babies were so small they could get lost in their own mothers' fur. History was the study of those animals who were now extinct. Mrs. Dugas taught evolution, made all the children remove their shoes and contemplate their fifth, finlike, useless little toes, which would someday disappear. Her favorite subject was science. The same day TV had stepped into her classroom, Mrs. Dugas introduced two rats who would help the students understand the dangers of Coke and potato chips and candy bars.

They wrote in their experiment diaries. One rat would be given vegetables and cheese and milk; the other would eat Bugles and Fruit Loops and Orange Crush. TV was grateful for the rats, as they held the attention that otherwise would surely have been directed toward him. The children named the control rat Batman and the junk-food rat Joker. On Friday afternoons the animals were packed off to different homes, each child promising to maintain the experiment.

The changes came quickly, Joker's white coat turning slightly gray, his tail losing its pink, his eyes their shine. TV had thought neither of the rats especially handsome but eventually, by comparison, Joker became ugly. Batman continued to look the way he had. Bigger, better. They sat in their two cages, next to each other, one eating an apple wedge, one a Frito. Both rats spent most of their time standing on their hind legs reaching for the screens that kept them caged. TV had noted that, though Joker *looked* worse, he didn't seem to *feel* worse. Moreover, it was Batman, the rat named as control, who ate the more exotic diet. TV couldn't remember when he himself had last eaten a raw vegetable. But, of course, that was Mrs. Dugas's point. When TV's turn came to take home a rat, he was happy to get Joker. He cheated, poking into the cage little cubes of cheddar cheese and a nutritious piece of wheat toast. Joker obliged by eating whatever was shoved his way. TV had worried Mrs. Dugas would not give him an opportunity with a rat. It seemed natural to him that she might have reservations concerning his character. But though he looked for fretfulness in her face the Friday he departed the annex with Joker in his traveling cage, she did not reveal any.

That weekend the temperature dropped into the negative. TV, believing Joker needed more space to move, turned him loose in a large cardboard box that had once held a microwave oven. He reinforced the top flaps with three volumes of the encyclopedia to make sure he wouldn't escape. In the morning he found the rat frozen, curled in what he assumed was a death position. He immediately thought of fleeing; he could not face Mrs. Dugas. Screaming his foster mother's name, he ran to her bedroom. He made note of the fact that he could see his breath.

"He can't have frozen," his foster mother told him, groggily following to the box. The rat lay where he'd been, scraggly and dead. His foster mother squatted, laying her forefinger warily on the animal's chest.

"Hibernation," she diagnosed after a moment. She carried the box to the floor heat register in the hallway and set it down. "He'll thaw," she assured TV, then giggled. "I'd like to call the landlord and tell him even the rats are freezing."

But TV found nothing about the situation comical. He watched Joker slowly come to. When he fed him, later, he

made sure the food was bad, a lidful of red wine, a few chocolate chips.

In the end no gesture would have made any impression
whatsoever. At the conclusion of the experiment, Week 10, a
man from a lab came and took both rats away. TV was
shocked. He had assumed the next step would be to rehabili-
tate Joker, record in their diaries the bringing back of his shiny
eyes and coat. The class asked if they couldn't take the rats
home to keep as pets. Mrs. Dugas explained that experimental
animals had to be destroyed. Joker and Batman went together.
As consolation, Joker's leftover box of Cracker Jacks was
passed around the room for the kids to eat.

TV's new foster mother said, "I wonder which lesson will
stick? You Are What You Eat? or, Life Sucks?"

But TV began loving Mrs. Dugas then, trusting her to judge
him without sentimentality. She did not, it was clear, feel sorry
for anyone.

T V had moved in with his new foster mother just three
months ago. He was, actually, unsure he would stay with
her. The last foster arrangement had not worked out; the
committee deciding his future had tried an opposite approach
this time, placing him not with a large family, as he had been
last time, but with a single woman. This was intended to
replicate his natural situation, though in his real life he had
also lived with his grandfather. Joanne Link, his new parent,
had another month left on trial time. She could turn him
back, he understood that. He was trying to behave. She was
preferable, mostly, by default. TV felt Joanne sometimes
watching him. They had discussed his mother a few times,
approaching the subject delicately, Joanne only too eager to
back off. She did not ask him questions point blank, pretending she wasn't interested in the details. For instance, TV
had heard his mother and her boyfriend Wade planning to kill
TV's grandfather. The old man had been sick for a long time,
peeing his bed and screaming at people. In more lucid moments, he would apologize, saying, "I forget myself." Wade

wanted to inject him with an air bubble. Apparently, air could kill you.

TV had stood on the landing in his old house listening to his grandfather wheeze in an upstairs room, his mother and Wade talking in a downstairs one. He had no idea what to do. His stealth in returning unheard to bed gave him a headache, which he nursed through the night into genuine illness. The next day, however, he did not want to remain at home with his grandfather, afraid he would be included in the conspiracy, participant or victim.

But his grandfather lived for months following TV's eavesdropping. TV had convinced himself it was a nightmare, had been on the verge of confessing this to his mother when he came home one day from school to find his whole life turned inside out; that is, what he'd held close and fought in himself suddenly was free, open to anyone's inspection.

Though Joanne sympathized with him, he could tell he made her nervous. She embarrassed easily and, when driven to exclamation, would not say *Shit*! but *Sugar*! She was likable, that way. But alien. She provided TV with a generous allowance and, on weekends, let him loose and seemed happy not to know what he did. They shared a small apartment in a dirty neighborhood miles and miles from Hamilton Elementary, which was by reputation one of the best schools in Wichita. TV rode the bus.

MRS. DUGAS made it standard policy to invite the children to her home once during the year. She lived near a drainage canal and after the twenty-two fourth graders had consumed Dixie cups of orange juice and a sesame rice cake each, a rabbit-watching expedition embarked. Three mothers—the drivers—opted to stay in Mrs. Dugas's living room with a tag-along toddler. Mrs. Dugas herself changed shoes and tied a peach chiffon scarf over her hair so that she could join the search.

"Do we frighten rabbits?" she asked the group before opening the gate between her tidy yard and the wild canal. It was late spring in Kansas, but the sky looked as if it could still threaten snow. Houses precisely like Mrs. Dugas's lined both sides of the cement-walled canal, and TV imagined them sliding in, crumpling, all of them except Mrs. Dugas's. The dank odor of stagnant water drifted in the air. "Do we frighten rabbits?"

"No," the girls in the class answered.

"Do we jab sticks in their homes or throw rocks at their tails?"

Again, the girls chimed no.

"Do we take nature as we find it, not as we wish to manipulate it?"

A few girls, shivering, eager to get on with the hunt, having sensed the general direction of this line of questioning, answered once more in the negative. Mrs. Dugas raised her eyebrows. TV's heart lurched; he could make out the little quiver her lip made toward smiling. It was her eyebrows, still black despite her silver hair, that most intrigued him. She knew something he wished to learn.

"Yes, yes," the girls amended.

Mrs. Dugas opened her gate. She had shared with them her secret method of watching the rabbits, the way she had discovered them years ago by coming to the canal to think—about what? TV wondered desperately—sitting down among the broken pieces of concrete and holding perfectly still until she became part of the picture, the life already there soon forgetting her presence and getting on with business. "They see the world differently," she told her class. "They rely on movement, on instinct." She could wiggle her nose, a gesture that meant disapproval. She could hear, from one end of her fourth grade annex to the other, the illicit whisper of notes being passed, of secrets on the verge of leaving lips. Hostile looks, cast between enemies, reflected unerringly from the satellite of her sharp eyes. TV would watch her eyebrows, the lift that signaled unspoken intercession.

He followed her down the canal. Some days it mattered to him what the boys thought but other days he couldn't remember to care. They had been a group since kindergarten, neighbors and Cub Scouts together, summer camp initiates. TV's acceptance into their midst was based on his mother's celebrity, his own frankness concerning her crime and incarceration. Around Mrs. Dugas he felt a twinge taking advantage of his mother's notoriety, so around her he pretended the boys had not accepted him. He pretended he had higher matters on his mind, the same matters, coincidentally, that Mrs. Dugas seemed to have on hers—rabbits, today, perhaps a pheasant.

True to her anecdotes in the classroom, Mrs. Dugas soon settled on a broken piece of concrete and proceeded to stop moving. She had changed her clear lenses for sunglasses. The last motion she made was to secure the chiffon scarf's knot under her chin. TV knelt a few yards from her. While she waited for rabbits, he stared at her.

ON TUESDAYS, after school, TV took his regular bus home, then boarded a city line to his psychologist's office in a medical complex that resembled a strip mall. For a while, the psychologist had discussed adopting him. Then his wife had gotten pregnant and the idea had been dropped. They talked about Joanne a lot, the psychologist making sure she was better than the last family, assuaging his own guilt. They'd made jokes about General Patton, the name they gave the father at the first home. TV's own name was not short for anything less ridiculous, simpy TV. It was his mother's little joke on her father, whose name had been Terrence Valley Mitchell.

TV's psychologist liked the fact that Joanne was studying to be a psychiatric nurse, though he worried openly about her weak financial setup. "It's true you can't buy happiness," he told TV, "but you *can* buy better odds."

After their sessions, TV walked across the street to a Russell Stover candy shop and bought a chocolate turtle. Waiting for his bus home, he rewarded himself for another week safely passed.

★ ★ ★

DURING the time TV squatted in the dried weeds growing from the upended chunks of canal concrete at Mrs. Dugas's, he devised a plan. He would invite Mrs. Dugas to lunch next Saturday. He would take his saved allowance and meet her somewhere he could reach by bus. Soon it would be summer, he would leave her classroom forever. His love for her frightened him; he did not want to kiss her or see her naked. He did not know exactly what he wanted but he felt a hunger, a physical depth of daily need for her that was going to be denied him.

On the ride back to school, in the cramped quarters of a foreign station wagon, a few kids claimed to have seen rabbits. The boys, in fear, in respect, out of anger, asked TV if he'd seen any.

He shook his head, though in truth, he had. Mrs. Dugas, without turning around, had lifted her arm slowly so as not to seem out of keeping with the rest of the animal's picture, knowing TV was behind her, knowing he would follow the point. A small brown rabbit sat terrified between the rocks.

HE PHONED her while Joanne was still at the hospital, hanging up on her husband the first time, feeling ashamed when she answered—as if she knew—the second.

Before inviting her he thanked her for the orange juice. She told him, formally, perhaps with irritation, he was most welcome. He would have hung up if he had not heard her turn the receiver away and cough, once, a moist sound that carried through the line and gave TV a window of vulnerability, a shot.

"Can you go to lunch with me?" he asked. "At the . . ." he blinked hard at the Yellow Pages he'd found, the penciled line he'd drawn beneath the ideal establishment now invisible. "Depot!" he cried. "The Depot, on this Saturday, at twelve noon?"

Her pause sent sweat streaming down his ribs. He imagined

a most amorphous Mr. Dugas turning a newspaper, receiving his wife's curious raised eyebrows with a smile. He heard the rustle of wild rabbits in the dry grass. TV sat on the floor heat register, the only square of warmth in the whole apartment, sat there in Joanne's director's chair asking his teacher for a date. The lead of the pencil in his hand snapped, the Yellow page tore, his rubber-soled hightop shoes melted onto the metal register and lifted the cover when he raised his feet. He panicked, thinking immediately of fire, of having to roll in the frayed and undersized Oriental carpet runner in the hall. The cover banged down in place just as Mrs. Dugas spoke.

"What?" TV nearly shouted. "I—"

She repeated, "I would be pleased."

HE MADE a dry run on Friday after school. The day had been difficult, the subject of murder having come up during a lesson on buffaloes in the Wild West. But it came up everywhere, and it always would. Later, at the tornado drill, TV had abstained from attempting to peek up Mrs. Dugas's skirt with the other children, girls as well as boys, while she canvassed the halls, checking for exposed necks or proximity to windows. In his anxiety, he had not looked her in the eye all day, not wanting to give her the opportunity to cancel.

After school, he leapt from the school bus and ran hard for the city stop, taking the first downtown bus that came. Not until it was too late did he realize he'd chosen an East-West line instead of a North-South. He wound up at the transit station, a mile from his destination, near tears. This dry run would predict tomorrow's outcome, he felt. He did not want to fail. After calming himself and then consulting the elaborate city map on the wall, he took off running once more, ducking in and out of the rush-hour traffic, taking shortcuts through alleys. TV had grown up in his grandfather's old house on the east side. Wichita's downtown, though not large by any real measure, still was daunting. TV crossed a set of railroad tracks without realizing a train, moving slowly, had been approaching, the red lights of the crossing flashing, the bells

ringing. A flagman, free hand on his hip, shouted out, wanted
to know if TV was trying to kill himself. He ran on.

The Depot, true to its name, was located near the tracks.
But it didn't appear to have existed for very long; it had never
been a real depot, the only concession to authenticity a blue-
and-white sign announcing its name. TV had counted on atmosphere, a romantic setting of shoeshine stands and antiquated
arrival and departure charts. Its awnings, maroon, full of water, were torn. A Christmas scene, months or possibly years
out of date, had been soaped onto the front windows and never
washed off. TV entered, setting an alarm buzzing which ceased
when the door slid shut.

"We are not opened," a voice shouted from the kitchen.
"Our door is, but we aren't." TV took stock of the restaurant
where he would, tomorrow, meet Mrs. Dugas. They could sit
in the farthest corner, the small table under the one clean
window. TV saw that the window was clean because it had
been replaced in the recent past, dried caulking still left on
its edges, hundreds of white fingerprints framing the glass,
suggesting a frantic coded message. Nevertheless, he and Mrs.
Dugas would sit here, she facing the window, TV the restaurant. It seemed to be a totally functional establishment, not
one part charming.

"We're closed," a woman said from behind an opening in
the cheap paneling between the dining room and kitchen. Over
her head were the words PICK UP; on the other side, over a
second opening, ORDER. New problems confronted TV.

"I know," TV said. "I'm just looking."

She leaned out and made an angry swipe at the iced tea
dispenser before disappearing into the back once more. TV
stood in the empty fluorescent-lighted restaurant ready to cry.

H E   D I D   N O T sleep well. Joanne came to his room
more than once in the night, frumpy and sour-smelling, sitting
next to him on the bed, sleepily trying to make him feel better,
misunderstanding his fear. She reminded him that he would
be able to see his mother soon, that she, Joanne, would never

prevent his seeing his mother. Yawning, she informed him that his grandfather had lived a full life, a prosperous life, that he had loved TV very much.

TV counted while she spoke. First he simply counted, and then he counted by twos, threes, sevens. His mother had struck his grandfather just once, killed him for his money. TV counted the number of strokes Joanne idly made on his back, the way her thoughtless hand fell just between his shoulder blades and ran in a perfunctory line to his waist, over and over. She was thirty-seven years old, unmarried, studying to become a psychiatric nurse. TV wanted to stay with her because he knew he could be placed in a worse situation. His first foster home resembled a halfway house, a full family of orphaned or delinquent children, an ex-Marine running the show like the military. Names were stenciled on towels and bedsheets and clothes. Joanne was not a bad sponsor; she tried to do the right thing. It just always turned out like this backrub, without any more than superficial thought of how he might feel receiving it.

Then he bagan counting rabbits, imagined himself standing above a field of them as they darted, barely visible, through the blowing grass.

J O A N N E asked him in the morning if he was part of the 69ers, a young gang in the neighborhood. Their Friday night graffiti was the apartment building's topic of conversation each Saturday morning.

"I'm not," he told her, though he had run with them just last weekend. They, too, stood in awe of TV's past. For some reason, TV could not keep the information to himself. He tried, it wasn't that he didn't try, but it spilled, always. The 69ers had become famous for drawing the sexy yin-yang symbol of their name, a linked, naked circle, man and woman.

Joanne said, blushing, "I don't object to nudity, myself, but some people, the older ones in the building, find it offensive. I would rather you didn't hang out with them, okay?"

"I won't," TV told her.

"You get enough sleep?" she asked.

"I'm fine."

"Let's do something together," Joanne said suddenly, brightly. "Want to?"

TV looked at the clock over the stove, calculating rapidly. What could she have in mind? Why today? And how long till it was satisfied?

Now Joanne scrutinized him, crossing her arms over her scrappy bathrobe. "Are you in that gang?" she demanded.

"No!" TV croaked.

She sat back and a full minute ticked by. Then she said, more confidently, "The only thing we have going for us is honesty."

"I swear to God I'm not!"

The phone rang. For a second, when Joanne didn't move, TV believed his lunch with Mrs. Dugas was not the only thing hanging in the balance. Then, after the third ring, Joanne pushed herself away from the table and scuffed to the telephone.

TV grabbed his skateboard as a prop, held it over his chest to show her his intentions, this Saturday, were wholesome. He waited for her to nod, hoping she would not note his pocketful of fives and singles, saved allowance.

She met his eyes as he threw the front door locks, then looked away, talking to one of her parents, who made her defensive. TV slipped out.

He made the same mistake he had the day before, boarding the wrong bus. He rode along hitting his thigh with his fist to prevent tears. He yanked his grandfather's handkerchief from his pocket and wiped mud off his hightops. At the transit station a cool rain began falling. He ran, his skateboard banging at his hip.

Mrs. Dugas had not arrived when he entered The Depot. He took the opportunity to claim the corner table, rolling his skateboard under it. He used the bathroom, throwing his hair over his head to dry, again and again until he was dizzy. The mirrors were not glass but aluminum, like at a roadside rest stop, as if someone might want to break them. His image was wavy and blanched, unhealthy looking. He slapped his cheeks for color.

Mrs. Dugas wore green slacks and carried an umbrella that had a map of the world on it, half a globe. She stopped at the doorway and, backing in, shook the umbrella before releasing its spring. She touched her silver hair.

"Good afternoon, TV," she said. She stood at the table until he rose, then nestled into the plastic chair across from him.

"Hello," he said. He wanted her to like him so badly he felt sure she could read it in his eyes, like a dog's. Knowing she would have other students, he other teachers, pained TV the way irreversible facts always did. "What do you want to eat?" he asked.

Mrs. Dugas squinted at the signs over the Order window. "A Monte Cristo," she told him.

TV stood and pulled his shirt down. He went to the Order window and waited, hearing the clanging of pans in the back. He cleared his throat and said, "Excuse me." He tapped the counter with his fingers. Mrs. Dugas, her back to him, appeared to be watching the rain, which gushed through a hole in the awning like a small waterfall.

"Put forth," the woman from yesterday said, motioning with her hand for him to speak.

TV ordered a Monte Cristo, french fries, two waters and ketchup. She did not write any of it down. He started to reach for his pocket to pay but she told him he paid when he picked up. He returned to the table with a playing card, the seven of hearts, which he was to insert in the napkin holder.

"But we're the only ones here," Mrs. Dugas laughed.

He laughed with her, eager to find this funny. "Did you drive?" he asked.

"My husband dropped me off. He's lunching at the Shrine Club, around the corner."

"What kind of car?"

She rolled her lips and said, "A moderate-sized blue one."

"I rode the bus."

"Did you?"

"I only got wet because the stop is a ways from here."

She nodded, raising her black eyebrows.

"I liked those rats," TV told her quickly. "That was a good experiment."

"Have you been eating better?"

TV flushed, horrified at what his lunch of french fries would reveal.

Mrs. Dugas lowered her chin and looked up at him in what was supposed to a teacherly manner. Yet her lip twitched, and TV knew she did not really find fault. "Never mind," she said. "Someday it will register. You know, I don't believe I've ever had a lunch invitation from one of my students before. I've had hundreds of students—it's not my habit to exaggerate—and not a single lunch. I once went to a birthday party and another time I attended a funeral."

TV nodded, hoping she'd keep talking. If only she would just keep talking, he thought he might catch up, he might find his bearings in her voice.

"The birthday I enjoyed but the funeral, well, it was predictably depressing. The pallbearers were your age, so solemn in their suits. One of my students died, a few years ago. Actually, more than a few. Of all those hundreds, she's the only one dead." Then she added, "That I know of."

TV thought of the cemetery his grandfather had gone to. It did not allow vertical headstones and so resembled a golf course, marked every few feet by flat bouquets of plastic flowers. Only the American flag could be upright at Resthaven.

Mrs. Dugas said, "She wasn't wearing a seatbelt, though that is another lesson my classes generally learn. Along with food."

The woman behind the counter shouted, "Seven of hearts?"

TV jumped up. "I'll get it," he told Mrs. Dugas, though she'd made no move to help.

On the way to the Pick-Up window TV realized his money was gone. He reached for the pocket and could feel the bulk missing. His handkerchief was gone, too, probably worked loose during his dash to the restaurant. All he felt was his warm leg beneath the wet corduroy of his pants. Still, he continued to the counter, hoping something would occur to him, hoping he'd trip over a solution on the sticky linoleum floor.

"Four seventy-three, with tax," the waitress said. She was without heart, TV saw.

He took hold of the tray on which his and Mrs. Dugas's lunch rested. "I lost my money," he said quietly, looking into the woman's hard face. He could not bear what was happening to him. "Please let me pay you tomorrow."

"You lost your money," she said skeptically, loudly. TV turned to meet Mrs. Dugas's eyes. She had heard; her eyebrows perked.

TV looked back at the waitress. "I lost it on the bus. Or running. I lost my grandfather's handkerchief, too."

"Big whoop," she said, twirling her finger in the air.

He said, more softly, "He's dead."

She stared, unfazed.

"My mother killed him," he was whispering. "With a hammer. The handkerchief was stuffed in his mouth."

The woman cocked her head, finger still in the air. "You're saying you're that kid?"

He nodded.

"No way. Really? And her boyfriend helped, right?"

He nodded again, already sorry. Mrs. Dugas had turned back to the window. TV did not know whether or not she'd heard him. Then he saw her shoulders rise, a shrug accompanying a sigh. She had heard, once again.

"Please, I promise to pay you back. I'll leave my skateboard here for collateral."

"Get some money from grandma."

"What?"

She nudged her head toward Mrs. Dugas.

TV pleaded, "I came here yesterday."

She seemed to understand that he meant he would come back tomorrow and finally released her side of the tray. "You're lying," she said. TV blinked. If only he *was* lying. But maybe she meant about the money.

TV set the tray on the table. Mrs. Dugas picked up her sandwich and briefly smiled at him. But it was her bad smile, the one she used when she'd been disappointed. Last week she had smiled that way before bodily seating John Coffey and stretching masking tape to bind him to his desk.

To TV, between bites, she quoted, " 'What you suffer does not defile you; what you do does.' "

TV ate his french fries without tasting them, working not to choke on their greasy mass, imagining his psychologist's office and the only *file* he knew anything about, the manila one with his name on the tab, crammed full of his bad life.

HE FOUND his handkerchief on the way home. It lay like a hamburger wrapper in a muddy puddle. TV made a strangling noise when he saw it there, wrung it out, and pushed it in his pocket. The money was gone but he didn't care. Mrs. Dugas had refused his offer to walk her over to the Shrine Club to meet her husband. She opened her purse at the end of the meal and TV had started to tell her not to pay when she pulled out an envelope and then a stamp, leaving them on the table like a tip. She'd had no intention of producing money.

"I'll see you bright and early Monday," she told TV. Forty-eight hours, he thought. He'd waited until she was gone before taking his skateboard to the waitress.

"This ain't no pawn shop," she told him. She pointed at his and Mrs. Dugas's table. "Gimme that envelope." When he had obeyed, she penciled an address on it and handed it back to him. "Don't forget," she warned, then laughed for the first time. She rolled her eyes, leaned through her Pick-Up hole, and spoke out the corner of her mouth melodramatically. "Just send me the fin, kid."

When he arrived home Joanne was sleeping, curled under a man's coat on the living room couch. Watching her breathe, it was not hard to imagine the ease with which a person could be killed. TV stood for a moment contemplating her, wondering if he would ever love her. Then he went into the kitchen and quietly shut the door. He washed his grandfather's hand-kerchief in the sink, using plenty of dish soap and scrubbing it between his knuckles until they stung. He rinsed it, running his fingers across the navy monogram, then dried it over the heat register, standing with his feet spread so as not to melt his shoes. His lips parched and his eyes burned. Afterward, he folded the wrinkled cloth to fit the envelope.

ADOBE

I HAVE reached the age at which I no longer expect men to come to me as lovers. One resigns oneself, having lost two husbands to younger women. Men will come as dear friends and ex-husbands, acquaintances and neighbors, as merchants and salesmen, and, most recently and startlingly, as employees. I stand at my kitchen window watching men I've hired construct my new home, thinking that not one of them is entertaining the thought of me in bed with him. It could be self-pity but I'm hoping not to dwell in that region. Further, am *I* entertaining the thought of one of them in bed with me? No. I simply will miss the luxury of believing I inspire lust. I achieved forty years earlier this week, arriving atop the peak of my life alone, and anticipate the downhill slope (which I can all too clearly see) to be manned exclusively by those I listed. My new house, this one singularly mine, takes shape while I reacquaint myself with the fact that life never fails to present me with what I want at the precise moment I no longer want it.

I had always dreamed of designing my own house—who hasn't? And for a little while, just after the second divorce, I could be enchanted by crude floor plans sketched and revised over and over, by discussing with my contractor the wheres and hows of cabinets, arches, doors, nooks. I lived then, as I do now, by myself in a trailer on the desert. Outside on my sandy hill I drew with a stick the shape of my house, smoothed a wide blanket over the space where my bed would someday rest, and sat down, staking claim to the view. This spell, this insulated waking dream, cracked when my sister, four years younger than I, made a western sojourn. She broke down weeping, openly distressed. Is there anything worse than the pity of a younger sibling? Coming from Chicago, she had expected the Southwest she saw on television tourist ads, saguaros and palm trees, golf courses and grand canyons, swimming holes. New Mexico has a closer kinship to West Texas than to Arizona, a fact I've grown to love—it's an acquired taste, this landscape. I tried explaining to my sister.

"It's beautiful," I said, spreading my arms to include every woeful knoll and scrubby mesquite tree, "for its lack of human interference."

"You're disappearing out here," she wailed. "Look at you, you look like a tumbleweed." The day she spoke these words the wind blew ferociously, rocking my little trailer like a lunch box, and I could see she thought I might literally dislodge and bounce away. It must have appeared all too expendable an environment. I worked to refuse, and still do, to see the tragedy. I felt I had given up, as an adult must, the notion of place or station to be self-defining. I was not running from Michael or Barry, not shamed by their desertion; rather, I was stepping from the skin I'd formerly inhabited, shimmering out from under that frantic, frightening epidermis. In Chicago I had wanted too much, been tempted too strongly to collect—furniture and books and food and friends. It had become an occupation in itself, the searching out and bearing triumphantly home, the displaying of and constant supplanting with the new. Here, I took what came to me, my kitchen windowsill a shrine to the desert, its broken glass, occasional quartz, scorpion husks, the fine crisp chamber of a rattler's tail. Things you might bring home unaware in your pants' cuff.

And soon the trailer will be shed, too, and I will take up residence in this solid fort I've commissioned. First the men dug a trench, snaked rebar throughout, and poured footings. They laid the adobe, grudgingly. They would have preferred the faster method, the cheaper frame-up, the one used all over the country. But I wanted a house that belonged specifically here, that couldn't have been constructed just anywhere. My contractor is Anglo but his crew is Chicano. Every morning a group clusters out front, some holding sleeping bags, one with his small child—girl? boy?—waiting to see what work they can get. Those turned away head into the valley, to the cotton or chile fields to make money picking, instead, or, too late for piecework, they resort to sitting at the chain-link entrance to the gravel quarry down the road. I own a hill, and they climb it each morning. They appear in the east with the sun, their shadowy images moving as if toward battle, tools or coats borne on shoulders.

I watched my contractor, Luke, for a week as he decided on workers before I finally interceded on behalf of the man with the child. He'd come out every day. He obviously had obligations.

The little son—I recognized his sex one day when he stood alongside his father at the edge of the clearing, hips thrown forward, chest puffed like a small threatened bird—maybe four years old, wanders around my property, circling the trailer and jumping up to look in the windows. As barren and poor a lot as this is, he's still able to make me squirm with the knowledge of our separate places in the food chain: My money feeds him. His hair, when he leaps, flies out straight and thick. I open the back door and step down onto the cement block that serves as stoop.

"*Buenos días,*" I say to him. The February day is clear and still. To the southeast grows the distant brown cloud that is the sprawling border between Juarez and El Paso, but in all other directions the blue sky reverberates clarity like a set of clashed cymbals. My eyes water.

He produces his coy profile for me, not speaking. His father has stopped laying adobes to make sure his son is not bothering the lady. (They call me "lady," a practice I don't quite know how to discourage.) I wave in his direction, indicating that I welcome the boy's company. Eddie Apodaca returns to work, still looking up now and then with anger in his set mouth. He is too harsh on his son, too quick to tug him upright and swat him. More than once I've seen him whack the child's backside, the comic accompanying puff of dust.

When I ask the boy's name, he will not tell me. He has shuffled closer and closer, never directly but more in the progress of a sidewinder, choreographing evasion. He sniffs at the bait that is my friendliness. But what, then, would be the hook? His timidity makes me sure he has been struck harder than the slapstick I've witnessed from his father. Where is your mother? I ask him, not loudly enough for anyone but him to hear my shabby Spanish. The question drives him running to his father's crotch, where he hides, explaining something in his ear. The father looks at me from the far wall of my half-constructed house, frowning with his brows and forehead. He's not yet thirty, still among that young dangerous sector of the populace, of the age and sex that sends insurance rates soaring, which has the shortest anticipated lifespan, which most often commits crimes. Young men. I have no doubt Eddie has seen his share of bad behavior, but what it has resulted in has yet to make a mark. There are no visible scars, no knifed face or missing digits, but his tough cynicism, his mild sneer, communicate to me across the rubbly site. It is not unlike flirtation in its effects: I shift uneasily, wondering how my tumbly hair appears, whether I'm attractive to him— because he would have to make some fairly complex leaps in order to be drawn to me. I'm no longer pretty, and young men, as I've said, have been the first to cast me aside. So I haven't a clue as to how to measure Eddie's stare.

On the other hand, on those days when I have job interviews in the city, I open the door without looking at the men, knowing they are staring with approval at my hose and heels and hemline, wondering why I don't look this way every day. Their eyes follow—they watch without willing it, without thinking about it, trowels and hammers and saws momentarily forgotten—as I cross the cloddy yard and step into my Jeep. When I work hard enough, I can put on the costume of an attractive woman, a sexual woman. Doing so does not feel false so much as desperate: I desire that transfixed stare. And to do so makes me angry; in turn, the anger makes me resent them. But these men, maybe all men, don't think in such wandering second-guessing ways. They think I'm sometimes beautiful. They are fooled.

I LIVE three and a half miles outside Las Cruces. Two years ago I purchased a knoll with my first divorce settlement (hoarded like forbidden candy in a separate account the duration of my next marriage) and then bought an old goat-herder's trailer with my second, smaller, divorce payoff. I think the goat herder was soft on his kids: The little aluminum home still holds the sweet odor of a hay-fed animal's stool.

When I bought the acreage, the hill and its skirts, it seemed an offset bump on a marginless plain. If this property were covered with water, as it once undoubtedly was, my hill would float like a little island, far from any others. I bought it quickly, without giving it much attention, more worried that I might back out and run home, make a fool of myself if I didn't stake a meaningful claim. I was newly arrived from Chicago, freshly spurned for a younger woman, and this seemed not only the middle of nowhere but nowhere near the middle. I felt, for a while, like a footnote, lost down near the bottom of the country, a small point one of my ex-husbands might inadvertently reference. I hung on. Now, with the half-finished home resting on top, my hill appears central. I drive toward it in the evening with a notion of destination. When I step out onto my trailer's cement-block stoop, the landscape spreads itself at my feet, equidistant in all directions. The sun sets dead center of the horizon. And so I have come to find myself unique.

Though alone. Should my sister ever express interest (and she won't, since I seem somehow defensively entrenched), I could explain that the world had grown paralyzingly homogeneous in Chicago, without depth or width, latitude or longitude. I had been traded up, in my husband's climb, and the sameness of his desires, the recognizable collecting impulse, had seemed about to swallow me. The shiny appearance of a correct life had worn away; I'd been left with the less attractive asset of judgment. I judged my life small and coglike, and left it.

The railroad tracks run not far from my property, which also abuts the wide ditch that once was the Rio Grande River, reduced now by Elephant Butte Dam, north of here, to a stagnant stripe of water, a sad impotent thing. A sort-of tent village full of transients lives on a sandbar of the river, a dozen or so people at a time, mostly men. Their poverty, however, contrasted with that of Chicago, seems a more bearable plight: the water, the sun, and, at night, the smoke from their fires sending up the woody nostalgic smell of camping.

My neighbors, such as they are out here, make a trip up my hill one evening to warn me about what Hugh Dugan calls a rash of break-ins.

Lois corrects her husband. "It's not exactly breaking in, hon, since the doors have always been unlocked."

Her husband rolls his eyes. "They took a shower, cleaned out the refrigerator, and left a dirty diaper in the trash. They're there without permission, I call that breaking in."

"No forced entry," Lois tells me. "Police as much as said we were asking for it."

Hugh snorts. "Come on in," he says, miming a welcoming motion from the snug fold-out couch that, at night, is my bed, "take off your shoes, use my towel and my deodorant."

I laugh suddenly, thinking of the Dugans' modest double-wide, the gaudy flocked wallpaper in their bathroom. Hugh smiles and shakes his head. "I thought I didn't have much."

"I know what you mean," I say, thinking of Eddie Apodaca and his son. "Did they take any glass?"

Hugh and Lois are in the stained glass business; they'd offered to design an octagonal window for my new bathroom. We've had a few awkward conversations about it, my tastes being a little at odds with theirs. Lois likes dragons and unicorns, and Hugh, having been born again, leans toward sunny pastures, lambs, and lions. They're in their late forties, starting on this fantastical new life after fleeing the claustrophobic Northeast.

Lois adds, "Somebody's been eating our garbage, too."

"That's right," Hugh agrees. "Lois left a half-eaten donut out there, wrapped in a bag. Next day, I found the bag folded up on my well cover. No dog'll do that. Gotta be those folks down at the river."

"Now we don't know what to do with our food we want to throw away."

Hugh smiles. "I'm afraid to insult them by leaving it next to the cans. And I sure don't want to make them root through the trash like an animal."

Lois says, "So we've ended up letting our leftovers sit in the fridge til they turn green. Isn't that the living end? So wasteful, but I can't think how to do the right thing."

"They might just come on in and find it in the fridge," Hugh says. "They already did that once. Shoot, eat my lunch, I don't care. Long as they don't take my glass, it don't much matter. That diaper, that was the kicker. Leaving that old diaper under my sink."

"Our sink," Lois corrects.

"I hate thinking there's a baby," I say. "You really think there's a baby?"

Lois rises and puts her fists on her small hips. "You worry about yourself, hear? I got old Hugh here, but you got nobody, not even a dog. Desperate men will do anything."

"That's right," Hugh says. "I got a mean bark." He illustrates with a poor imitation of a howl.

When they've gone I peer from my sink window at the half-wall of the new house, staring so long I think I see movement inside it, as if a man were lying there, staring at me.

A WEEK LATER Eddie Apodaca unloads the second load of adobes, which had arrived bumping down the dirt road on the long bed of a large semi. He and another worker unload each brick by hand while the driver sits in his cab smoking cigarettes. They establish a rhythm, Eddie on the truck swinging the mud squares to his co-worker, who stacks them. Each adobe weighs a good thirty-five pounds, and Eddie's naked back ripples like water as he swings. There are more than a thousand bricks on this load; more than five thousand will be necessary for the house. The sheer heaviness of my new home, the thickness of its walls, its weight on the sandy layer of earth, makes me feel happily substantial, makes the temporary aluminum trailer I'm living in seem just that: temporary, assailable as a beer can. Every time I look up I see Eddie's brown hands unloosing another hefty brick. In a few more weeks, it's his hands I watch smooth plaster on the chicken wire covering the walls, his body flattened against an outer wall smoothing and layering, using his trowel as adeptly as if he were spreading the mixture with his bare palms. The color of the mud, named Natural, reminds me of skin. Perhaps it is intended to. No accident, then, that the houses made of adobe are not square but slightly curved—the ceiling vigas, once live trees, bend occasionally like human joints—or that the complicated arterial network of electric and water and gas lines is slathered right into the wet mud.

My contractor and his son, Luke Senior and Junior, have appointed themselves the roles of father and brother in my new life. Luke Senior comes out once or twice a week to look things over. Luke Junior sometimes makes the trip. The son is the least ambitious man I ever met, forty-five years old and still living at home—not because he can't move out, he just hasn't the inspiration to do so. He will inherit the business from his father, falling into it out of inertia, out of an obligation toward keeping the same name in the phone book advertisement.

His father always hires strictly Chicano crews, and Eddie Apodaca has achieved high standing with Luke Senior during this project. It's Eddie he singles out to give instructions to the whole crew, Eddie he can count on to arrive every day. While Luke Senior follows Eddie up a scaffolding to inspect the house, Luke Junior and I sit at the trailer booth, watching as the men point and explain, Luke as mystified as I at what they do.

"Look how skinny my dad is," Luke laments. He lowers his chin to his chest to contemplate his own pudgy, unworked body. Not five minutes later he dumps sugar and cream into his coffee, begins eating seconds of the banana bread I've offered. He does only what he enjoys in life: eating, reading, and getting high. He tends to study a subject until he's exhausted it. Most recently he'd been interested in matters of the law. He's sat reading textbooks for years, his excuse not to go into construction with his father. Luke Senior respects studying; it baffles and impresses him the way house-building does his son.

Back in November, when my house was an ever-evolving floor plan on tissue paper and the Lukes had not yet been inducted as family, Luke Junior and I tried to be in love with one another. It's unfortunate that we couldn't have been content to be buddies; our attempt at intimacy still sometimes wanders into our friendship and makes things taste sour. There's nothing like failed love to destroy mutual respect. Since we were unable to make one work, relationships as a topic are completely out of the question. There are long pauses in our conversations where between merely friends there would be the discussion of whom each of us was dating or desiring.

"What's with the kid?" Luke asks.

"Tito?" I follow Luke's clean fingernail as he points outside. Tito Apodaca has set a plank of wood on a rock, walking it up and down while it teeter-totters below him. "I don't know. I keep wondering when his mother is going to show up and take him the hell away from all this hammering and sawing."

"Where do they live?" Luke watches Tito, who runs faster up the board, racing down the other side, leaving the wood vibrating.

Though I've asked, Tito won't tell. If I want to talk with him I have to play by his rules, which means not asking questions of him. I find things out indirectly: If I accuse him of not having a mother, he tells me he does so, she lives in Juarez; you don't know what a sister or brother is, I say, and he responds by saying he has two sisters of his own; when I tease him that he hasn't a home, however, he comes up short, blinking. He runs to his father and hides in his pants legs.

"Follow them sometime," Luke suggests.

"They walk. I'd be awfully obvious, trotting along behind."

"Ask Eddie."

I shake my head, nervous with the thought of speaking to

Eddie Apodaca, let alone inquiring about something personal. The longer he works building my house, the less sure I am the finished product will belong to me. He is putting his seal everywhere on it and, though I pay him, though I hold the deed, the place in some fundamental way—the way of sweat equity—must really be his.

THE DAY Tito falls on my concrete pump foundation and breaks his wrist, Eddie admits he and the boy live next to the river, sharing a tent with a drunk.

"El Borracho," Tito says, trying to get his father to smile. We are bouncing along the dirt road toward town, toward the emergency room at Memorial General, Eddie holding Tito in his lap. The boy won't cry. His stoicism makes me crazy, makes me burst into tears myself when I look at the little bone that ought to be insulated by tissue and skin, his hand unhinged. The injury is such that no blood has appeared, making it a surreal blue.

I pull over. "You'll have to drive," I tell Eddie, pointing at him and then miming the steering of the wheel. "I can't see."

Eddie lifts Tito out and waits for me to come around the Jeep and settle in the passenger seat, then sets the boy on my lap. He's large but light, like a mannequin. I feel him adjust to fit in my arms, those minor unconscious shifts to make do. I try to let him find his own comfort. He smells like the clay soil of my knoll. He is warm and dry, though I sense the price he pays in withholding tears. "You can cry," I whisper to him. "It's good to cry." When we hit rocks, which is frequently— Eddie drives like the young man he is—I absorb the shock, holding Tito's elbow to keep his wrist perfectly still.

At the hospital I call Luke Junior. Tito and Eddie have been taken to X ray while I complete paperwork. "Should I lie?" I ask Luke. "I mean, should I just make up stuff? I'm going to pay, it seems like I ought to have the buyer's right to lie. What do you think?"

"You sound kind of nutso," Luke says after a pause. I can hear him inhale marijuana.

"I don't know his mother's name," I say, staring at the impossibly narrow lines I am supposed to print the information between. "His address is a tent on the Rio Grande. They may be illegal aliens. I had to take an oath and give up a credit card before anybody'd even look at the kid's wrist."

"Welcome to America."

"You better tell your dad—somebody asked me about work conditions and insurance. I mean, I don't think it would happen, but what if I'm suable?"

Luke exhales, coughs. "You could use an interpreter," he says. "Or maybe that's *interloper*. But I'm on my way."

"Don't forget the Visine. And brush your teeth. That's all we need down here, you reeking of pot."

TITO'S wrist was broken cleanly; it looked bad but apparently this is the preferred way of injuring a bone, completely. His cast makes a circle around his thumb, then travels up to his elbow. He holds it in a sling, studying the X rays the doctor gave him as a gift.

"He can't stay in a tent," I declare on the ride home.

Luke, hunched and jostling in the back with Eddie, translates. Tito, riding shotgun, has arranged the X rays on the windshield, where the setting sun cuts a searing hole in his fractured arm.

Luke leans over the seat and says into my ear, "He says the mother is a whore in Juarez."

For a few blocks I listen to the word *whore* repeat itself in my mind. "Is she really a whore, or does he just want to call her one?" I ask.

"Does it matter?" Luke says. "The boy has nowhere to go."

"Tito will live with me," I say. "I have the other bed."

In Spanish I hear my invitation presented to Eddie. I hear Eddie be persuaded and finally agree, reluctantly. He's been defeated during this episode, one that he might or might not recognize as being a turning point in his growing up. I must admit to the guilty gratification I felt in seeing his defensiveness turn against him at the hospital, his anger absolutely useless and without power, even the fluorescent lights conspiring to make his skin a stricken shade of mustard. Everyone spoke to me, not him, about the injury, as if Eddie had come along just for the ride. And now I'm going to keep his son.

At the trailer, Eddie somberly shakes Tito's uninjured right hand, a gesture that makes me want to shove them together in an embrace. He walks off to the river, hands stuffed in his jeans pockets. That first night Tito sleeps the sleep of the dead, drugged on codeine, and I imagine his father still walking, maybe taking one hand from his pocket to thumb a ride far away.

But the next day, Saturday, Eddie comes wearing yesterday's clothes, and takes the boy. Though I offer a ride to town they refuse, walking down my hill in the morning, the white cast reflecting the bright sun, and returning at dusk.

The second night Tito falls from the bed, something I don't discover until morning, when he greets me with a whimper from the floor, still not crying, though his broken wrist has obviously struck the linoleum.

"Tito, for God's sake, please cry!" I flit my fingers on my cheeks to indicate streaming tears. *"Duermo,"* I command, then realize I've ordered him to sleep, or perhaps said that I myself am sleeping. In my arms he is stiff and light, like the skeleton of bones in his X rays.

"What shall we eat?" I ask, setting him on my bed while I unmake his, turning it into the breakfast table once more.

He shrugs, smiling at me. Sitting there, sweet and frightened, he appears a gift and I look long into his eyes, squelching the desire to run hug him tight. Shouldn't I hold fast to something so tenuously given? Instead, I busy myself with French toast and bacon, which he eats with his fingers. In the middle of the meal, one I have considered a success, tears finally begin sliding down his face. I dispense the baby painkiller the ER doctor prescribed, but it's obvious that what hurts him is my strangeness, which, though friendly, is still strange. I want to provide him with substance: food and comfort and home. But what he needs is less substantial. I push into his side of the booth, sitting close and holding his uninjured hand. We wait for Eddie.

DURING the week, while the crew buzzes and pounds and shouts and drops boards, Tito and I watch *Sesame Street* and play with the kitchen utensils. We make cookies and take the men a batch. They stare at the chocolate chips as if I might have used cyanide, waiting for Eddie to okay a taste. Tito doles them out and Eddie eats his in one bite. The other guys laugh in embarrassment, cookies being something they perhaps are no longer supposed to enjoy.

Tito delights in this success. He is a good-natured boy, brave—a characteristic I never before put much stock into. He is enchanted by the ordinary magic of domestic life. He likes to watch bread rise in the tiny lighted oven. He enjoys the television remote. And one day I fill the goat herder's water tank with warm water and, with his broken wrist set on a towel on the rim, give him a bath outside—he in the tattered underwear he refuses to remove—a treat he has never had. His pleasure in these simple things makes my eyes fill. But I ask myself for whose benefit is it, really, that I play this danger-ously encumbering role? Tito's? Eddie's? My own?

AFTER the adobes have all been laid and plastered, a cement truck chugs up the hill and the men spend the day pouring a bond beam along the house's top. For the past week two of the crew have devoted nearly all their time to chopping the knobby limbs from thirty twenty-foot pine trees. They swing their axes in an awkward sideways manner to chip off the bark, then plane and sand the poles, finally painting them with a thick coating of linseed oil. My hill is so covered with pine trees it looks as if I intend to live in a log cabin. A storm develops one afternoon and rains on the whole site, driving the crew into the tiny goat shed and leaving the air smelling of pine and linseed, an odor very much like urine.

On the day after the bond beam is poured Luke Junior joins me at the boothlike kitchen windows once more to watch the vigas go up. Four men stagger beneath the first tree's weight, moving it awkwardly off the sawhorses. Eddie and another man have the heavier end, balancing it on a two-by-two. Once they reach the house, they must figure a way to hoist the thing.

"What's the M.O. here?" Luke asks.

"Doesn't seem to be one," I tell him. "Things just sort of go up or in or on. Very spontaneous."

"It looks like an accident waiting to happen out there."

I agree, looking toward the little TV, Tito sitting gape-mouthed on the couch in front of it.

"Those things actually going to bear weight or just be decorative?" Luke asks of the vigas.

"Weight bearing," I tell him, but I'm not familiar enough with the procedure to really know. The next viga slides off the two-by-two and onto Eddie's foot. He leaps, holding his boot, shaking his hand. Luke scoots out of the booth.

"I can't just sit here watching this fiasco," he says. "They need a pulley. It's the principle of displaced matter, or something."

"They'll do it," I tell him. "Watch. They do it every time." Luke sits again. We watch as three men cluster on the scaffolding while the fourth, Eddie, climbs on the bond beam and ties a rope on the broad-end of the viga.

"No way can he lift that," says Luke.

The three men heft the viga and Eddie lifts the rope. One man jumps off the scaffolding to grab a four-by-four and lodge it beneath the viga, extending the push. With their arms raised, the three men below show their taut bellies; above, Eddie's back is bare. They tremble, exert. The log finally nudges onto the beam. The men laugh, sweating, shirts covering their skin again. Their caps come off, a cigarette is lit. One yells something in Spanish.

"What'd he say?"

Luke smiles. "He says only a woman can make him work this hard."

"Me?"

"Well, no, actually it seems to have to do with sex." Luke nods uncomfortably. "Yeah, that was the implication."

"Oh. That."

E D D I E knocks every morning, a rap rap rap, and then waits for Tito to come out. I always watch Eddie through the small window over the sink, the way he looks off toward Juárez, thinking. His face is broad, the skin tight and brown, marked by small dark freckles around his eyes. He is skittish, always on the verge of flight. I worry that he will take Tito away from me, but every morning, after a short intense talk with his son (I imagine him asking if the lady has treated the boy well), he lets him loose and walks with his back to us as he starts in on the house. I've tried to offer coffee or a meal, but he shakes his head, squinting as if understanding all too well my timidity in offering. Always he surveys me, eyes flicking down my body as if taking stock: mouth, breasts, thighs.

When I present Tito with a new set of clothes, his father is finally forced into the trailer. When I see him stooping through the door, I am not sure this hasn't been my purpose all along, to bring him into the house he isn't building, to set him at a table and make him take a delicate glass of wine in his rough hands.

He pushes Tito stiffly in front of him, kneeling in his crusty pants to coach him.

"Thank you for the gift," the boy recites. Eddie nods in agreement, still frowning with his forehead.

"*Siéntense*," I say. "*Por favor*." Eddie sighs but they both back up and sit on opposite sides of the booth, facing me on the couch, which is my bed.

Needing something to say, I remark on the progress of the adobe house.

"Yes," Eddie says, nodding.

Suddenly I know I will give him and Tito the trailer when my house is finished. It is not Eddie's style—not even his size—but it must be preferable to living outdoors. I begin, hoping to remember *accept* or *take*. I settle on *live*. I try to make clear that I want Eddie and Tito to live in my trailer, a sentiment I seem to manage to convey. I am happy for about two beats, flushed and virtuous. Then realize they have no trailer hitch and no car. That the place they would have to park, the sand bar, will not bear even the minimal weight of my trailer. They must assume I mean for them to live here, in what will soon be my new backyard.

Eddie has been nodding, a confused expression on his face, trying to decide if I know what I'm saying. He's not a handsome man, his facial features too hard in the places where they ought to be soft, the eyes and mouth, and then soft in those where hardness would be best, the nose and jaw. The dark freckles around his eyes suggest illness, a permanent rash. His mouth makes a kind of kissing wrinkle: He would like to spit—on the gift, on whites, on women.

"*Puedes*"—I reach and then invoke my usual hopeful cognate—"*decidir mañana. O más tarde.* Okay?" But do I know what I'm asking him to decide in the near future?

Eddie stares deep into my face, and I blush, wondering again what he sees. I don't know how he reads me and, moreover, I don't know how I want him to. I do know I wanted to see him bend, come through the trailer door. Beyond that I'm as lost as he.

He says, "Okay," and then speaks with Tito in Spanish, too quickly for me to follow, though I hear mention of a woman, a bed, a moon, his mother.

I BEGIN to imagine that Eddie disappears. In this dream, I keep Tito. He lives with me and I don't have to think about his father. My inclination is to make the little boy forget all his life prior to this one with me. Forget his mother, the tents, the cast on his wrist. We would have our problems, this brown child and I, white and with a distinctly poor grasp of Spanish. Tito's transience, the way he and his father live unrecorded, unknown, homeless, makes me want to claim him, to write his name next to mine, to buy him a fortune's worth of toys and put him in a beautiful safe room. I'm afraid all of Mexico appears this way to me, a place where children lose their mothers, where addresses are not registered but found only incidentally.

Suppose you are taught, all your life, not to think of yourself as the universe's center? How can you make any one thing the center? I owned a knoll; on top of it rested a new, heavy, two-bedroom house. It was the center of something, but it wasn't fair. Really, a human can fill only a few square feet of space at any given moment.

W H E N all the other men have left, when I've fulfilled the monetary end of my agreement with Luke, Sr., and tell him I cannot afford to have him do the finishing work, I'm left at last alone with my new house. And the two Apodacas. Eddie will finish the interior. Tito's arm, castless, is a pale puny thing, white. He eyes it suspiciously, as if the rest of him might fade, too. He has remained as my guest; the longer he stays the more mine he becomes, a delusion I nurse along on the flimsy dream of squatter's rights or common-law marriages, made legal by sheer endurance.

I suggest to Eddie that the three of us drive to Mexico to purchase tiles and fixtures—an adventure!—but he shakes his head and does not explain. Simply, he won't go. Annoyed, I buy them at U.S. prices, hiring Eddie nevertheless to do the work. At night, he stays in the new house, sleeping on a second-hand couch. The Rio Grande has been allowed to rise for the growing season, and rumor has it the tent people have moved on. Like an abused or wild animal, Eddie has been coaxed closer to my hospitality, occasionally eating meals with me and Tito, smiling when I attempt to talk to him in Spanish. He will not, though I don't believe cannot, use English.

When the monsoons come, my house has been under construction for six months and I love Eddie's son. My love may spill over to include Tito's father. I have a job, and now come home happily to find the Apodacas there, Eddie forever looking over the house, critically evaluating his progress as if this will keep me from doing so. When it rains, we sit in the tight

booth, the two of them across from me, and watch the water
break against the windows, shake the trailer.

With the money he earns, Eddie purchases a most horrible
black motorcycle. He's young, I remind myself, and the young
like shiny objects. At my insistence, he makes Tito wear a
helmet—his broken wrist a blessing in its way of lesson—
though Eddie will have nothing to do with the larger matching
one I bought for him. We disagree over tile color and light
fixtures and paint shades. Eddie suggests a red and black bathroom, sharp and bright; I prefer the peachy white of old clay
tiles, the thousands of minuscule cracks on its surface like
broken capillaries, a road map of age. Our decorating ideas
have been stolen from opposite cultures: his from 1960s Las
Vegas, mine from nineteenth-century Mexico. Otherwise he
gives suggestions only if I ask, and I continue asking, hoping,
in vain, his answers will begin to approximate my own taste.

On the day he finishes hanging doors, the last of his projects,
I return from work to find the house done, Eddie and Tito
nowhere in sight. Desperate, I calm myself by remembering I
have not yet paid him this week, that he would not simply
disappear without his money. But dark approaches and he is
not home. I pretend Tito is my only concern, the sweet boy
who deserves a more reliable life.

They roar up on the motorcycle at eleven P.M. My lights are
off yet I sit, dressed, watching them through the window. A
third person is with them, a slender woman who catches hold
of Eddie as she dismounts the large bike. She laughs drunkenly
and Eddie, with a look at my dark trailer, covers her mouth
with his hand. He sends Tito toward me and though the boy
complains, whimpering, he complies and trudges slowly to the
door, opening it quietly, stepping in without a sound.

"Come here," I whisper.

He sits beside me and removes his helmet.

"Is that your mother?"

He shakes his head. The girl, he tells me, is his mother's
sister. They've been riding around the city looking for her
boyfriend but now she's tired. They'll try again tomorrow.
While interrogating him, I watch the couple progress from the

bike to my finished house. Eddie guides her with his hip, his arm around her shoulders. For a moment, it's possible she's simply drunk and he's simply the helpful brother-in-law. Then on the porch they embrace and Eddie kisses her. My rage is a complicated thing, sifted as it is through reason and logic. He works for me, I pay him. He did not ask me to take care of his boy or to give him my trailer. I have imposed the circumstances that might dictate gratitude. Eddie has asked for nothing. The girl giggles, falling off her heels. Once they're inside, the bathroom light comes on, then goes off. There's nothing more. I can say for certain because I watch most of the night.

IN THE MORNING Eddie asks his first favor of me. After only a few hours of sleep, I listen without inviting him in for coffee. The girl sits, unintroduced, on the motorcycle. She is pretty, savvy, unthreatened by another woman, tapping one heel on the rear wheel guard impatiently.

"Will you take care of Tito for today?" Eddie asks me, in English. Tito has already cried over this arrangement and now stands near the motorcycle glaring at his aunt, who teases him. Eddie won't really meet my eyes, his shame clear but its origin not entirely obvious. Is he embarrassed in front of me? Or in front of the girl?

"Don't bring her back here," I tell him. "You know I'll take care of Tito, but don't bring her back."

He gives me a long idling look, then briefly smiles. "Okay," he says, nodding. His smile makes me want to launch into a long account of his rights as a guest himself, but something tells me the less I say now the better. So I let him drive off with the beautiful girl. I play with his son, wondering at what point my affection had become a package deal. Eddie returns without her. Neither of us ever mentions it again, yet it stays as a moment between us, the moment Eddie recognized his peculiar place in my heart.

One night not too long after this Eddie takes me in his arms. We stand outside, observing the moon. I had gone to empty trash, caught on my way back inside by the beginning brilliance of the rising moon. Its beauty insisted on an audience and so I had called him from the dark of the new house to come see it rising over the Organ Mountains, so brightly launched from their crags that it looked painful, like birth. His quaking decides me; I could not refuse affection so seriously given—nor so seriously needed, a fact I realize only after we press close and my eyes tear in welcome desire. Whatever emotion I have held toward him—pity, condescension, respect, anger—melds now into one much larger and more foolish. A young feeling, thoughtless and unevaluated. I believed it wouldn't happen again, yet here it is. That he is wrong for me in a hundred ways, and that I am to be deeply hurt, I dismiss by an act of will. He holds me, and I fall into the dark shelter of his intelligent hands; I cannot help but see him at work, swinging an axe, layering adobes, lifting with superhuman strength the first and every subsequent viga, planing the lumber of my ceiling, shaping my walls with his palms, preparing all along to house me.

HERE ON EARTH

"**THIS** is where we bought the pregnancy test," Darcy's mother told her. "It was positive the next morning. Your father didn't believe it. I brought it to him in bed, little test tube of pink urine. By then, we had our furniture."

"Huh." Darcy watched the grungy drugstore pass, unwillingly imagining her parents walking out the door together, sack between them, the two of them the next morning in bed with no clothes on. She was thirteen years old. She didn't want to hear about pregnancy tests at all, but especially ones involving herself or her mother and father. The word *urine* hung in the air like a bad smell.

Reclining in the front seat of the rental car, Darcy fantasized they owned it and she lived here in Chicago. Busy and fast, trains rattling through and people rushing on the streets, the sky a ponderous, profound gray. Apartments stacked on one another, lined up on endless blocks, all the red bricks it had taken to build them: the overwhelming sense of numbers and density. Of never being able to know it all. She felt herself opening up as the kitchen and bedroom and living room windows rushed by, this life, another life, yet another on top. How many beds must there be in one high rise alone? And just behind them, Lake Michigan, another stretch of the mind's capacity for volume, a lake that might just as well have been the ocean, full of fish and junk and sunken ships and drowned people.

Darcy had never been to a city like Chicago, old; it thrilled her as much as it made her resentful. When she demanded to know why they'd ever left such a worthy, wondrous place, her mother gave her an endless account of the worst public schools in the nation and ungodly bad weather. They'd moved to Arizona when Darcy was two. She felt badly treated, taken against her will, bereft of her birthright. Chicago seemed like home. She'd thought so since they landed at O'Hare. The three teenagers who'd sat in front of her and her mother on the flight had talked nonstop about the radio stations in Chicago, how much they'd missed the music during their visit to Phoenix.

"We just did it all wrong," her mother explained. "We bought when we should have rented, we took the first job your father got instead of really thinking about day-to-day things like could we stand to live in a place where people have to clean up after their dogs. We were young. We had a dog." Her mother laughed as if she'd said something funny.

Her mother had been sent by the Phoenix City Council to Chicago to attend a seminar on recycling plastic containers. She had to present her findings next week. Darcy joined her because the airlines' promotional pitch this summer was to offer free trips to children. They were staying at the Ramada Inn next to the airport, a disappointing location. From their window, Darcy's mother was quick to point out to Darcy (as if she were three instead of thirteen), they could watch the planes land. Driving on Michigan Avenue, in the heart of the city, Darcy had seen many more intriguing hotels in which to hold a conference.

"I can play hooky today," her mother had told her that morning. "They're talking about recycling tires." So they'd decided to tour the old neighborhood, Rogers Park, on the far north side. Darcy navigated, astonished each time the street on the map would materialize in front of them. They visited the Loop, then sped up Lake Shore Drive, onto Hollywood, past Touhy, circling back to Sheridan. Her mother pointed out landmarks: the place they'd bought a television, an air-conditioner, the buildings they'd looked at apartments and condos in, the office her obstetrician had occupied. Apparently, the whole three years in Chicago had been, for her, a time of becoming a mother. Her memories had little else in them.

"And you went to day care right there," her mother said, pointing at what Darcy had learned was called a brownstone. "You loved Debbi. Remember Debbi?"

"No, why should I?"

"First you said Mommy, then Daddy, then Debbi. Your grandmothers were hurt. Debbie cried when we moved away."

"Maybe we should go back downtown and eat lunch on top of the Hancock building. Maybe it revolves."

"There!" her mother exclaimed. "Right there on the corner!" She pointed to a brick apartment building with a fake turret on top. "That's where you were conceived!"

Not "That's where we lived" or "That's our old condo," but, "That's where you were conceived." Darcy felt like jumping out the car door. She looked at the building, giving her mother the silent treatment. The turret was a mossy green and had leached its color down the drainpipes surrounding it.

"We only had a futon for the first week, and we were painting everything white. Your father wanted it all white, so it would look bigger than it was. But I insisted on one pink window. After you were talking, you could say, 'Pink window.' "

Someone honked at them. A black man gave them the finger as he passed, yelling things in the vacuum of his air-conditioned car interior. Darcy felt her face heat like fire. There weren't many blacks in Phoenix; she felt this man had superior claim to the road and was embarrassed when her mother, white, ignored him. Her mother leaned over Darcy to ogle the building some more, her head nearly in Darcy's lap. Darcy stared down at her mother's coarse, cantankerous hair and made a face.

"The first thing we said when we looked at the place was,

"It will be fine as long as we don't have kids." Nine months later, boom, there you were."

"Ironic," Darcy said. "Could you move? Your dandruff is getting on me."

Her mother sat up and looked hurt. Now ashamed, Darcy tried to make amends. "Where was I born?" she forced herself to ask.

Though she didn't say anything, her mother began driving again.

"Didn't you say there was an earthquake the day I was born, Mom?"

"Yes."

"Isn't that kind of weird in Illinois?"

"Yes." Her mother had set out on today's adventure with Darcy enthusiastically, but her eagerness had waned. One thing that kept Darcy on her toes was her mother's sudden mood changes. Now she began cursing other drivers. Darcy, conversely, had cheered up as she made conversation. She was just on the edge of discovering the push-me, pull-you relationship she and her mother would share the rest of their lives together.

After thirty minutes of circling and reading signs, they gave up on the hospital search and went to an Italian restaurant her mother remembered ("They love kids, always gave you crayons and cookies") but which had turned into a foreign-auto repair shop in the intervening eleven years. They sat in the parking lot while her mother squinted in deep thought, muttering the names of streets she could remember and swearing over the ones she couldn't. It was almost perverse how her mother's anger made Darcy feel better.

"Let's have a picnic instead," Darcy suggested. "We can go to that store." On the corner at an angle from them was a small grocery that advertised lottery tickets and bourbon. A bum (a drug addict, Darcy thought) sat on the curb. Her mother looked skeptical. The trash in the streets only made Darcy feel sophisticated; Phoenix was so *sanitary* compared with this. She felt real here. "Come on. We'll get Vienna sausages and American cheese slices and circus peanuts."

Her mother finally smiled. These were things she was not, as a grown-up, supposed to enjoy.

"When I was pregnant with you," she said, "I made your father buy me circus peanuts in the middle of the night."

"Yeah, I know."

"Don't forget to lock your door."

"Duh."

With their groceries, they drove south along the lake, looking for a suitable spot for a picnic. The wind blew and the water was a deadly, churning gray. Darcy could not get over the fact that you could not see to the other side.

"When I was pregnant, I cried about anything. One time, taking the train down to the city, I saw these three boys standing over a grave in the cemetery. They were skinheads, you know, shaved skulls and black jackets and what not. I burst into tears. The woman sitting next to me got up, she thought I was a nut. Other times I'd cry over TV commercials, little babies playing in toilet paper. I kept thinking the dog was going to quit breathing. It was an emotional time. Raging hormones."

Darcy flinched at the mention of hormones. Her mother could tell a perfectly presentable anecdote and then ruin it with certain uncomfortable words. Sometimes Darcy believed this was intentional, that her mother liked to embarrass her, liked to put her in situations in which she'd have to prove her frank relationship with her mother: See, they could discuss hormones. Darcy resisted, annoyed with the obviousness of the ploy. When she was young she loved to hear about her birth and prenatal activity, but lately the more biological details kept cropping up, forcing her to imagine herself inside her mother. At this rate, she would not be able to stand any of it in a few years. It remained a story her mother never tired of telling. "I don't expect you to be grateful," she'd say, cheerfully. "I'm still not grateful to my mother for having me." Darcy had been a surprise baby, "a happy accident," an active kicker in the womb, a frustratingly late delivery, the one redeeming thing that had happened to her mother and father during their three-year stay in Chicago.

"But if we hadn't lived here," her mother said, "if we hadn't bought that tiny condo or that miserable futon, we wouldn't have gotten you, so I can't really regret anything we did. You see?"

"Uh huh."

"And sometimes I think if we'd never left here . . ." She trailed off, though Darcy followed her logic, silently. She thought this way, too. If they'd never left Chicago, her father might still be living with them. He might not have a new wife and another family, a new baby daughter. In Chicago, there used to be just the three of them, crowded in a one-bedroom apartment with a big dog. Now, everything had flown apart. Even the dog had died.

Their car was the only one near the Loyola Park Beach. Darcy experienced the cold wind and the freezing water as something to retain for later, when she was hot in Phoenix, when even swimming couldn't cool her.

"Look, Dar! Tulips!" Her mother pointed at three straggling flowers. She found amazement in the most peculiar, ordinary things. She stared lovingly at the woeful red tulips bent sideways in the gusting wind. "Every year I think flowers are more beautiful. I must never have noticed them, growing up. I never noticed trees or gardens or nature. I look at them now and can hardly stand how spectacularly beautiful they are. How did it all happen?"

"They're bionic," Darcy said. "Little super wires in their stems. Let's eat." She sat and opened the sack, pulling out their deli sandwiches and the soda her mother had made certain was in returnable bottles.

"Doesn't it just astound you?" her mother said, joining her, biting into her pastrami. "To get something from nothing?" She chewed, not needing or expecting an answer. Darcy was, as always, a captive audience. And the only one left to listen to this upcoming particular story. "I just couldn't believe when I was pregnant that you were going to be born. Two people, your dad and me, and then a third one, you. Something from nothing."

"Not nothing," Darcy felt obliged to point out, however

distasteful the thought of sperms swimming in semen toward the fat, waiting egg.

"Microscopic dots hardly constitute something real," her mother scoffed. She went on, but Darcy tuned out. Her mother could wax incredulous for a long time without needing a response.

When Darcy was younger she would request proof of her mother's love for her. If you had to choose, she would say, would you want me to die or you? Her mother always gave Darcy life; after all, she explained, she'd already led her own, and Darcy's was not yet filled in.

Darcy worried she might never grow into making such a choice, the choice that was, by virtue of its generosity, obviously the right one. It was not yet possible for her to imagine she would give her life up for anything or -one. (She would not, for instance, choose her mother's life over her own.) All the other parts were unthinkable, too, the getting married and having children parts, the putting things in her and the getting them out.

When she'd asked her father whose life he would choose, he told her the question was ridiculous. He asked her to please provide a realistic scenario in which one of their lives would be taken or spared over the other. "It's indulgent," he told Darcy, "to think that way. I'm not going to be a party to it." Her father also thought it was indulgent to tell over and over the story of their first years together, the Chicago years. Because she was half his, Darcy could be persuaded to believe he was right, that reminiscing and saying "what if" led nowhere. Still, there was that part that was her mother's.

She finished her sandwich and lay back in the damp new grass. Lake Michigan rose and dropped a few feet away. Darcy looked up, into the only hole in the wide, solid mass of clouds that filled the sky. A window of blue, directly and distantly overhead. She blinked, her heart thudding suddenly as she thought this might be an invitation from above, an ovation she alone would be offered. She would fly away—she felt the sky pulling her—watching her mother and their lunch litter recede below her. But what was the password? She was frightened to think she might possess it. She wanted terribly to shoot away into that hole, to float above the city, to see the world in a piece. On the airplane she'd pressed her face to the glass, aching to see more, to escape the constraints around her, to pry out the glass, to climb through the porthole and stand on the wing, to see. Anyplace, no matter how wide and open, could give her claustrophobia; she sometimes felt her skin to be a kind of straitjacket.

Darcy stared into the blue until it vibrated, swearing to whatever power had pushed open that hole in the sky that she would exchange her life for a glimpse. No science, no ship, no oxygen. She would not even expect the exclusive rights to the story; she'd die immediately (implicitly part of the bargain) and not tell a soul.

She thought of swimming through mute air, the earth at last comprehensible and whole beneath her. But of course she would want to tell someone. She deflated, gravity quickly binding her once more, and watched the gray clouds overcome the clear blue. Her moment passed. She knew the receipt of such a gift ought to have been more gracious than wanting to brag, but there was no denying she would want to *tell* somebody, report back on the miracle.

"When you were little," her mother was saying, here on earth eating sticky orange circus peanuts, "you loved to say 'double-you,' the letter of the alphabet, over and over again. You'd get on the phone and say, 'Hi. Double-you. Bye.' "

"Really brilliant, wasn't I?"

"Yes," her mother said. "Yes, you surely were."

FIRE SEASON

I N T H E middle of the movie Kidder's new girlfriend gripped Kidder's arm with one hand and covered her breastbone with the other. "I can't breathe," she whispered strenuously, paddling her legs under her seat as if fighting a riptide. The woman sitting in front of them turned to shush her. Kidder said, "Bite it, bag," and Paige, despite her breathing problem, took a moment to slug his arm.

Onscreen a ripe young woman shaped her mouth around fragile bubbles of the French language while the mumbled guttural of English sounded out. Everyone's footsteps clopped a beat too late and too loudly. The protagonist's husband had been murdered by a pack of men over a poker debt and now the wife—coy bitch—stealthily hunted the killers, wooed them, made them want her, love her, then put them to gruesome vengeful deaths. Its lewd black logic suited Kidder and he was enjoying the film, bad dub job and all. Paige's illness befell her before the final murderer, the bald-headed kingpin, in prison and thereby a more complicated victim, got his deserts.

Though they'd only been seeing each other for a week, Kidder already was skeptical about Paige's high theatrics, the way she took running leaps into adventure, her discomfort elevated to *pleurisy* during the short ride home in Kidder's Jeep. Their first night together, last weekend, she'd said, "I'm assuming you'd tell me if you had a disease."

Having fucked twice by this point, Kidder found her remark laughably and hopelessly young. "The word is '*pre*suming.'"

"Huh?"

"I'm clean, you lucky dog."

Now he suggested, "Maybe we should consult a doctor before we start calling it pleurisy." He did not sneer; after all, he needed her.

"I can't breathe," she complained raspily as they drove to her parents' house. The folks were on vacation in the Bahamas. Easter break. Kidder had met her at a party; friend of a friend of a friend, that kind of party, as darkly impersonal as a bar. He'd been bumming all winter, trying to live for nothing until fire season started out west; there was good money to be made in burning. For now, he bummed. This wasn't hard; he was handsome, gracious, attentive. But he'd gotten slack and been kicked out of his previous arrangement, Judith's mobile home in St. Louis. Paige's place, hands down, was the best he'd found. Maybe not old money, but old ornaments: high ceilings, good liquor, crystal. Hollywood in the Midwest. Her father the dentist kept a spool of dental floss on the coffee table in a little gold pot. Kidder'd looked inside expecting rolled stamps. He had no problem taking advantage, drinking that liquor, borrowing shirts, sending letters on stationery monogramed *R.W. "Skip" Lundstrum, DDS*. The odd thing was, Paige was just as happy as he to join the game. The two of them had been sleeping in the master bedroom, under the master chandelier, between the master silks.

"Take it slow!" Paige demanded on the steps of her house. Kidder obliged, hand steering under her elbow. She had heft, pockets of flesh distributed like ballast. The neighbors stared baldly from their front porch glider, sliding pensively forward and back, arms aggressively crossed, dark glasses reflecting the setting sun in four square little panes. Kidder felt caught. He wondered if they had been instructed to keep an eye on the place.

Paige trembled so at the front door he had to take the key from her and unlock it. The neighbors, heads righteously turned to watch, might assume he had a gun to her ribs, that her deep inhalations were their signal to sound an alarm. When the door swung open and Paige had tumbled, bent over, through, he raised one hand to the couple on the glider, trying to appear chivalrous, suitorly.

"Who are they?" he asked Paige, who'd fallen on the first couch she'd come across in the cavernous living room.

"Who're who?" she gasped.

"The Pumpkin-Eaters, next door."

"Don't . . . make . . . me . . . laugh," she said on the crests of small exhalations.

"Hey," Kidder said, taking real note of her blanched face now that they were indoors. "What do you think, the E.R.?" A light on the other side of the room switched on when its sensor read their presence. The whole place ran itself on automatic pilot, obsequious electronics.

Paige lay on her side, tilting her top hipbone forward and throwing her head over the couch's edge. "I feel like I'm being squeezed, like my ribcage is being crushed," she told him upside down. "Maybe some water?"

He made his way through the dining room and butler's pantry to the kitchen, alarming himself as usual in the pantry's panorama of mirrors, his criminal posture and hostile eyebrows. No wonder the neighbors stared. He was twenty-eight years old and though he could appear all-American when he put on the right attitude, when he wasn't thinking he looked pissed off. A stint in the Merchant Marine had left him a long distance behind his peers, struggling as though through quicksand to reach them. They were graduated, self-started, fattened, and financed. Where was he? Still balancing the book of his life, weighing the times he'd gotten the raw end against those times he hadn't, keeping that debit column accordant with credit. Fighting the combustion of his discontent. He realized nursing Paige, fetching water and asking what to do next, would tidy a lopsided score.

"I know you think I'm pretending—" she started.

"I don't."

"—but maybe you could carry me upstairs? My lungs just won't take the exertion."

"I believe you." Kidder hoisted her with his knees bent— she was heavy, truth be known, hippy and liquid—and moved up the creaking steps. He imagined Skip the dentist doing this—carrying not his daughter but a voluptuous highball— lulling himself as he played the song of the stairs, the song of what he possessed and each night put to bed.

"Watch the newel!" she warned as they rounded the landing, nuzzling into his shoulder like a sheepdog. When they met she'd been drunk, a boisterous silly girl whose off-center face belied a sense of humor, a knowing, a weakness for pithy sarcastic remark. She needed a ride; he needed a place. He'd slept with her that first night and felt he was in a perpetual cool slide down the side of the marble moon, listening to her self-conscious laugh when they bumped buttocks, heads. In the morning he lay sweating on the silk, blinking as if blinded by the jeweled land in which he discovered himself. Shy, dismayed, Paige rolled herself in the topsheet and hopped to the bathroom, reappearing in a tightly knotted bathrobe, the sheet folded like a reprimand on her arm.

"Princess," Kidder said, sitting on the bed with her now. She was nineteen years old, pretty but not in the way that was currently popular. Her hair too short, curly as a black sheep's, the skin beneath it too fair. Moon-faced, ironic. Making love, she pretended to know more than she did, delighted by her own rapid panting. She would mug a passionate expression that twisted her sweet features rubbery and grotesque.

Another light ignited itself in the hall. More than once in this house he had expected doors to swing open without his pushing.

"Like servant ghosts," he said.

"*You're* what's scary," Paige told him, her eyes all pupil.

"Little late to worry."

"That's the scariest part." She withdrew herself from his enclosure and adjusted her ribs for easeful breathing, lying with her mouth wide open. Her teeth, of course, were pristine.

"Pillows," she said, distantly, as if from a dream.

Kidder placed them where she indicated, between her knees, rolled under her neck, bracing her backside. He removed her shoes, lifting each one idly to his nose a second before dropping it on the floor. Talcum, sweat, damp leather. A low-wattage light on her father's spare and masculine dresser blinked on like a warning. The furniture in here was all shoulders, broad and square. No mirrors, but Kidder still had the uneasy sensation he would startle himself.

"Eyes," he whispered to Paige, "opening up to spy on us. On me. Like those neighbors."

"Hmm," Paige murmured. "Forget . . . the . . . neighbors."

"An orgasm would relax you," he said, tapping the metal buttons of her jeans' fly with his fingertip, his own pants tightening.

"The thought," she sighed, "of you on top of me . . ."

"Yeah?" He smiled, a tingle ricocheting between his ribs and major organs.

"Well, I'd just plain collapse," Paige said flatly. "I can hardly draw breath as it is. Frankly, I can't imagine anything worse." Kidder's silence made her add, "No offense."

"I don't have to be on top of you."

She shuddered her shoulders to illustrate the unthinkableness of anything having to do with sex at a time like this, her respiration shallow and quick. Was she acting? "Do me a favor," she said. "Don't let me quit breathing tonight, okay? I'm going to sleep, but I'd like it if you just made sure I kept at it."

He stood at the doorway and looked at her, wondering what it was in him—or what he lacked—that made him feel only that he was wasting this moment, that her lovely vulnerability could be nothing more than an invitation to violate her.

H E snooped. Not through diaries or files or photos, but through rooms, over carpets, across threshholds, fingers riffling coat sleeves, umbrella handles, a dying bouquet of day lilies. The family cat followed him and he stroked her, scratched that peculiar sexual itch on her back no cat could resist. He toyed with an analogy: He had this same touch with women. Like Janet, whom he'd lived with in Connecticut for six months, paying no rent, providing no helpful labor. He was good to her, though, he listened, he made jokes, he would dance. Women could turn so cold in a heartbeat, so icy cold. Their gift was right-brained, wordy. That Janet could spit forth a litany of his faults so articulate and well-considered had silenced him, left him fumbling toward the door without a comeback. His clothing and belongings—a bottle of brandy, an electric razor, address book—contained in a beer case, packed as carefully as a bag of groceries, sitting on the stoop. So cold, taking the time to button the buttons and fold his shirts while she seethed. The thing about women was they tried so hard and expected so little—at first. Then slowly the whole situation managed to turn itself inside out—during which time a man could be counted on to change not one hair, not one molecule—until the woman was trying hardly at all yet expecting the world.

The sweetest aspect of this chapter called Paige would be departing while she was still trying. How ideal if he could always savor the luxury of a quick exit.

He had not quite perfected his timing.

This reminded him to post a few letters, stoke his contacts and safe havens across the remainder of the Midwest. Outside the front door, he lifted the mail slot and clipped his envelopes on. At the neighbors' house all was quiet, the steady blue flame of television burning between the blinds' slats. It was only Paige's request that he check on her that kept him from popping through the poodlelike privet hedge separating the two houses and doing some damage.

In Skip's basement he stretched himself the length of the pool table and lay his cheek on the felt. Chalking his cue, he took hold of the family's life, feeling the dense substance of the house overhead, the breathing daughter in the master bedroom. He was going to steal things they wouldn't miss, not the old man or the wife, not the party-boy son nor the married daughter with kids. One white linen jacket—if it hadn't made the trip to the Bahamas, its absence would never be noted. A small marble statue, a naked woman on her knees, an objet d'art Mrs. DDS probably despised anyway. A few cassette tapes. Television remote control. Two wine glasses, a single serving set of silver, perhaps a ceramic egg cup he'd admired this morning on the shelf. Spare change and discarded singles. A spool of floss. Liquid soap, shampoo, maybe the odorless starchy powder he now rubbed into the webbing of his left hand.

Thinking, shooting pool, Kidder ran the one through the nine balls as if he knew how: as if he knew where the cue ball would end up, as if the ivory diamonds could guide him. It was the distracted man's lucky grace. He was settling debts as he debated shots. These people had money, more money than people he'd ripped off worse, and, furthermore, were strangers. His brother had been left in much poorer shape than what he planned here. And Paige's illness provided ideal freedom for fickle browsing. Her family's lifestyle—lighting itself up throughout the house, sprinkling in the yard, coursing in the walls—spoiled him, responding indiscriminately as it did. He wanted to leave his peculiar brand.

Yet he could not take offense in this house. There was something confrontational everywhere he looked—in the dark polished wood and the quiet carpet, in the muted colors and dense drapes—but he could not muster anger. He could empty the place, and still it would stand above him. He had been denied this, he told himself, and deserved it. But no one here would miss any of it. They would not be the wiser.

So he shot brilliant pool and made no move toward harm. Every ten minutes or so he found himself standing beside the bed of a cream-fed stranger, breathing a little hard himself from taking two flights of steps two at a time, looking down on an ordinary pampered sleeping girl, her lips open at an unattractive kilter, waiting quietly for air to continue its dutiful process in her.

★ ★ ★

"THE problem with eating," Paige said in the morning, "is that it makes you hungry." Kidder couldn't disagree.

"How's your pleurisy?"

She hesitated, resting her bacon on the table while she took a lungful of air. "Mostly gone," she said, thumping her chest. "I forgot about it."

"You have me to thank. I didn't sleep a wink for looking at you."

"Really?" She blushed, titillated by his devotion. See how little it took? She had difficulty keeping her bathrobe cinched or her legs together, the way a ten-year-old girl might, trying to learn ladylike behavior.

He smiled at her, running his slick palms down his thighs. "Now, when are Mom and Dad due back?"

"Are you leaving me?" In a flash her brow was furrowed, her hands on her hips. "Saturday," she added.

"I don't see me staying here with Skip and Lindy, no."

"Lindy will love you," Paige pleaded weakly. "She always wanted another son. The first one . . . well, and Skip . . ." She bit into her bacon again and switched tacks. "I could have met you at school. You could be one of my professors, passing through town on your way to . . ."

"Fiji."

"Right! Fiji on a Fulbright."

"Professor of what?"

She studied him with a smirk on her face. "Economics."

He laughed uneasily.

"Or food," she said. "Doctor Cholesterol."

He laughed again. She nodded, happy to have pleased him, her mouth gleaming with bacon grease. They had a week in this larder that was her home.

"I USED to steal things," Kidder told her in the afternoon. Early spring heat had suddenly broken out like a red rash in Kansas, prickly and sullen. Next door the neighbors played a radio, twisting the dial in search of talk instead of music, as if their lives were backwards. In the west, rain and floods, fire season still pending. Birds clacked down irritably from trees. Paige and Kidder had nothing to do but investigate each other. Her college textbooks lay like bricks, collecting dust. When they tired of the bedroom they moved downstairs to the living room. The postman came and went, his fingers briefly and grotesquely inside the metal flap in the door, Paige and Kidder coupled half on the couch, half on the floor. He thought fleetingly of his letters, his words, traveling ahead of him, marking a future trail. Then he turned back to Paige. The couch grunted as it was nudged a few inches. Making love with her was like cleaning up syrup, necessarily slow, thorough, sticky, and unfinishable. Kidder had developed a theory of civilization based on the relative laziness of the rich: out of their boredom, they fucked until they used up one partner—then moved on, living life faster, getting more for their money. Feeling virtuously inexperienced and proudly poor, he decided to tell Paige he was a thief; besides, he wanted to know if she had guessed.

"What'd you take?"

"Money. Credit cards. A sheepskin rug. A step-van. Necessities."

"Uh-huh." She bent forward to look under her legs, lifting a wet thigh. "You stained the couch," she announced. "I know for a fact semen stains."

"We," Kidder corrected her. "We stained the couch. Vinegar will take it out. It takes out anything."

" 'We' nothing," she said. "Wait here." Kidder leaned back, expecting her to return with a damp sponge. Instead, she dropped a pile of clothes on him.

"I want you to take them." Her father's shirts, the linen jacket. Skip's stifling musk. "I have a trust fund, too. I can lend you money. And this"—she knelt and pressed into his hand a key—"this is to our condo in Vail. You can stay there." Her eyes shone with naughtiness, with the excitement of collusion, with the expectation of gratitude.

Kidder's anger surprised even him. That smell—aftershave, deodorant, fruity fluoride, age—an insidious odor that remained regardless of laundering. He wadded the shirts around the key and threw the tangle across the room. The jacket fell short, lay on the carpet like a limp body. Wiping the backs of his hands on his thighs, he called her a few things.

Her head was lowered and her scalp showed between curls in a crosshatch of white lines like scars. Her posture, he noted, was that of the marble statue's, the one he'd admired. Seeing this, the statue was ruined for him.

"Stupid," he added. When she would not look up, he said, "I have my pride."

She snorted, then asked, philosophically, "You think it's bad to love someone for money?"

"I don't love you."

"But you think it's bad, never mind you and me?"

"Yes."

"How about for sex?" She rose and lifted herself against him tentatively, one affable rolling movement like a surfacing sea beast, slowly up on his lap, one leg, then the other, heavy young girl, and he looked into her face. She really wanted to know.

He took hold of her big soft bottom with both hands. "Goosebumps," he said. "And in this heat."

"I like how you bend in the middle," she said, leaning back and folding his semihard penis upward painfully.

"Resiliency," he said with care, "is my middle name."

She laughed, and Kidder felt not only forgiven but glad of it. She took his face between her cool hands and looked into him, right to the bottom of him. He felt her presence like an icy lethal drink, like liquid nitrogen. Oxygen was being supplanted; to breathe out was to lose it for good. She looked until tears ran down her own cheeks. She insisted they fuck while she cried. When she came she sobbed and sobbed.

What *is* this? Kidder heard himself asking himself, underneath it somewhere, what the fuck *is* this?

★ ★ ★

"YOU didn't rob people," she said over steaks. They'd eaten steaks every night, side by side on the Italian leather dining room chairs. Why not? Skip had every conceivable edible in the freezer, half a cow packaged in clean white butcher bundles, venison, Peking duck.

"Red meat is an aphrodisiac," Paige told him. "I'm fairly certain."

"Blood," Kidder agreed.

"You didn't rob people," she went on, "and there was never any other woman."

"I withdrew cash on my brother's plastic," Kidder said lamely, the urge to confess commensurate with her refusal to indict.

"You did not."

"I stayed at his house and never washed a single dish."

Using her baked potato peel, Paige finished wiping her plate clean of the clear red juices of her steak. Now she took the plate and broke it on the table, three equal wedges. "Nuh uh."

"How rich *are* you?" Kidder couldn't help digressing.

"Well, he's not an orthodontist or anything. You're familiar with the middle class."

"I wanted to sleep with my brother's wife."

This she considered. "But did you?"

"No," Kidder admitted.

Paige stacked her dish parts, three triangles. They'd left televisions on in four different rooms of the house for company and she focused now on the news of a hurricane near the Bahamas, her face brightening in anticipation of drama.

"She turned me down," Kidder said triumphantly, but Paige wasn't listening to him.

HE allowed her to bathe him, standing haunch to haunch in a cool trickling shower, to navigate her father's oval bar of black soap along his throat and under his arms, glide across his ribs, beneath his navel, inside the legs. She pulled his penis through his thighs and behind him, unmanning him, slicked his blond pubic hair until the soap's black lather left it dark as her own sleek obsidian curls. Then made him reach behind and hold his genitals himself so she could step back and look. "You men," she said. "So funny looking without your John Thomas." Kidder let his spring forward. She laughed. "And even funnier looking *with*. But I like this big clown . . . with his little smile and his silly hat." At her fingernail's prompting Kidder's foreskin shrugged. Under the steady tepid drizzle of the shower she lowered herself and began to coddle him, letting him feint and bob, tucking him warmly away, accepting into her mouth all his merry antics.

THAT NIGHT she got on her hands and knees, insisting on rear entry. Did she know what she was doing? Her pain, which she breathlessly denied, seemed to put out heat, a heat that Kidder then felt as pain, though he did not hurt. Hotter and hotter, fiery air. He lost direction, and did not come so much as boil over, reach a point and cease. Pass out. He rose in the night to pee and could not locate the bathroom door, could not, apparently, emit enough presence to light a lamp, slapping the cool ungiving walls like a blinded man. Retraced his trail and could not find the moving currents of the fan, the silk, or Paige. When she threw on the light, the room's imposing dark furniture and walls swung tauntingly around into their proper places and he found himself crouching between the closets, precisely opposite where he'd previously believed.

"Lost?" she asked drily.

IN THE MORNING he was alone in bed. Kidder thought he could have discovered Paige hanging in the closet, slumped over cereal, dead in a hundred nightmarish ways. She was not an ordinary girl. He found her following aerobics on the sun porch TV, covered in lively Lycra.

"Sex change?" Kidder said, relieved, peering at the effeminate little guy dancing on screen.

Paige laughed and fell out of rhythm. "I need to get in shape." She grabbed a handful of flesh to illustrate.

"I have dreams about padding like that." Though he liked the looks of bone, he liked the feel of fat. Lean was for aesthetes; cushion for the working man.

She blinked at him, trying to find the compliment, then turned back to her show. Offhand, she said, "They ever hire girl fire fighters?"

"Yep. I lived with women last year, two of them." Amazons, he did not add, dykes.

"You have to have training or something? Fireman school? How to hold a hose?" She stopped rotating her shoulders long enough to imitate a man urinating.

He nodded, wary of her direction. "Do I smell coffee?"

"Oh, I thought of something else you could take with you, these gold rings my father used to make for me and my sister. Solid gold from old fillings he replaced. We must have two dozen of them."

Kidder held up his index fingers to her face, crossed as against a vampire.

"You know what else? I have a secret, too," she said from her squatting bent-kneed position, hands slapping as she swiveled to the TV's canned music. Her thighs quivered with effort.

"What's that?"

"This isn't really my house. I'm taking care of it for a friend. She's in the Bahamas with Skip and Lindy. What do you think of that?"

"I don't believe you."

"So I can go with you." She threw her arms wide, clapped them together.

"You're in the pictures."

"That's not me."

"The portrait, the *oil* portrait, in the hall."

"Nuh uh."

* * *

THAT NIGHT it was Kidder who could not breathe. Just as she'd described her pleurisy, he felt squeezed. The house was spacious but where was the air? They did not make love, though she offered the open-ended smorgasbord of her goods. She slept like the moon, remote, white, contented. It was not in him to accept such a gift.

When he pulled out of the dentist's driveway he had not one thing with him—he'd even considered bequeathing her the Jeep, leave the keys on her soft sleeping stomach and run, run, run until he reached the tortured flaming mountains—not a speck of gold nor silk or silver, not even his own pile of soiled laundry (presents, loans, thefts). Neither his coffee thermos (his unseduced sister-in-law's) nor the aged spiral notebook (lifted in a long-ago student bookstore) that held the names and directives of less willing accomplices, friends of friends and friends of enemies, the tenuous roping linkage of names, names he'd once believed might, someday, in the long haul, prove useful.

GOODBYE, MIDWEST

EVERYONE needs a friend like Roxanne Titan, someone who serves, by being constant, as a reminder of how much you have changed. There is Roxanne, twenty-eight years old, the same long, layered-look frosted blond hair pulling in a swirl away from her face as if she'd styled it in a headwind of hairspray. Around her eyes is the teal blue color we favored. Her clothes are more expensive replicas of what she wore in high school ten years ago, muted sweaters, tapering blue jeans, heels. She wants to be young, off balance, teetering purposefully next to her husband, drinking something serious like bourbon. Though I knew its contents, I opened the envelope anyway. I hand the photo to my two-year-old daughter, who delights in pictures. She names all women Mommy and says it now of my old best friend.

Last week in an elevator someone said "Roxanne" and I found myself turning reflexively, on the verge of responding, as if I'd heard my own name.

I met Roxanne when I joined Blue Birds in third grade. Blue Birds was an organization less famous than Girl Scouts but with superior, natural-fiber uniforms. Ours was a smart navy-blue skirt and vest, topped by a baseball cap bearing our emblem, a one-eyed representation of a flying bird. Roxanne wore hers like a catcher, her white bangs sprouting like straw from the adjustable leather strap. I envied her freckles, the white band across her nose where summer sunburn had left a scar. I was a nervous and paranoid child, socially awkward, I thought, because I had no siblings. Roxanne's befriending me continued to, alternately, confound and flatter me. She must want something, I thought, but what? She seemed to have it all already. My memory is that our house was connected to the deal, that I had to offer it and its spacious dining room table as a kind of dowry to the Blue Birds. Every Thursday afternoon we would burst into my kitchen, myself transformed from virtual unknown into chatty hostess. I was, if nothing else, an expert on the subject of my own house. It wore me out giving tours, leading the troop up back stairs, through the basement, into the coal cellar and the tiny drafty room that was the bottom of an empty elevator shaft. I told them the house had twenty-six rooms, which was strictly true, counting all five bathrooms, two of the larger halls, and the dank wine cellar.

Roxanne would disappear. I once found her in my parents' bedroom and I stood watching without letting her know I was there. The way she took inventory of the dark messy room— touching their dresser scarves, bending to sniff my father's bathrobe that hung from a bedpost—made me feel under scrutiny and I worried that she would discover, through my parents' effects, my true unworthiness. Without turning around, she said, "Cool house. I like it."

I was thereby approved.

My mother, skeptical of anything traditional or conformist, would not come inside until the Blue Birds had all gone. She would park in our garage (once a carriage house) and read *Middlemarch*, which she had stashed in the glove compartment for just such occasions.

Possibly the troop thought my family was wealthy. We were not. My parents were academics and the house, a monstrosity in a part of town that would go to seed first and then, slowly, commercialize, was leased from my father's parents, who, at the time, wanted to sell it but could not get a decent price. Throughout my childhood the house would go on the market. The real estate office would call to set up appointments. Fine, sure, any time, my father would say expansively, as if we were just waiting around for an opportunity to show the place. Then he would hang up and rub his hands anxiously. He and I would race through the house throwing things in closets, vacuuming and dusting furiously, opening and closing key curtains so as to present each room in its best, dim or bright, light.

Our visitors would not fail to get lost. My father and I would sit at the kitchen table, listening conspiratorially until the inevitable, embarrassed "Yoo-hoo, where are you?" would sound. Most often they would be on a landing, confused between floors. The back entry and stairways were made of inferior pine and had fixtures of unpolished brass. These were the servants' quarters, nearly half the house, a modest home unto itself. At one time there had been two complete families living here, owners in the front, help in the back. I prefered the less magnificent rear side of the house because the scale was more my size, the ceilings nearer and the doors lightweight. A banker had built this house in 1911 and my father's family was only the second owner, a fact I could be proud of without knowing why and repeated, as I repeated many such adult facts, frequently to the Blue Birds. My bedroom was on the third floor, my bed lodged beneath a dormer window. At night I could crawl out on the sleeping-porch roof and be among the mulberry trees.

Roxanne began spending Friday nights with me. I expected to relax into our apparent close friendship, to feel like the sister I was sometimes mistaken for. Instead, I continued to tread lightly, wary of her choosing me, which, among the fickle young, is a choice made new each day. While I was transfixed by Roxanne, I sometimes wished for someone less, someone calm like myself who enjoyed dressing dolls or concocting sweets or reading song lyrics aloud. Roxanne's attention span was so manic and alien to me that our dashing from one activity to another seemed as random and unsatisfying as running an obstacle course. After a typical overnight, beginning when school let out Friday and lasting until late Saturday morning, I was exhausted from following her frenetic rhythms. It took the remainder of Saturday to recover my senses and slow down.

For ten years this was our pattern, every Friday night during the school year, whatever else may have changed. Her parents divorced and her brother, never quite normal, went crazy and was driven to a hospital outside town. Roxanne's mother remarried and moved to the suburbs, claiming that our neighborhood, where she and Roxanne's family had lived for many undisturbed years, was too full of—she'd whisper the word—negroids.

Even as a child, I understood that Roxanne's mother, Fran, worried about the wrong things. She cared too much about money and glamour, praising expensive cars and clothes. My own mother was a different kind of snob, shunning glitz but helpless before the likes of sarcastic intellectuals with mean wits. Hers was a harder elitism for me to recognize, whereas Fran's was fairly elementary.

She insisted, for instance, that Roxanne wear a dress at least one day a week, as if a bodice or ironed pleats might ensure femininity. Fran took her on excruciating shopping trips and provided her with charge accounts at extravagant dress shops, things I envied. I would have been a good daughter for Fran, in this regard, as my shape and metabolism were better suited to frills. But Roxanne was a tomboy then, an athlete, a girl who needed physicality the way the rest of us needed air. She wore shorts beneath her mandatory skirts, carried sneakers in her school bag. When the time came for bras, Roxanne wore undershirts. Before it was popular, she ran every afternoon at the park. By then, I'd quit trying to keep up. I would come along with our dog, Mitch, who was blind. Roxanne called me his seeing-eye person. Around the bike paths she would jog, miles and miles. Mitch and I would stumble about, sitting at the tennis courts or next to the fenced swimming pool, getting drinks at the fountain or pushing neighborhood children in the swings, while Roxanne, breathing in through her nose, out through her mouth, concentrating on a fixed and ever-distant point, ran and ran.

In high school, Roxanne made the track team as a freshman. She had hard tanned legs and pale-blue satin shorts. Her mother refused to attend meets. Instead, Fran had become a real estate agent in her new husband's office and was busy climbing society's ladder. She'd bought a silver Camaro and I took great pleasure in emerging from it in the North High parking lot twice a week. Fran did not approve of Roxanne's and my friendship. College people like my parents, she believed, were revolutionaries, hippies, troublemakers, drug and sex advocates. All Roxanne's truancies she liked to blame on me, despite what anyone said to the contrary. I had a big vocabulary I liked to throw around and knew how to use "lie" and "lay" properly.

It's painful to recall how tightly I clung to those amulets of superiority.

When Fran picked me up, I had to be out on our corner at 7:50 A.M., sharp, waiting for her or she would speed on without me. That happened more than once, causing hard feelings between her and my parents. This seemed to be her lesson to me on the ways of the real world: No one waited. She would slow down in traffic, the door would pop open, I would jump in next to Roxanne, and we'd be rushing off before I had time to pull my coat in or slam the door.

"Hi, Mrs. Titan," I would chirp, though her new name was Mrs. McBride.

"Uh huh," she would say. She was an aging beauty put back together with a few false parts—eyelashes, fingernails, nose job, tucks—and as vehemently different from my mother and her uncoiffed hair and frumpy sweatshirts as I could imagine. I was thrilled to ride around with Fran. "Mr. Stud," she called the Camaro. Going somewhere with her was an event; everyone else on the road was engaged in a conspiracy to keep us from arriving. "Cut off Mr. Stud, will you?" she'd say to the presumptuous driver trying to pass her. Swerving maniacally, she'd wriggle the car through tight traffic the way Roxanne wriggled into jeans. She liked to give other drivers the finger. "Do I make myself clear?" she'd say. Big hurry, same hyperactive urgency as Roxanne. Her lipstick-rimmed cigarette butts filled and overflowed the ashtray. Roxanne did not like to touch her so the two of us sat on each other in the passenger's bucket seat. When we got out at North, we imitated the hard thrusts of Fran's shifting, up our fists went into first, down to second, humming over to third, finally leaning hard into fourth, cruising. Sometimes I could almost feel whatever it was that was chasing Mrs. Titan, I could almost understand the imperativeness in keeping it at bay. It was not unlike the elusive, exciting thing that dangled ahead of Roxanne when she ran.

IRONICALLY, it was Fran McBride who eventually sold my parents' house, albeit reluctantly. She did not like to show older homes, preferring the new models outside the heart of the city, fresh paint, golf course–like lawns and silky-smooth window sashes. A developer bought it. Our yard was paved into a parking lot and a mini-mall opened inside. In my suite of rooms on the third floor, the servants' apartment, someone now sells expensive kitchen utensils.

ROXANNE was a wonder at track meets. She was so beautiful I realized she'd been designed for this and this alone. Her races became personal events, the crowds obliterated, the other runners obscured: Toward her focal point she would hurl, pissed off. Everything womanly about her seemed a hindrance, and as I watched, cheering from the bleachers, I understood she should have been born male, unencumbered by breasts and a low center of gravity. Records got broken right and left. There were no marathons in those days, not in the Midwest, but had there been, Roxanne would easily have won. She was the team's kingpin. Most runners did best at either short sprints or long runs, but Roxanne excelled in both. Her nature had always been contrary, two-sided. On the one hand, she was a tomboy, indignant of even the mention of personal appearance, ignoring the dresses in her closet, intolerant of the girls she called "girlies."

On the other hand, she needed boys as more than teammates or friends. They had always liked Roxanne. When we were in elementary school she was without fail among the first picks for kickball or dodgeball. Their respect for her was not limited to her wide-ranging athletic talents, either; she would not settle for merely being a pal. They told her their secrets, she was one of them without nullifying sexual attraction. She was pretty and smart and good at sports. She had it all.

Then she lost some of her advantage. The pool had widened exponentially when we moved on to North High, variations of female competition Roxanne had never dreamed of. Though she was a track star, the honor was low-profile in these postpubescent days and did not particularly register in this land of cheerleader and pom-pom uniforms. Roxanne, dissatisfied with being a smaller fish, introduced the idea of hitting bars our junior year. She found the one that did not card, and then dressed us both on those Friday nights, made us up and blow-dried our hair into the windswept look that was then popular. Obediently I sat on the toilet lid while Roxanne highlighted my eyes and downplayed my wide, cheeky face. This was alchemy learned from her mother, the wizard of such enterprises. Off to The Library we went. We would conquer new territory.

The Library was near the college where my mother taught and where my father would pretend to write and research his physics dissertation off and on for many years. Though I knew they never went to The Library (they went to bars, but this one was a jock bar and not to their taste), I still worried one of their colleagues might spot me there. My parents did not have a lot of friends—my mother had no patience for social rites and my father was as awkward around his peers as I was around mine—but the mere proximity of the college made me queasy.

A complete transformation took place in Roxanne. It appeared that this was her other element. Flirtatious, sexy, joking with college boys as if they were younger than she. Her athlete's body she had sheathed in tight boy's jeans and one of her mother's expensive cashmere sweaters. This became her trademark throughout high school and college, simple and elegant and completely flattering on her. My body was more difficult to present—breasts were my long suit, legs my unquestionable weakness, especially compared to Roxanne's lean ones. I generally wore dark pants and oversized, low-scooped sweaters the color of my eyes, hoping to draw attention upward rather than down.

It was in The Library that Roxanne hit the peak of her life. I did not realize this until much later, of course, and then felt bad for her, because it was such a hollow success, so full of teenage lies and misguided romantic ambitions. Nowhere but in the suffocating dark of the bar was any of it real. We wanted to be loved by foolish college boys, who wanted to sleep with foolish underage girls.

At the time, however, I envied Roxanne with a nearly homicidal intensity. In the guise of friendly criticism, I began questioning her bar costume, raising my eyebrows at her choice of boyfriend, getting off little jabs whenever possible. We had always teased one another—it was part of being unsentimental and entertaining, of not being "girlies"—calling each other nicknames that were just this side of unkind, but now the banter upped a notch in hostility.

To others I maintained my possessive loyalty for Roxanne, defending her dubious reputation as if my life depended on it, telling the rest of the track team she only drank water at The Library, lying to Fran on Friday nights when she'd call to check up on Roxanne. "She's in the bathroom, Mrs. Titan." Then I'd phone Roxanne at Jimmy's or Andy's or wherever and she'd return her mother's call. As my friend, Roxanne defined me, so I provided alibis, but to Roxanne, I would say innocently, "Don't you worry about being called a slut?" The worst imaginable fate. I once drove her to Andy's and sat in the living room eating pickles with his roommate while they went in the bedroom. The roommate and I had nothing to say to each other: me, silenced by the blunt magnitude of what our friends were doing; him, bored by his hostly duties.

Afterward, I lectured Roxanne on the drive home, pulling into our driveway to find Fran's shiny Camaro parked there, Fran in a rage. She flew out the door screaming as we drove up and I simply barreled by her, hearing her palm smack Roxanne's window, pulling under the carport and out the other side of our circular driveway, half conscious, beneath my terror, of how pleasingly ironic it was to leave Mrs. Titan on the curb.

After that, Roxanne ran away from home. Fran, idiotic as always, had prohibited Roxanne from doing the one thing in her life that was good for her, running track. Roxanne was grounded for a month and could not see me outside of school. I drove her to the bus station during lunch and waited with her for a while. We shared vending-machine food. She would go to Lake Tahoe on a two-day ride. Her aunt, who loved her, would be glad to see her. When she got there, she would call me collect; if everything was fine, she would be herself, Roxanne, and I would not accept the charges. If anything was wrong, she would be Lolita, and I would say, yes, operator, I'll pay. We loved the subterfuge of these kinds of useless tactics.

"What do I tell Fran?" I asked.

"Say squat," Roxanne said. "Say you haven't seen me since first hour."

Roxanne had always put me in difficult situations with her mom. I'd come to expect them, bearing up giddily under the peculiar pressure of deceiving an adult. But even my parents, who withheld opinion on most grown-ups I wished them to condemn, thought Mrs. Titan a bad mother and somehow sanctified my disrespect. They weren't wild about Roxanne, but they understood the psychological origins of her problems and were at least sympathetic. What astounds me now is that they trusted my judgment enough to let me be her friend. It's more than I can imagine allowing my own daughter to do.

I had to rush to get back to sixth period. Aeronautics class, and no Roxanne to crack up with. She often tried me, I thought, but what would I do without her? That train of thought always led me to speculate what part I played in her life. It was possible she only needed me to watch her, a thought that depressed me.

The phone was ringing when I got home; my father sat at his desk reading one of his enormous texts, pencil in hand, ignoring the noise.

"It's rung roughly a hundred times," he said without looking up. "My guess is it's for you."

No operator in the world let a phone ring a hundred times. It had to be Mrs. Titan. I hung up my coat and stooped to lift Mitch from his safe and dirty spot by the study door.

"Dad, would you do me a favor?"

"No lying," he said, taking the chewed pencil eraser from his lips but still reading.

"Okay, what if I step outside and you tell her I'm not in?"

He finally looked up. "Roxanne's mom?"

I nodded, sighing loudly, shaking my head wearily as the phone rang on. He smiled in his young goofy way. My father was only nineteen when I was born and had braces on his teeth. In all the grinning pictures of him with me, his silver-filled mouth reflects the camera's flash. Braces and acne. When he smiled, his underbite (less severe these days) still made him look like a silly leering boy.

"Just this once," he and I said at the same time, his voice mimicking mine. I dashed out the front door, hugging Mitch and listening as my father picked up the phone. No, I wasn't home, no he hadn't seen Roxanne, no he wasn't protecting anybody. He hung up without saying good-bye.

"Thanks, Dad."

But Roxanne was back in three days. As soon as she'd gotten to Tahoe her aunt had stuck her on a plane home. She hadn't even had time to make her collect call, hadn't made it within sight of the lake before she was at the airport, waiting for a flight out. The only real consolation was the scandal her absence had caused at school. She got counseling, thereby missing a few classes, and Ms. Leavitt, the reputed homosexual track coach who was supposed to have a thing for Roxanne and of whom Roxanne made merciless fun, pleaded personally to Fran for Roxanne's reinstatement to the team. Life went on.

W E played a game called Dump or Drive. All we needed was a place to sit and a street to watch, my front porch, most often. Cars passed. "Dump," we would say of a family wagon, meaning, should this car be made a miraculous gift to us we would cash it in. "Dump" to the ubiquitous quarter-ton pickup truck, "Dump" to the lumbering sedan. Night would fall. Behind us, we would hear my mother shut the front door against the cool breeze that rose after sunset. Cicadas, distant sirens, shouting children, cars. I would drift philosophically from our sitting selves and look at Roxanne, wishing she were a boy so I could be in love with her; even then I knew I was no Ms. Leavitt. Roxanne lifted up to slip her hands beneath her, separating her pad-free rear end from the cold cement steps. "Life is too full of Dumps," she would say, grinning.

W H E N E V E R we could borrow a car, I drove the twelve miles to Mount Hope while Roxanne ran on the road's shoulder. We went to see her brother, Leo. Leo was three years older than Roxanne and they had not been close when he lived at home. Nevertheless, he had promised us when we were making the big move from middle school to high school that he would introduce us to people, meaning boys, and that he would see to our status among the right groups. This was wishful thinking on Leo's part, though I'm sure he would have done whatever he could to ensure safe passage, but he was one of the great North High unknowns. He adored us. He thought we were even funnier than we thought we were. A sweet and dumb boy, he was handsome the way Roxanne was but hindered by having no sense of himself, no cockiness or pretense, as placid and innocent as milk. "Lights on, nobody home," Roxanne would complain. Their mother, Fran, said of him, "He sways with every breeze," ruffling her fingers on either side of her face. He swayed into acid. After he overdosed his first year of college and never quite snapped back, Roxanne took interest in him at last.

"Did you hallucinate?" she asked, sitting on his rollaway bed, stretching her toes to keep herself from shin splints. At Mount Hope the floors were waxed and furniture was on wheels, giving the impression that things could slip out from under you at any moment.

"I got very interested in my hands," Leo said, smiling sheepishly. Honestly, I couldn't tell that he was much changed. Same guileless eyes, same elapsed response time. "My hands looked so cool, I thought I could do anything with them." Getting a drink of water, he had shattered the glass and then tried to repair it with his fingers, working ambitiously while the sink filled with blood. Raised scars from his stitched cuts covered his hands like small white slugs.

Roxanne shook her head impatiently. "No, I mean did you see things that weren't there, like God."

Leo laughed in his languid way, overly amused as he always had been by Roxanne. "I thought God was in my hands," he told her.

"I guess that could be a hallucination," she said speculatively. "Do people smuggle drugs in here?"

Leo shrugged, still smiling. It was obvious to me that he would be among the last to know if anything covert was happening at Mount Hope.

"Let's walk," Roxanne said. She wore her track shorts and sleeveless jersey. She smelled like salt. Leo's floor was all male and Roxanne liked to create a stir. I wasn't above feeling jealous that even here they all preferred her. At Mount Hope, she was "Blondie" and I was "Blondie's Friend." The one she wanted, J. D. Bain, never even looked up from his bed as she went by. Dark and moody, he became an obsession with Roxanne, and after her original interest in her brother, our visits to Mount Hope were really to see J. D. After the requisite chat with Leo, she would search him out.

J. D., like Leo, was a voluntary. He checked himself in and out of Mount Hope every few months. J. D. had nothing but good looks going for him, and they were very standard, film-idol good looks, a type I had never trusted or been attracted to. He was twenty-four and when he wasn't sick, he lived above a garage in the city. Roxanne took me to visit him there once a few years later. But at Mount Hope, when he finally acknowledged her (a long and annoying process), the two of them had a hushed affair—sex was not permitted there—and I was dispatched as lookout. I sat in the hallway outside J. D.'s door and watched for hospital staff, never sure what I would do if one came along. Create a diversion? Sometimes I would return to Leo's room, just down the hall, and talk to him from the doorway.

Leo liked Mount Hope and he seemed to fit in, though his roommate hit him up for money all the time. The staff was friendly and when he couldn't sleep they gave him pills. "Good medicine," he said, "keeps you from having dreams."

"Really?" I said, glancing down the hall.

"Really. I can't wait to go to sleep. You know what J. D. did?"

I said I didn't.

He crooked his finger so I would come to him. I checked the empty hall again and went. "Accidentally killed his best friend," Leo said reverently.

"When?"

"When he was a kid, playing with rifles. Don't tell Roxanne. He said it in group and that's confidential."

Not to tell Roxanne anything was ludicrous, a fact even Leo must have known. "See you next time, Leo."

I resumed my post outside J. D.'s door, excited with my discovery. She emerged later flushed and giggly, unlike herself, though what she was doing was what she always did, breaking rules, pushing limits.

"He killed a boy," I told her on the ride home, nonchalantly. We both rode in the car going back, Roxanne at the wheel.

"Big whiz," she said, giving me a withering look and successfully cutting off conversation. We were easily doing eighty or ninety miles per hour.

MY PARENTS, academics, escaped the Midwest heat every summer and went to Oregon. Until I was eight years old and my thinking was corrected, I believed everyone worked under a nine-month contract and had the summer off, choosing, inexplicably, to stay put during the broiling months of June, July, and August.

Off we went to Oregon, where my mother's family owned a beach house. I could have invited Roxanne along, but even then I think I understood that there were parts of myself I could not share with her, aspects of myself that I knew instinctively would clash. Oregon was the biggest of those secrets. Also secret was my true affection for my parents. In the summer, we played three-handed bridge or took parts and read plays to one another. We discussed current events. My parents were friends and I sometimes worried I would not have a marriage that would meet up to theirs.

On the beach, near the water too cold to swim in but fine for wading, I felt a cleanness wash over me with every falling wave, a clarifying light that rinsed away the cloudy nine-month winter of the Midwest. I woke in my small and spare bedroom every morning to the sound of seagulls and the ocean. I wrote Roxanne dutifully, daily in the beginning of the summer, then less frequently as I slowly lost contact with our intimacy. It was as if the waves pulled part of me away with them, the difficult, childish parts. I would grow, it seemed, outreach the confinements of school and fashion.

When we returned, I hated those first few shrinking, frustrating weeks in late August when Roxanne and I did not have easy access to each other.

But we came around, reshaped our changed selves to mesh once more with the other. I let Oregon submerge. Years later, when we fought and failed to make up, I believed that I was the one who'd always had to adjust, that Roxanne had been simply Roxanne, immovable, stubbornly inhospitable to changes she did not initiate. For example, during our first year in college, as roommates in the dorm she had chosen for us, we were not likely to be asked to rush. I wanted to be invited to join a sorority. I didn't necessarily want to become a sister, but I wanted to savor the option.

"Like Blue Birds," I coaxed. Roxanne would have none of it. She made it clear she would have none of me if I rushed. Our friends now were mostly men. Roxanne never had women friends unless they were the dates of her men friends. As a group, we all took a class called Space and Adventure, which she enjoyed the way she had enjoyed Aeronautics in high school, making bad puns, exchanging witty notes, cheating aggressively on tests. Any genuine interest in the subject was laughable so I hid mine.

The university was only three hours away from our hometown. When we came home, which was often during our first year, Roxanne would plan to stay with my family, but then would always end up with J. D. He cast a spell strong enough to supplant our friendship, our Friday nights. Her mother would have disapproved if she'd known, but Roxanne never told her or her stepfather she was in town. There was no reason for them to think she wasn't safely away at school. Truthfully, I believed Mrs. Titan had been disengaging herself from Roxanne over the last few months. Understandable, I thought, since she'd delivered Roxanne intact into legal adulthood. Enough, after all, was enough.

So that first weekend we went to J. D.'s without the threat of discovery hanging over us. I went just because I had always gone when Roxanne visited him at Mount Hope. His shabby garage apartment smelled of the parked cars below. J. D. Bain was the only man I ever knew who made Roxanne tongue-tied, and aside from his being unpredictably hostile and a tease, I think I disliked him for turning Roxanne unsteady and timid, qualities that did not suit her and that made me impatient. I counted on her to be the leader. But perhaps I was only jealous. Or maybe I hated what he managed, by metamorphosing Roxanne, to cause as a reaction in me: I became the strident wet blanket. Roxanne sat on his lap, blurrily high and deferential, while I huffed angrily. Could I have been tapping my foot?

"What's your beef?" J. D. said at last, giving me a sly smile.

"Nothing."

"Too good for us?" He continued to smile. They both got high, first thing, then began their slow move toward sex. Eventually, I would have to leave, pace, today, in the parking lot below. At Mount Hope, at least, I had an assignment and the implicit understanding that what was going on inside was a willful but knowing violation of rules. But in the lengthening shadows of the downtown buildings, I stood alone and apprehensive, aware all of a sudden that my presence was not necessary. No one would step in to reprimand them. The illicitness of their love had disintegrated with age, so that the only thing left up there, behind the aluminum window sash and tacky American flag curtains, was Roxanne and J. D. I felt dumb walking around in the broken glass and rubble. It made me sad, this liberation, but I was abruptly and obviously an anachronism and so I got in my car and drove home without her.

I AM ashamed of what followed. My interests led me to art and literature and political science classes, while her schedule filled with health and athletics and education classes. My style was duplicitous: The Serious Intellectual versus Roxanne's Best Friend. They were mutually exclusive roles, I knew that, and I decided quite consciously which one I believed to be more worthy of my fidelity.

It was terrible. By now, our third year away from home, we were sharing an apartment. Roxanne had selected a two-bedroom place in a brand new shoebox building while I was away in Oregon for the summer. I'd requested an apartment in a Victorian house, which our small college town was filled with, but Roxanne put our money down on this place, pale green and smelling of its new carpet. Worst of all was the fact that our boyfriends reflected more concretely the directions each of us had taken. She still saw J. D. Bain, but at school, three hours distance from him, Roxanne, with effort, had upscaled her image and gotten another boyfriend. It did not occur to me until much later that she might have done this to please me, offering up a compromise. I didn't think that way about our friendship back then.

Whatever the reason, now she wanted clean-cut, wholesome. Her new man was blond and muscular, a member of the rugby team and a bartender at one of the frat bars. Mine was a dark-eyed cynic who chain-smoked and wrote for the college paper. They met in the mornings over the city news-paper, Roxanne's studying the box scores while mine made pithy remarks about the crappy right-wing editorial board. In all hindsight honesty, mine was worse, but whereas he was my first serious boyfriend, the first one I'd slept with, Roxanne's was the latest in a line of men, excluding J. D., no more serious than Andy from The Library five years earlier. I thought I deserved more tolerance since mine was the superior love.

We came to blows, but under surprising circumstances. For once, just the two of us were in the apartment, both dressing to go out that night, Roxanne to the bar where her boyfriend worked and I to a Russian movie alone, a plan I had been congratulating myself on all day. I had never been to a movie by myself before.

Roxanne came out of her bedroom wearing her usual jeans and sweater, hair a luxurious tangle around her face. "Have you seen my peach shoe?" she asked, stopping at my doorway. She cocked her head and narrowed her eyes accusingly, which did not make much sense. Though we had exchanged clothes in the past, our feet were different sizes.

"No," I said coldly, the word full of indignation.

"Come on," she said, shaking her blond head. "I'm missing two shoes, from separate pairs, and I know you took them."

"What?" I had quit trying to decide what to wear by this point, standing at my closet holding on to the sleeves of shirts.

"Give me my shoes," she said.

I told her I didn't have them. I laughed at her, though it took work. Why would I hide her shoes? What kind of child did she take me for? I was nothing if not a grown-up.

"Come on," she said, letting her cool surface heat a little. "You go in my room while I'm not here, you use my bath-room stuff, why shouldn't you take my shoes? Just give them back."

It was true I went in her room, but behind her door was the only full-length mirror in the apartment. Otherwise, she was full of shit, which I wasted no time in telling her.

"You know what else I hate," she said, still leaning at my bedroom door. "I hate how you yell at those kids."

"They're brats," I told her. Our landlord's children pounded up and down the fire escape when they got home from school every day. I'd had enough and stood on our balcony telling them to shut up.

Roxanne said, "And why do you wear those nasty old used clothes?"

"Excuse me?"

"How can you stand to put on clothes someone else has sweated in?"

With tremendous adult presence of mind, I said, gently, "Maybe you need to start running again. Maybe you'd feel better." Surely she could see that this nonsensical outburst hid some deeper anger. At least, I decided it did.

She rolled her eyes. "Don't patronize me. You and your mother, just alike."

Again the self-control I proudly maintained, unwilling to sink to the level that would allow me to bring *her* mother into the conversation. "Did something happen, Roxanne?" I asked, hurt and concern in my voice.

"Fuck you. Just fuck you, you're so hot, your parents are so hot, your goddamn house is so hot. Fuck you." She pounded the cheap door frame and walked away. "Fuck, fuck, fuck you," I heard, her cold wrath thrown over her shoulder. My face was painfully hot and I shut my door with false calm. I sat hard on the bed, though, heaving with self-pitying, quiet tears. What had I done to deserve this, I asked myself, and later asked my boyfriend. But I wasn't as wounded as I pretended, feeling in the deepest recesses of my snobby soul that she had been right to accuse me, even if she'd misidentified the reasons.

I moved in with my boyfriend; her boyfriend moved into the shoebox. I had cried, true, but it was all so fast in dissolving and I was so relieved that I understood the break had been coming for a long time. Roxanne and I did not speak to each other again.

★   ★   ★

I TRIED explaining my confusion concerning Roxanne Titan to my mother when I came home for Christmas break the year we quit being best friends. I left out the squirmy self-incriminating parts.

"People change," my mother said. "You and Roxanne aren't done with each other, you're just taking a breather. In time, you'll make up." Some sentimental little bit of me wanted to believe her, but the majority claim was on forging ahead without her. Onward into my new life I would go, forsaking those frivolous years I'd wasted knowing Roxanne Titan.

I almost married my first boyfriend, that cynical reporter. All of my romances nearly led to marriage. I didn't fall in love often, but when I did, it was in dead earnest. I invested everything I had in relationships, expecting lover and best friend wrapped up in one parcel. As with Roxanne, eventually I would feel myself pulling away from them to take a good hard look, criticizing obliquely, and then coming to that moment when apprehension cast its shadow, like the night in the parking lot downtown outside J. D.'s. I would learn this man's weakness, his annoyingly human nature, my part in his private agenda. What would begin as a pinhole in the fabric of flawlessness I would nurse into a full-blown rip. What use did I have for imperfection?

As was always the case with Roxanne, she continued to lead the more troubled life. When we were young I would come home from Oregon full of stories for her about my summer, held up for her inspection, her approval, sure I could impress her at last. I'd gone this far with a boy, drunk that much one night. Whatever my miscreant accomplishments, hers were grander. During the summer of my first mushroom trip, she'd had an abortion. I didn't speak to my father for a week; she moved out of the house and lived with J. D. Bain in the garage apartment. I barely squeaked through Biology; Roxanne flunked out of the university completely.

She consistently took harder knocks. I heard about Roxanne through one of our teachers from North. Both Roxanne and I

had fallen in love with Johnny Pierpoint and were his best
students in Government, a class we'd excelled in because we
worshipped him. Roxanne thought he was good-looking and I
thought he was hilarious. Those were our respective require-
ments for love; we rarely shared a recipient. Johnny Pierpoint
was one exception.

He was married now and when I came to town, I looked
him and his wife up. It pleased me to be able to say that I got
along better with my teachers from high school than the other
students. As always, I brought the conversation around to
Roxanne. Johnny and his wife exchanged a glance, and my
heart quickened. They told me Roxanne had been raped. This
was after our fateful junior year, the year of the shoebox apartment and her flunking out. Overwhelmed by the university,
Johnny told me, she'd moved back home with her mother and
stepfather. Fran, more neurotic than ever, somehow got it in
her mind that Roxanne was flirting with her husband, Roxanne's stepfather. I balked at the idea. Dreary Ned, we had
always called him. Bland and CEO-like, who but Fran would
want him? After a horrible fight, Roxanne had moved into a
duplex on the south (bad) side of town. Her rapist had followed
her home from work and picked her back-door lock. Sleeping
with the TV on, she'd wakened when he sat down on her bed.

After I left the Pierpoints', I drove around the neighborhood
I'd grown up in, the one Roxanne and I had explored together.
My parents no longer lived here but the renovation of our
house was not yet complete so it stood empty. Roxanne's and
my friendship came back to me everywhere I looked—the
dinner theater where we'd waited tables only one night and
then been fired as a unit, the corner where my dog, Mitch,
had gotten hit by a car and the stop sign from which my fingers
could not be pried in my hysteria, the Catholic church we
sometimes broke into and prayed for suave boyfriends. I realized I hadn't thought of Roxanne in any whole way (that is,
as a whole person whose life went on under the same clock
and calendar as my own) for years. Maybe I never had. This
possibility distressed me, that I had misread our friendship
and her needs entirely. Eventually, I stopped at the twenty-

four-hour donut shop we used to go to when we weren't quite through with a Friday night—cream puffs, bow ties, hot chocolate, playing Dump or Drive from a window booth—and tried to imagine phoning her, tried to convince myself I wanted to hear her familiar, ironic voice.

I HAD not been vigilant in my defense of Roxanne to myself. I was not selfless in my love. But I was young and still learning these honorable traits. My excuse now is that it is too late. These days, I have successfully re-created myself. Most of the people I knew when I was young are strangers to me and I take a proud pleasure in the fact. When we visit my hometown, I claim to my husband that I wish I knew them— in the mall, that woman looks familiar—but how idealistic and impossible a wish! And, most important, how dishonest. I cling to my new sunny life in California, a life that reminds me of my family's cleansing summers in Oregon, and I promise myself not to let such catastrophic oversights, insensitivities, occur in my future. Good-bye, hometown, good-bye, Roxanne.

She married a man twenty years older than herself. She was his mistress for the last years of his first marriage, a short pirate of a man who makes a lot of money and who looks ridiculous next to leggy Roxanne, a man with three grown children who don't like her. She drinks. She had a nose job, forever rectifying that white slash of sunburn scar. She, too, left the Midwest, and now lives in a wealthy Dallas suburb. Sometimes she takes business classes at the local college. I believe she'll pine for J. D. Bain and have affairs and be lonely, but what do I know? I married a man who became my best friend, just what I thought I wanted. I don't want to know Roxanne.

It would not have surprised me to learn that she had killed herself. I woke one night certain that it had happened or was about to. In a frenzy, I tried to find her address, her phone number, some slip of paper that meant I had a connection to her, my obligation to my insight obvious: I had to reach her, to save her. But I didn't know how to find her. Eventually my anxiety subsided—I let my husband talk me out of it—and we went back to bed.

And he was right, she didn't kill herself. She got married in the Bahamas, an event recorded in a set of photos she sent to me two years ago along with the announcement, out of the blue. She found me. No friends or relatives in attendance, just the happy couple and a few cheerful native islanders, everyone surrounded by flowers, turquoise ocean behind them. They're dressed exquisitely, she and he, posing in all the traditional ways: approaching the alter separately, somberly, watching their feet as the ceremony proceeds, arms linked afterward, pushing cake into each others' mouths. But for what audience?

The photos were with the first announcement. I didn't send a gift. I justified this by asking myself what they, people with money, could need. With our tastes so insistently at odds, what could I give Roxanne? I considered the question for a long time, aware that, however awkwardly, she had put the ball in my court. Still, I did not respond.

The second wedding announcement arrived three months later, a gently coaxing provocation, or perhaps an oversight— I remember well enough the stamp-and-envelope confusion of invitations, acknowledgments, congratulations, and thank yous. But Roxanne's announcements, expensive and ornately ugly in a way I associate with the ostentatious side of Texas, embossed with rose petals and raised cursive silver wording, continue to come. Another, and another, sometimes with a photo, like today's, sometimes by themselves, arriving at my door in the steady, mindful way of unpaid bills, outstanding debts.

INERTIA

T H E squirrel paused on a high branch in a bare winter elm, his tail twitching thinly, suspiciously. Though the sun reflected blindingly on car hoods and broken glass and the three rails of the elevated train tracks, the temperature hovered near zero, and the squirrel's front feet, under his chin as he stood on the limb, quivered with cold. He slowly blinked before taking another jump; his eyes closed as if he might be driven to hibernation there on the spindly branch. Then suddenly he streaked through the intricate network of tree limbs scaffolding the alley, coursing along them and onto a telephone wire as if carried by an electrical current.

The phone line to the bakery was frozen, ice encircling it like extra insulator casing. When the squirrel took the last leap he would ever take, he grabbed the thick, slick cable with all four paws and hung on, spinning like a gymnast, around once, twice, inescapable inertia sending him looping a third time, then throwing him free. He landed on his back on the roof, which was also icy. There'd been a kitchen fire two nights earlier in the bakery and firemen had soaked the old roof to keep it from igniting. Water had been shot indiscriminately so that now icicles hung like stalactites from everything surrounding the storefront. The squirrel lay blinking up at the bright morning sky, his heart beating visibly in his small chest.

Hope Daniels, witness, felt her own heart accelerate in response. She had watched the whole thing from her sewing room window. Her niece was staying in the room. On instruction from her brother-in-law, Hope was searching the girl's room for evidence, for clues, for reassurance. So far she had found nothing strictly incriminating, though the girl's diary, painstakingly hidden beneath a drawer, was a tempting short-cut. Hope could not bring herself to read it, could not decide either whether to present it to Monty, the girl's father. Considering this dilemma, Hope had been standing at the second-floor window reaching for her own past, trying to call up that distant fifteen-year-old self that might inform her, when the graceful but unlucky squirrel caught her eye.

For an instant Hope believed his accident came from her desire for him to be punished. She could not deny that his flirtatious nonchalance in the serious face of gravity had made her feel heavily earthbound and vengeful.

"Monty!" she yelled ahead of herself as she ran down the stairs. "Monty, get your coat, hurry, there's a hurt squirrel."

Hope was grateful Monty geared into motion without questioning the mission. Her husband would have made her explain herself before becoming involved. This particular excursion he would have seen as futile from the onset, though, to give due credit, he would have come along if Hope insisted. She grabbed the first coat she could lay her hands on, a parka of her husband's that he called "Off in Antarctica." Its hood was lined with synthetic fur that appeared meant to resemble gray wolf.

"What happened?" Monty asked once they were outside. The air was so cold Hope's first inhalation seemed to freeze-dry her nostrils. Monty wiped his watering eyes as they ran toward the bakery, Hope telling him about the squirrel, circling her bare hands to illustrate the animal's rotation on the cable.

Because of the fire, the bakery was closed. A hand-lettered apology on the front door promised a quick return to business as usual and thanked its loyal patrons. On one side of the bakery was a drive-thru bank (a woman's flat, institutional voice could be heard, amplified by her microphone, saying, "Push the button to send the tube, *push* the button") and on the other side was a hardware store.

"He's alive," Hope said. "We have to rescue him." Though she could not see the squirrel, she knew he still lay on the roof blinking into the sky. Animals had no conception of time; the squirrel's mind might obliterate all that had come before, certainly all he might have had ahead of him. Now there was the fathomless brilliant cold sky and, undoubtedly, pain. Did animals have tear glands, Hope wondered, did they cry when hurt? Or might that have been evolutionarily unwise? She could not bear exiling the squirrel to his fate. "We have to do something!" she said to Monty.

Her brother-in-law focused on her tone of voice now for the first time. Hope saw him weigh her anxiety against reality, not judging her, as her husband might, but simply taking note.

"I could call the owner," Hope went on. "You could see if the hardware store has a ladder. *We* might have a ladder." She turned to look at her house, as if its rear face might remind her of the odd and forgotten possessions inside. The second floor window she'd stood at was close enough to the bakery to have made out the rapid rise and fall of the squirrel's chest. That window right there. Hope saw Lisa's diary leaning against the glass, a large ox-blood–leather book with none of the childish accoutrements of a typical girl's diary: no little laughable lock and key, no gold-scripted title on its cover. The seriousness of its looks and hiding place had convinced Hope it would yield the information she and Monty wanted. Yet she had not opened it. Now it waited, hastily and stupidly left in the windowsill where anyone on Western Avenue could see it. If Lisa came home and found this, Hope would not be able to forgive herself.

Stomping from foot to foot on the sidewalk beside Hope, Monty said, "I could check next door for roof access."

Hope had her hands in her husband's coat pockets and now realized that in her worried and cold condition she had completely and unconsciously shredded some receipts or, possibly, dollar bills. She pulled out the limp orange remains of two unused tickets to a play she and her husband had planned to go see in November, three months ago. Hope could still read the printed price, and though her husband had gotten them free, Hope understood he hesitated in throwing away something clearly valued at twenty-five dollars apiece.

"I'm going to call the humane society," she told Monty.

"Good idea!" He sounded surprised and impressed. Since he'd come to live with Hope she'd realized incrementally the extent of his stunned reactions to the world. He'd forgotten how to manage. He had not known how to go about getting his mail forwarded or his utilities cut off. He'd simply left his house in Milwaukee, walked out the front door and driven himself and Lisa to Chicago.

"Yes, call the humane society," he said. His words appeared in puffs of white steam. Calling the humane society would have been Hope's husband's first plan of action, a fact Hope could only recognize in hindsight. It was the kind of revelation that made her see she often sold him short.

She ran past the ice-filled trash cans behind the bakery and through the alley gate. Another squirrel balanced on the fence separating her yard from the alley, staring menacingly at Hope as if she'd threatened it. For a second Hope realized the sheer number of squirrels in the world, thousands of millions, no doubt. It was foolish sentimentality to work at rescuing the particular unfortunate one of the bakery roof; look, here was another, adequate enough. Between his paws this one held an empty plastic peanut butter jar, glaring at Hope as if she might steal it from him. She could not imagine how he planned to transport it, or even how he had gotten this far with it. His stubborn clench and paranoid demeanor were irritating: such fruitless perseverance. "Scat," she hissed at him.

The back door had not latched shut when she and Monty had run out, so now the kitchen was freezing. Hope paused for a second listening: What if some enterprising burglar had slid in while she and Monty had been on their valiant mission? The refrigerator motor came on at this point and Hope could not sustain any genuine worry over its placid innocuous hum. She lit the oven before heading upstairs.

In the sewing room, she lifted the journal (she had to acknowledge that it was not a diary) from the windowsill and put it back in the base of the night table. With the drawer removed, the journal slipped right in. Hope replaced the drawer of socks and underwear, ashamed at having agreed to search the room at all. But in the last few days Monty had been emerging from his stupor to take notice finally of Lisa, of her unusual silence and long acquiescent stares, the sleepy circles under the opaque eyes. His alarm had set off Hope's; they had to act.

Finding a package of pills or some other sign of average delinquency, honestly, might have been a relief; the real danger, Hope knew, lay in reading what the girl might be writing. Lisa's mother, Hope's older sister, had killed herself in November. She had done it in her car, had driven at a high speed and without any sign of resistance directly into a bridge abutment, her obvious desire being that Lisa would—*could*, anyway—think her death accidental. That later Lisa could say, "My mother had an accident." Hope and her husband had planned to go to the theater that night. The unused tickets in the pocket of the parka had been to a comic production put on by a theater group whose office shared a parking lot with Hope's husband's office in the city. When the phone call came, Hope had been rolling pantyhose up her calves, singing with the radio, enjoying the elaborate ritual that constituted Going Out. The phone rang but she was sure it would be a computer; they always called at supper time.

Her husband answered downstairs and Hope waited, smiling, to hear him snarl his standard reply—"I do *not* talk to machines." But instead he said, "Oh no," in a voice saturated with utter defeat. Hope heard everything in those two words, the fact that he was absorbing a blow for her, that it was the end not of his world but hers. She sat on the bed wearing only her pantyhose, her hands crossed over her chest defensively, cupping opposite shoulders, waiting for him to come tell her.

Hope shut the drawer with resolve; it was none of her business what Lisa wrote, but then she was afraid she was masking cowardice with false and selective affinity to a rule of privacy:

The truth was, she did not have the necessary character to take on Lisa's suffering. Its potential width and depth and girth overwhelmed her. She went to the window and looked down at the bakery.

Monty was on its roof. He'd found access and was making his way slowly across the ice, moving on his haunches, his fists and hips swaying in an exaggeration of equilibrium. From where she stood, Hope could see the squirrel's chest still moving much too quickly. He blinked, paralyzed for any number of reasons.

Suddenly Monty slid—Hope put both palms to the cold glass in reflex, as if to buttress him—then righted himself. The roof sloped very abruptly toward the alley, and Hope realized Monty was in danger of falling, landing on *his* back near the garbage bins. How was it the squirrel did not slide? His staying put had been misleading evidence of a flat roof. Hope nearly rapped on the glass to warn Monty, but caught herself: He startled so easily, snapped from deep concentration with visible regret and fright, shaking himself, coming to. A sudden noise might send him over.

Hope let out her breath when he reached the squirrel, though of course he still had to make his way back across the roof if he intended to rescue the animal, and this time without the balance of his arms. Relief was not yet in order. Moronic, Hope thought, of herself and of Monty; what made them believe this effort useful? Her husband's rational approach, calling in the experts, was much the superior one. Yet there Monty was, edging the last few inches, bending over the creature.

He had squatted deliberately beside the squirrel, lowering his ballast. The wind blew and the trees in the alley, stiff and heavy with ice as they were, creaked. It was the coldest winter Hope could remember. Monty's hood flew back and his long blond hair whipped across his face. Hope decided that when the squirrel fell it was the inevitable secretions of a living body which had stuck him at once to the ice, the way a moist fingertip will stick to an ice cube. Monty was crying. His hands moved in absolute futility, for naturally the squirrel was firmly frozen to his imminent death. Now Monty raised his eyes and met Hope's, across the alley and through the glass, as from an ice floe to a receding land, and Hope knew for the rest of her life she would come again and again precisely to this instant and move no longer forward.

How must it have seemed, she wondered later, from the squirrel's point of view? What were his last, not *thoughts*, but *impressions*? A man's unthinkably large face appears above him, descended from the replete sameness of the sky and of the pain, shocking him so thoroughly, so physically, his heart— self-protective and wise to the survival of species—ceases altogether? A face, contorted in its own rite of despair, presented without referral, without worthy context or sequence: The squirrel, in all likelihood, had never seen a man so clearly, so near.

FAIR HUNT

J A M E S had never killed an animal before. There were other facts he could have been wrestling but this one found him on his back porch at twilight, head at a thoughtful angle, thumbnail between his teeth. His hands smelled of the soap he'd used at the hospital, of the paper greens he'd worn, of the mask, smelled of the essence of illness itself, which he believed to be fear, and not at all of his wife. Surely he'd struck an animal on the road? For he'd driven countless vehicles, in the country and without caution, for over thirteen years. But nothing came to him, no jackrabbit, no snake, not one worthless grackle, a bird he might have killed without remorse.

He'd never hunted either and yet, as of this afternoon, he owned a gun. Driving home from the airport, he had stopped at the garish turquoise building whose excited sign—GUNS! AMMO! BEER!—had become so familiar to him that he nearly drove by when searching it out. The proprietor had been held up and shot with one of his own hand guns not too long ago, a bullet through the lung, he told James. Just made him mad. But he kept his eye on James, possibly thinking James's complete ignorance in the line of firearms suspicious. It was rural New Mexico, after all, and men owned guns.

Another thing, James thought, removed from the porch, past the can-opening routine that marked his recent meal-making, now eating his dinner in front of the television: He'd never fired a gun. He had studied the act, indirectly and repeatedly, via TV, but had never, to his knowledge, taken a gun in his hands, wrapped his finger around a trigger. His parents were pacifists; he'd been ten years too young for Vietnam. He hesitated, holding his soup spoon above the bowl, cocking his head and staring upward and to his right, the same pose he'd assumed earlier on the porch, the one his wife had told him all people take when trying to remember the past. This was something about Dee: her ability to make him self-conscious, like a hidden camera. She studied him and then fed him her findings. He was, she let him know, curious though worthy material. James stared purposefully down into the floating debris of his soup. There was no gun he could recall.

The secondhand shotgun lay, for lack of a better place, on the couch beside him. He had tossed it there trying to make it appear natural in his home, like a sweaty hat. Dee hated guns, had not long ago planted a homemade anti-NRA sign-board in the front yard which had been promptly shot full of holes. Now the bravest of her stray toms suddenly jumped to a cushion, startling James, and sniffed along the instrument that tomorrow would be used to kill him.

"What do you think, Cat?" James squeaked and so had to clear his throat and repeat the question calmly. He'd never been in the habit of talking to the animals, either, another abberation Dee would have pointed out to him if she'd been home.

THEY were bad farmers, not really farmers at all, their garden eaten by rabbits, their chickens overrunning the out-buildings because Dee had declared herself, and James, ex-treme vegetarians, unwilling to consume animals or their byproducts. So eggs were permitted to hatch. Coyotes, perhaps hawks, served to thin the group. James and Dee had come to the country first generation, both raised in suburban Houston, where crows and giant cockroaches constituted wildlife. They had bought a small cotton and pecan farm and allowed the meager acreage to take its own course. Tumbleweeds now filled the untilled cotton fields; the pecan trees bloomed and dropped their husky nuts and spread their summer canopy without interference. The county provided irrigation water which James could not remember to take advantage of. Both he and Dee worked in El Paso, across the New Mexico state line thirty miles south. They were happy enough to come home at night to the country, which was filled with the noises James had always associated with longing—coyotes, the relentless wind, train whistles and the accompanying clack of wheels—except, could it be longing, if he was here? Their animals accumulated as strays will, sent packing by intolerant adjoining farms, adopted by Dee, who turned each into a character, comical, harmless. Soon they owned a self-destructive goat who ate not only feed dishes and barbed wire but her own fur as well, her rump as bare and smooth as a human's, prone to excema. She would ram her head into a wall until she passed out. From the litters of skinny cats in the fields, Dee fed kittens who became older and less wild, who soon moved under the house and then in, never somehow forsaking their outdoor habit of pissing wherever they happened to be standing. The chickens had begun with a single hen who'd walked up their washboard road one morning ("Like some old white-trash church lady," Dee laughed), fat and insolent, and had stayed, content by herself in the tin outbuilding, wandering only often enough to produce fertile eggs, busy creating her own quick empire of chicks.

The peacocks, two arrogant fellows who lived to outshine one another, had been won in a small-town raffle. Dee had a habit of winning prizes. They strutted, they preened, they presented their butts as if witholding the superior beauty of their plumage. Dee exalted in their cockiness, their purely natural conceit.

But she loved them all, without favorites, like children, loved to create their tales and salve their infections. It was her nature to rescue things, James came to understand. She kept a cardboard box of veterinary supplies beneath the bathroom sink, and more than once he had heard her through the closed bathroom door, convincing an unwilling animal to let her render aid.

I N the morning it was the goat James decided to sacrifice first. She was a loud nervous beast, large enough to make James uncomfortable at the prospect of her watching him slaughter the rest. He led her into the pecan grove, over the cracked topsoil, ducking under low limbs. It was a windy spring morning, the kind of day Dee would have announced by saying, "I hate the wind." The trees' shadows, bending, frightened the goat; she balked at his lead. Or perhaps he put off some odor of desperation. James certainly felt desperate, and he was sweating heavily, the hand holding the shotgun slick.

Dee had been away so long now that James had grown used to mourning her absence; it was practice for her death, which was coming, a heavy blanket worn over his shoulders. At first, it had been worse, more sharp and random, prodding him when he was most vulnerable. But now loss simply characterized him. He was thin and unhappy; his house seemed sinister, the landscape malevolent. Moving from morning to night, he felt his own will tested. Dee would die, he knew that, though no one would say as much. A sterile home would prolong her passing. She came to him in small, tenuous images, Dee lying submerged in a tub of cloudy bathwater, islands of her pink flesh, breasts and belly and splayed knees. Dee disparaging the local newspaper, Dee sitting against the south side of the house, sunbathing, her face held up to the light, and afterward, sunburned, James tamping pungent Noxzema over her shoulders while she winced.

Superimposed over these images, however, was the more concrete one of Dee in a hospital bed. It seemed to James that merely being there had made her twice as sick. From nowhere and for no good reason, she'd begun fainting, exhaustion coming on her so quickly she sometimes could not make it to a chair or bed. She'd always had headaches but she started suffering migraines, spent hours at a time weeping with pain. Between attacks were whole days she walked delicately through the house, her neck held as if her head might tumble off. Then she would be subsumed once more. Pain had turned her ugly, impatient. The peacocks' noise made her shriek in fury. James once found her lying on the bed slapping her own forehead and cheeks, fighting what hurt her. The next day she'd had two black eyes.

They had loved their quaint and endearing rural life, treating it ironically and with good humor, but James suddenly felt enraged with local doctors and the slow resignation they offered as assessment of her complaints. Dee, afraid of the worst, pretended for a time to believe them, that she needed rest more than anything.

Eventually a hematologist was consulted, and then an oncologist in El Paso, who sent her to Albuquerque and then Phoenix. James had just returned from seeing her, yet felt as distant as ever. Each transfer had taken her farther away from him, from their marriage, their home, from health. She'd even left her friendly name behind, was now called Dierdre. What remained of her seemed to grow transparent, like a healing burn.

James tethered the goat to a tree at the far end of the grove. The Rio Grande passed not far from where he stood; he could smell the swampy water, and its mosquitoes kept landing on his neck. He lifted the shotgun awkwardly under his armpit, elbow cocked in a clumsy position, and aimed at the goat's head, which was lowered as she tried busily to pull free of the rope. She was stirring up dust, braying, and James decided to just kill her fast. "I'm sorry," he told her, though she paid no attention to him, "but you're dirty." He fired and fell on his ass. The goat's first reaction was to sit on her bare haunches, too, as if to join him on the ground. Then she dropped her head, which hung unnaturally stretched and slack over the rope. Her front legs had not buckled, still stood rigid. James began crying when her eyes blinked open. He aimed again but the gun's trigger would not budge. He hammered the safety with his palm, whacked the barrel on a tree, then aimed once more, this time at the exposed patch of her brown chest, and pressed the trigger, missing the goat, who, during James's panic, had died, still sitting up.

★ ★ ★

HE HAD NOT thought about what to do with her body. Or any of the bodies, he realized, walking back to the house. He was hot and sickened but also exhilarated from adrenaline, from his sense of making progress. When he'd asked Dee's doctor what he could do, he was told to sanitize her home environment. She would be susceptible to any passing illness. Immediately James pictured germs the precise size of ticks and mites and fleas, the animals' combined stench, alone, enough to kill her. It was this image that had fortified him to shoot the goat, to take the first step. But it had not occurred to him how to get rid of the goat's large body. He was proceeding without any practicality, he realized, like walking blindfolded. It was Dee, six months older than he, who had set the tone of their married life, established in its three short years a policy of taking what came their way without prolonged deliberation.

After lunch he drove his car around the perimeter of the grove to where the goat still sat, head dangling as if hanged. Flies swarmed at the entrance points of the spray of pellets and at her open eyes. James put his hand to his turning stomach. He could not guess how to continue. Dig a hole? But it would have to be six feet long, probably six feet deep, and the earth, unwatered, would not give in easily to a shovel. He considered renting a backhoe, but operating one was another in an ever-growing list of things he'd never before done. For a second, genuine despair overtook him: He was ill-prepared for what he had to endure! It was not fair, to be so completely unqualified!

Again he smelled the foul Rio Grande. Behind the seat in his car he had brought his shotgun, as if he might have cause to defend himself. He stood until the sight of the goat did not nauseate him, until his necessary maturity caught up with him, then hit upon a solution.

He returned to the house for rope, and, finding none, settled on three leather belts from his closet. Back at the dead goat, he cut her from the tree, fashioned a kind of harness with the belts around her front legs and chest, then tied the lead rope

to his small bumper. Across the empty field south of his grove
he dragged the animal, careful to move so slowly there would
be no chance of the rope's breaking or the car's high centering.
He longed now for a rugged truck instead of his old 280Z, the
one Dee called The Penis Car. He watched the goat in the
rearview mirror, on her side, front legs erect with rigor mortis.
Beyond her, behind the car perhaps two miles, diesels passed
on the interstate, big shiny rectangles moving neatly across the
desert to El Paso. James stopped at the river and wondered
what he would say if someone came upon him.

He slammed the car door and surveyed the water, which
was now at its highest level, though it moved like lava, slow
and brown and hot. He hauled the goat himself, dragged her
across the broken beer bottles and desert scrub down to the
muddy bank. There she stuck and James lost a shoe pulling
his own feet from the slog. Tumbleweeds floated by, soda pop
and motor oil cans. The water at the bank was shallow enough
that James had to push the goat's body away, lying prone in
the water himself until the current finally caught her.

AT HOME the peacocks rested on the porch railing like
decoys, eyes in slits. This was the last he would see of them.
James showered. Afterward he found coarse white goat hairs
in the tub's drain screen which he flushed down the toilet.
Instead of getting on with the chore, James sat in the living
room smoking pot. He'd given this up more than a year ago,
when Dee had, but now he couldn't imagine what else would
stop the shaking in his hands. The stash he'd kept in the
freezer was stale and tasted like burning oregano. He got high
anyway and watched the dying sunlight turn the room a sentimental yellow. Pot made him melancholy and hungry. He
wished to be in a scene of ordinary past, Dee slicing tomatoes
and peppers and onions, crying from the odors, he poking the
bobbing ears of corn into boiling water. Dee's oaky hair had
been long and too thin, hanging down her back in a fringey
V, reaching just to the two dimples of her extremely wide hips.
She was flat-chested and big-bottomed, called most of her life

the Gourd by her brothers. She wore sundresses and went braless, her big strong calves rippling where her hemline stopped. Eye makeup was the only concession she made toward modifying herself, blue mascara, blue eyeliner, blue eyeshadow, the rest of her face freckled and ruddy, her eyes, she was convinced, too small.

James thought of her breasts, little more than big nipples on either side of her bony ribcage, an areola of pale downy hair around each. The only good thing about pregnancy, Dee had supposed meditatively to James one evening after sex, was that it might give some bust to her bust. But there had been no children, and now there never would be. It was possible she would die before the year finished, before they both turned twenty-nine.

Sometimes he gave in, weakened by the effort of keeping his thoughts pure, to the fantasy of another woman, a healthy woman. When he'd married Dee, his sister told him he'd made a mistake, that Dee was cold, dedicated to negativity. She'd predicted that it wouldn't work out and now, when James looked into the future, he thought of his sister's words as prophetic, saw himself with his next wife, the true wife, a woman he would know more profoundly than Dee, having lived with her longer, among children, no doubt. She might be beautiful; she might wonder about the tragic character Dee would become. He indulged this fantasy with only half his mind, the other half experiencing acute shame. There was some relief in imagining that Dee had been nothing more than a detour, that the future lay ahead, refreshingly far from the way he felt now. But he always came back, always came crashing head-first to the here and now.

Just as James passed into the dreamless sleep he'd smoked himself toward, he remembered he'd left the shotgun in the Z, the doors of both the car and the house unlocked, lights blazing. Come and get me, he thought.

THE SMELL of cat urine woke him. Sunday. Overhead a light burned palely in the sunshine from the east window. Birds twittered. On the cookie sheet on the coffee table the remaining marijuana bud looked like a scorpion. She would be home Tuesday, flown from Phoenix to El Paso, driven to her house by medical personnel. James had dredged up some lost bit of politeness and thanked the doctor in Arizona for providing curb service. "Actually, it's self-protection," the man had admitted. "Once she's out of our hands, there's nothing you can hold us responsible for." The tom Dee had named Opie licked himself sullenly at James's feet. He was orange and nearly always had, somewhere, a pus-filled infection from fights. Dee liked to open such wounds, using a sterile razor. An ear had been torn halfway off in a terrible scramble just a few months ago, giving Opie the lopsided look of a brain-damaged boxer. The urine smell propelled James from the couch and to the car, where he picked up the gun without taking time to feel its cool, dewy metal bulk in his hands. The cat had followed him as far as the porch door, and James took the opportunity to fire, recognizing the error of this instantly.

His ears rang with the gun's report, and he walked up the porch steps with a sense of unreality. The birds had hushed. He'd hit the animal's heart, just at the point where his front legs tapered down. One leg had been blown off, on the same side of the body as the torn ear, James noted. He stood sweating over the carnage, fur and blood and the leg's bone. It was seeing the concentric cross-section of layers—fur, flesh, muscle, bone, and, finally, the small inner spore of marrow— that gave him stomach enough to clean the mess. He soaked the porch with water, then let the hose run into a patch of dry ground behind the chicken shed. When the earth was saturated, he dug a hole in the mud and, using a broad-ended shovel, brought the shattered cat to his grave.

WISER, he soaked the ground and dug another hole, larger than the first, and put a makeshift barricade around it using sawhorses and blankets. Into this he threw all the chickens but Church Lady, who would not let him near her. The peacocks had disappeared, either smarter or more cowardly than the other fowl. James found himself both disappointed and relieved that he would not have a chance to blast their plucky, impertinent beauty.

He fired at the pit of chickens to shut them up, their hysteria shrill and childlike, fired until all movement ceased, removed the sawhorses and threw on dirt, stomped over it until the mound was solid. He shot the remaining hen on the run, down the road she'd arrived on. Too weak to dig another hole, he dropped her in a pile of old tires, covered her with a hill of rocks, and left her beside the driveway.

He realized one death made the next one easier, one killing leading more easily to another—shooting the chickens had reminded him of a carnival game—this massacre having giving him the stamina to find the last cats, the three who had hidden after Opie's death. Their mistrust of him, their unwillingness to be coerced from the cool crawl space beneath the house, built his sense of its being a fair hunt, the hours it took to lure and trap them justification. He killed them without pity, one shot each, killed them and felt Dee that much closer to coming home.

JAMES had gone gratefully to work on Monday, had purchased Clorox and Comet and industrial-sized sponges afterward and headed to the farm for the much simpler task of washing down the house. He was just outside the small town of Anthony, smiling to himself, remembering Dee's constant argument that he never helped with housekeeping, when a black-and-white dog dashed from the road's shoulder and was under James's front wheels before he realized it. He felt the animal pass under his feet, like a lump beneath a rug, then saw it land on the opposite shoulder. He lurched to a stop, the engine dying, and watched in the rearview. The dog did not move. Dee had never brought home a dog, a fact for which James felt sudden enormous gratitude. Could he have intentionally killed a dog? On the highway shoulder he waited for someone to come claim the one he'd killed accidentally, a young sobbing child to come running from the poor adobe house in the distance. But nothing stirred except the wind. He let loose the steering wheel and looked at his hands as if for blood.

When Dee phoned from Phoenix he was high again. Immediately he understood she could not discover this.

"So," he said, "everything friendly?"

Dee had acute myeloblastic leukemia, which had entered the bone marrow and turned it black. Or so James pictured it. The disease itself sounded like a weapon from a comic book. "Imagine little ray guns in your blood," he had suggested when the doctors encouraged Dee to use visualization. "Myeloblasters."

"I hate guns," was her response.

She'd had chemotherapy just to prepare her for the more difficult procedure of a marrow transplant. This new fluid, from her terrified younger brother, might save her but only if her body were completely amenable to hosting it.

"Not exactly unfriendly," she said tonight, "though I have a fever and everyone keeps whispering 'not pneumonia' like a prayer. I'm supposed to picture beautiful butterflies helping the transplant, I guess the same ones that were supposed to eat the leukemia cells. Not like they did such a great job of that, either. I think my imagination fell out with my hair."

James stood at the kitchen phone taking note of all he had to do. This dirt, like the animals, had come to equal Dee's disease, something to be forced from his life, the more thoroughly—the more violently—the better. "I guess I'm going to start cleaning up a little," James told her. "Scrape off the sheets and erase the plates. Ha, ha."

Dee snorted. "I'm so sick of this fucking place," she said suddenly. "I'm so sick of being sick, I could die."

He worked that night like a man possessed, first trying to vacuum the rug, running the Hoover over and over, later simply ripping up the yellow shag carpeting and, using a serrated bread knife, hacking it into chunks small enough to burn in the metal trash cans. After midnight, he stood overseeing the fire he'd filled with his and Dee's unsanitary belongings, the smoke laced with the smell of the rug's rubber backing.

He'd returned to the Rio Grande and tossed in the gun, followed with the leftover ammunition. It was primitive, this purging and burning and washing, but he believed it would free him. He even threw into the fire his aged marijuana and did not inhale the smoke. The house smelled so strongly of chlorine bleach, its stark cleanliness was so daunting, he'd decided to sleep outside. He lay in a sleeping bag watching the flames die. Some last bit of burning cloth floated in the hot air, a little brilliant chink against the night, light and languid. Watching it until it landed on the ground, safely extinguished, James saw the red eyes of a small wild animal, cat or possum or, possibly, peacock, hidden down in the shadows of the overgrown cotton field, looking at him.

SHE CAME HOME in a private ambulance, sterile all the way, deposited with care by two young men whose responsibility for her well-being ended at her own front door. They approached, one at each of her elbows, masks beneath their noses. James wore his, his wife hers, as well as a white turban wrapped round her bald head. It could have been a scene from a movie about the future, when the air is poisonous and resourceful humans have erected clear bubbles over their plots of life-sustaining land.

"Easy," he said to her, steering her to the porch swing.

"Home," she said, crying suddenly. "I'd rather die than leave here again." Of course, she could only pretend she had this option. Her chance of survival had been eaten away like a deficit pie: Within the sixty percent leukemia presented, twenty percent had to be cut, and then only for five years, if they were lucky. James had never been good at fractions, or at numbers at all. There wasn't much he was good at. He thought he'd been a pretty fair husband. Now he made his wife sit in the swing while he stood behind her and gently pushed. She was no longer Dee, he thought, her hair and heft gone, her gait timid and trembling, her insides radiated, expunged, replaced—and perhaps he would not have her long enough to discover who she had become.

James watched the ambulance roll slowly down the dirt road, sensing that its disappearance also marked the end of the lifeline, monitored night and day, that had kept his wife, himself, tied to procedure and authority. It was not until the vehicle's brake lights flashed one final time at the intersection of their driveway and the county road—a startling blast of red—that James realized his mistake of the last few days. Behind his mask his mouth went dry as dirt. Dee's shoulders swung toward him and he squeezed them as he pushed her.

Unbidden, the faces of a dozen people came to him, people who might have taken a neurotic goat, wild cats, chickens. The names of his neighbors reached him as if sung by an angel, McNeil, Tuft, Gutierrez, Gerard.

Stunned, he met Dee's eyes—so unnaturally, radiantly blue, housed as they were between the screaming white of her mask and turban—as she turned to face him. Just before she asked him, "Where are the animals?" he understood he might not ever convince her, he might not ever understand, himself, truthfully. He would live longer than she, and so have the opportunity to wonder at it for many years; he would never view peacocks without a certain unease. He'd killed her animals. But never once, until this moment, did it occur to him there was any other way. He had only done what he knew he had to.

HOW MUCH WE COULD SEE

T H E N , Telluride was a small dying mining town set in the cradle of a steep box canyon. On either side of Main Street, houses built by eager immigrants staggered upward like stairs, north and south, many of them empty and unworthy even of being boarded up. The half of town we lived in, north, was called the sunny side because the low winter sun reached it while the other side, what had once been the red light district, was left in perennial clifflike shadow.

The Everetts lived below us, and when they turned on their lights at night, we could see into their house. There were four children and the parents, Lucy and Earl. Earl had insisted all the children's names begin with E: Erleen, Emily, Eddie, and Ennis. I felt most sorry for Erleen, named in a desperate moment after the father, as if he weren't sure a boy would ever come along.

At one time, they'd run the barber shop, the movie theater, and the liquor store, different parts of one building downtown. They'd lived upstairs and used to sit in their windows over Main Street, watching pedestrians and cars going by. They never hired anyone else to help run their businesses; the whole family worked several jobs apiece. When we went to the movies, there was Erleen selling tickets and Ennis and Emily behind the concession stand handing out Dr Peppers and oversalted popcorn. Earl operated the projector. Their mother, Lucy, ran the nightly raffle with the help of Eddie, who got to draw names. Our family had begun coming to Telluride in the summers the same year I was born but I wasn't aware of the Everetts until I was nine, sitting in the theater during the raffle. My first memory of Eddie is of him on the stage reaching into the littered hopper, a grin on his face so menacing and wolflike I prayed the red stub with my name on it was buried deep in the basket.

When he drew my brother's stub the following summer, Lee refused to walk onstage to accept his coupon for a free haircut and Orange Crush. Eddie stood waving the coupon like bait and my brother continued to sit between my sister and me, pretending not to have heard his name. Finally Lucy brought the paper to the end of our aisle and it was passed down to us, from one hand to another. Walking home after the movie, I told Lee he should have gone up, that he'd made Eddie angry, that he'd made us stand out. We stood out enough as it was, with our Chicago accents and purely temporary presence each year.

Lee, eight years old, reminded me that he didn't like sodas of any sort and that Earl's haircuts made everybody in town look like a buzzard. It was true—he shaved the lower half of the head, leaving a flap of hair on top—but since I was a girl and exempt I felt Lee should try to adapt to the local custom. Instead, he let his hair grow all summer and suffered the further abuse of being called a hippie. It was 1972; hippies, we were told, would ruin Telluride.

Our summer house was much smaller than our winter one, plus we had no television in Telluride. We spent the evenings, after curfew, sitting at the kitchen table learning to play bridge. Lee and I would be partners, between us devising so complicated a system of cheating we might as well have followed the rules. We named this system Walter; my parents played Goren. My sister, six years old, sat happily on my father's lap waiting to be dispatched to get one of us something to eat.

It was a tight little boat, that old miner's house. Outside the air was cold and clear and entirely without sound, except for the river, which could be heard from six blocks away, pouring on and on down the canyon. The stars were so bright and close you could lose yourself looking into them. We returned at night from a movie or from long exhausting games of hide and seek with our cheeks and ears stinging cold. Eddie Everett would sometimes join those games; more often, however, he was reputed to be elsewhere, with older boys, breaking into abandoned buildings or setting fire to cats at the cemetery. Did he really do these things? I never knew for certain. But stories of his dangerousness made our lives closer to it—we wanted to hear all about him.

Inside our house a fire burned in an ugly metal stove that resembled a suit of armor. At bedtime the three of us would climb the steep narrow stairway that led to our shared bedroom. My father had built a long, low table beneath the pitched roof and set on it three single mattresses, end to end. Here we slept every night, a record player on the floor beside us, its extension cord trailing downstairs. Back home we each had our own room, our own friends, separate lives. In Chicago we never lay in bed at night listening to our parents' records, Arlo Guthrie and Janis Joplin, laughing about the peculiar locals that populated Telluride, the family of midgets all named Shorty, the bartenders and waitresses and clerks and mechanics who seemed, one and all, colorful and hilarious.

But before bed we drank tea, while my parents shared a bottle of wine, and learned bridge. In the wavering, fragile glass of the old window behind Lee, I tried to read his hand of cards.

WHEN I was fourteen the Everetts moved from downtown and built a house below us on the hill. Over the winter they'd sold the businesses and Earl had retired. Our first week in any summer was spent catching up on what had happened during the winter. The changes always seemed amazing, as if they'd taken place overnight instead of in the long course of nine months. I was appalled that the Everetts now lived so close. Not only had they destroyed a good vacant lot, but I would have to see Eddie every day.

Earl came out to wave at us. It would become an annual

tradition, his being the first to welcome us back. He yelled up, "What do you think of your new neighbors?" My parents waved to him. "Good-looking place," they said. It was a lie; later, sitting around the kitchen table, we laughed about their orange, prefabricated double-wide house. It stood out in the neighborhood of old mining homes, a flat one-story, split down the middle of its roof where the two halves came together. Three or four cars always rested in the yard, leaving rectangles of yellow grass when they were finally repaired and removed.

It was that summer that I invited a friend from Illinois to visit. For a few days we had a good time. I showed her everything I'd been telling her about for years. She wasn't very interested in hiking (she'd brought only sandals), and she thought the kids we hung around with were slow. But she loved going to the Alpine, a basement café that catered to teenagers. It was a place I liked to walk by or sit outside, close but not too close. Since she was the guest, however, I agreed to take her inside.

My brother and sister were too young to come. I began wishing my friend would go back to Chicago sooner than planned. I saw then that Chicago and Telluride were two different worlds—that I was a different person in each—and that they did not mix. I would have preferred being with Lee and Gwen, walking around town or playing Monopoly. Instead, my friend and I wore tight sweaters and pink blush and went down to the Alpine to sit in a booth watching games of pool. Eddie was always there.

Strangely, despite my stories about Eddie, my friend thought he was wonderful. He'd quit having his hair cut by his father, and I was surprised to see that it was actually shining blond; short, it had always looked rat brown. Tanned and cocky, he held his pool cue level over the table as he walked tightly around for the next shot. He was sixteen, and he seemed to have forgotten who I had once been. He flirted with us. He grinned at us after each shot. He bought us Dr Peppers and then, using his body as a shield between our table and Mr. Poker, the Alpine's owner, put a splash of vodka in our glasses. My friend loved it. Other girls from town gave us nasty looks.

After several games of pool, and almost to our curfew, Eddie suggested he and his friend should take us on a drive up Last Dollar Road. And, of course, we went. The curfew and my parents could be handled more easily than these boys and my friend.

Eddie drove a 1964 Cadillac, steel gray with one red fender. The seats were maroon and smelled of beer. Eddie and my friend and I sat in the front, Eddie's friend in the back. He leaned over the seat and breathed on us. His name was Eduardo Hernandez—called Dward—and he kept telling Eddie to go faster, bumping up against the back seat as if riding a horse. Eddie drove faster. He told us there were bricks in the trunk so he could take corners without slowing down, which he demonstrated. My friend and Dward laughed like crazy, but all I could think about was flying off the road, which I also thought might be a better reason for being late. A mild accident, no one killed, just a bunch of dumb kids. If I cried, my parents would say nothing about the curfew.

From the top of Last Dollar you could see Telluride's lights. The mountains all joined in the dark, a solid crack of black that took up half the world, the other half star-splattered sky. I was just drunk enough almost to say what I thought: We seemed to be in the shell of a broken egg, the cusp of a startling universe.

We all four sat on the warm hood of the Cadillac. Eddie pointed with his beer bottle toward town. "Great lights," he said. I nodded, expecting flashing red lights, my parents, and the Search and Rescue team.

Town looked bigger from a distance. I worked on something to say to Eddie. I considered telling him about Chicago's lights, the haunting blue dome downtown that I loved so dearly, but who knew what he might say in return? Somehow he had ended up next to me on the hood, and his thigh kept getting closer to mine. Our friends were talking to each other, and then not talking. Far below, in the tiny lights, I imagined Lee and Gwen playing cards at the kitchen table, Gwen in her pajamas. Lee would be letting her win.

Eddie said, too close to my ear, "You remember when we

were kids?" I said I did. He swung his legs and tapped the car's grill with his boot heels. "We had fun, huh?" He laughed and dropped his arm on my shoulders. I froze. The night seemed to take a breath with me. I could feel every move any one of us made on that car hood. Eddie threw his beer bottle into the dark and wrapped his other arm around me. It was awkward and hot.

Then he kissed me, and I let him. His mouth was cool and soft; I kept thinking of the hardness of the rest of him, the toughness, and I think that's why our kiss lasted so long: It was such a surprise.

EDDIE and I went out for the duration of my friend's visit, and it wasn't strictly because my friend wanted to go out with Dward, which is what I told Gwen and Lee. Eddie was dangerous; my parents forbade our getting in his car. They'd heard stories.

After my friend went back to Chicago, though, I began avoiding Eddie. Suddenly I was scared of him again. My friend had made driving around with him into an adventure, but without her, I felt as if anything might happen.

Eddie was not easy to avoid. He and his father were always fixing their cars in their yard, and he would look up whenever I came out of the house. He'd grin an awful, knowing grin, darting his tongue out to remind me how much I liked to kiss him, turning his tape player up, playing the same tapes we had listened to while making out in his car, Jimi Hendrix or Steve Miller. It gave me a stomachache.

Earl was slightly deaf, so when I walked by them he always shouted a hello to me and mimed an enormous wave. I never saw a man so wrinkled, and each deep line cut into his face was filled with dirt. Because he was a kind man, I felt sorry for him; it seemed to me he didn't deserve a son like Eddie. He deserved someone like Lee, friendly and naive. Anyone could take advantage of Earl. He always wore big snowboots with the buckles hanging open. These were for sloshing around with the hose.

"Hey there!" he'd shout over Eddie's music. I don't think he knew about Eddie and me. It was the kind of thing he wouldn't have noticed. He enjoyed teasing me, because I blush easily, so he was likely to say, "Your face is red!" and then watch as I obliged by turning pink. He'd stand there holding the dribbling hose, his feet pointing out, his workshirt covered with grease, smiling his pleased goofy smile—the most vulnerable grown-up I ever knew.

I always ducked my head in embarrassment and went on downtown, conscious of Eddie's wolf grin following my back.

I MISSED one summer in Telluride. The year I was sixteen, I went to Mexico as an exchange student. Any news that year had to be gathered from letters from my family. Gwen was the most faithful writer. She was eleven that summer and had become close friends with Eddie's sister Ennis, who was also eleven. Gwen's letters chatted, without punctuation, about catching and saddling horses, cooking french fries, riding sometimes in Eddie's car.

He still lived at home, and Gwen said she could see him through the windows at night, yelling and throwing things at Ennis. She said even his parents couldn't do anything about it. I felt, reading her letters, the same anger from past summers, but it was momentary. I was learning to live in Mexico, and that took up most of my time.

And when I returned to Telluride, the summer after, the usual, expected changes were doubled: new buildings everywhere, extending farther up the sides of the mountains than before. The mine had closed during the winter but the ski slope, built a few years earlier, was starting to expand, so some of the miners still had jobs. The others moved to Montrose and retired.

The new people in Telluride were different. From California and New York, they brought with them boutiques and speciality shops, art galleries and ethnic restaurants. My father said they bought the businesses away from the locals for hardly anything, but Earl Everett said he was sorry he hadn't waited a while longer before selling his building. The barber shop part had become a deli, the theater a dance studio, and the liquor store remained a liquor store, although Earl said the new people now stocked fifty-dollar champagne.

I suppose by that summer we had become more or less locals ourselves. On the Fourth of July, we invited the Everetts to come watch the fireworks from our porch. Our house was higher and we had a better view. They brought lawn chairs and hot toddies, and stayed for a long time after the display, watching the bats diving at the streetlight, talking to my parents. I thought they might realize how visible the inside of their house was to us, how much we could see, but they didn't close their curtains after that night. They didn't change a thing.

Eddie hadn't come up with them. Much later that night, I heard his Cadillac pull into their yard. My father had divided the attic into two rooms and Gwen and I were sharing the front half that summer. I slept directly under the open window. I lay waiting to hear Eddie get out, but after the engine stopped there wasn't another sound. After a time, I heard the door to the house open, and when I looked down, Earl was standing next to the Cadillac in his robe. He stood there, his hair silver in the streetlight, and then he opened the door. He said, "Eddie?" Eddie mumbled something, his voice drunk, hostile, floating up perfectly clearly in the dark.

Earl helped him out of the car and they staggered across the lawn, Eddie draped unconsciously on his father. When they got inside, their lights went on and I could have watched, but I turned away from the window, hugged my pillow, and shut my eyes.

B O R E D with retirement, Earl took a job as a custodian at the County Courthouse. He left early in the morning to raise the flags and pick up litter from the night before. If we walked by, later in the day, he might be outside painting trim or watering shrubs. He'd tease us about our dog, who followed us everywhere, a black-and-white mutt that Earl said looked like a sheep dog cut off at the knees. Or he might tease Gwen about falling from a horse or ask me if I still turned red as a tomato. He couldn't keep track of what year in college I was, so he just asked if I'd graduated yet. I said not yet.

Eddie and I had, by that time, a relationship peculiar to people who have known each other a long time but have no great fondness for each other. He'd ask about school; I'd ask about his winter. One winter he'd moved away from home, been arrested for contributing to the delinquency of a minor, been put on parole, broken it, moved back home, then had a car accident. Had I noticed the front of the Caddy? He said he'd hit a deer and then a ditch.

"Got him!" he said. "Bagged that buck!" His smile was the same, sly and infuriating, now marked by a gold filling in his left canine.

Another winter he became a father, but still didn't move away from home. Ennis told us the girl had put the baby up for adoption and now lived in a Ford Pinto in Montrose.

Stories about Eddie were always like that—he continued to walk away unscathed.

The Everetts came up for every Fourth of July after that first time. The summer that construction began on a house above our home, my father and Earl had a lengthy talk about Telluride's ruin. Earl thought that the newcomers were responsible for all the recent vandalism and marijuana use. Ennis and Gwen and I nudged each other, all of us ready to say, "What about Eddie?" My father said those kinds of things happened in every town. He was more concerned with the destruction of the wilderness; Earl, however, being a member of the Search and Rescue crew, said all the new roads up the mountains made it much easier to find lost hikers. They weren't talking about the same thing. It was one of those seeming conversations that are really two monologues pieced together in the form of dialogue.

After the fireworks, Ennis and Gwen and Lee and I went on a walk around town. The air was hazy with sulfur. Downtown was full of drunks and tourists in campers, driving back and forth on Main. We saw Eddie's Cadillac go by several times, very slowly. This was Eddie's kind of night, lots of new people to look at, girls to pick up.

On his fifth or sixth time by, he pulled over to talk to us. We were sitting on the courthouse steps, watching tourists and laughing. Eddie leaned out his window and asked if we wanted to cruise. We said no thanks. I was embarrassed for him; he was by himself and desperate enough for company to ask his little sister to ride around with him. Or maybe that wasn't it at all. Maybe it didn't embarrass him at all.

Finally Ennis agreed to go. She asked Gwen to come along but Lee and I talked Gwen into coming home with us. She accused us of being another set of parents, but I always felt better when we were all home together, safe.

Telluride didn't quiet down until much later. Gwen and I stayed awake talking in bed, listening to the last shrieks of people in the bars. I don't remember which of us fell asleep first; it seemed we both drifted off at the same moment.

But I woke first a few hours later when the Search and Rescue siren sounded. The siren meant all volunteers had to meet at the fire station. Gwen crawled into bed with me and we looked out the window. The Everetts' lights were already on, Earl's truck already gone. The Cadillac was also gone. Gwen whispered, "What if it's Ennis?"

Cars and Jeeps were starting up at a few of the houses near ours, and then we heard another siren, a softer one, heading out of town on the highway.

I WAS the first one up in the morning. The haze from the Fourth had cleared and the day was brilliant. I sat next to the dog on our porch with a cup of tea and a book, rolling up the sleeves of my sweatshirt.

At the Everetts' I could see someone sitting at the kitchen table, but the glare of the sun on the window made it impossible to tell who it was. The Cadillac was parked in its usual place, its grillwork facing me like a big metal grin.

Earl came out the door wearing his boots and jacket, as if going to work. Instead, when he reached the end of their walk, he turned toward our house. Our dog began barking. Earl hadn't looked at me yet, but my pulse doubled. I got up and started down the steps to meet him halfway. His face and wrinkles suggested a smile, but his eyes were bloodshot and shiny. He said, "There's been an accident." He told me Eddie had drowned at Woods Lake.

I became acutely conscious of the muscles in my face and around my eyes. In my torso. I did not know how to respond. We stood on the steps holding each other. He told me Ennis had tried to save Eddie, had gone out in the water again and again, and finally had to drive the car down the road by herself. "She doesn't even know how to drive," Earl said. "I've been meaning to teach her." He shook his head; we both stared at his unbuckled boots.

He told me to tell Gwen. He said he knew she'd be upset, but that Ennis would be okay. She was asleep now, he said, on the couch. "She didn't know how to swim, either," Earl said. "Neither of them did."

My father said Eddie had been self-destructive and, though the accident was a terrible thing, that it was fortunate he hadn't killed anyone else with him. According to Gwen, Ennis had kept telling him not to go into the lake. It was cold, and he'd been drinking. My mother said that his parents were enduring a nightmare. The natural pattern of death was that parents preceded children, she told us, and an upset in the pattern was doubly tragic and disturbing.

Their extended family came from all over the state. We watched the cars pull up, the people go into the house, and, through the windows, we saw them hugging, first Lucy then Earl. My mother made lasagna and sent Gwen and me to deliver it.

Earl gave us his watery smile and then hugged us together. Gwen began crying and he held us tighter. We'd heard that he hadn't slept since the Fourth.

I had never been inside the Everetts' house. It was roomier than it appeared from up on our hill. Doorways led off into hallways; a set of stairs went to the basement I hadn't known existed. I was surprised to see the living room filled with their belongings. I thought of Telluride as a summer home, so the permanent qualities—the mantel photos, the huge television console, the display case full of quartz crystals—threw me. This was their real house. I looked out the window to our house on the hill, our vacation house. My mother stood in the yard hanging laundry. I could make out my father's under-wear, Gwen's pajamas.

"I'm sorry," we told Eddie's relatives. It got easier the more we said it.

All the old-timers came to the funeral, even some who'd moved to Montrose. It rained, and the Catholic church smelled musty and sweaty. The Everetts stood together in the front, their heads bowed. Earl wore a dark blue suit several sizes too small for him. I could see his white socks. When I began crying, near the end of the eulogy, it was not so much for Eddie as it was for Earl, dressed in his best clothes.

For the rest of that summer, I half expected to see Eddie and his father out fooling with their cars. I was surprised again and again not to hear the tape player or their shouts to each other about what they were doing. Gwen said Ennis was wor-ried that Earl was breaking down. He hardly spoke, and some nights he sat smoking cigarettes in the dark, looking out the window.

When we left to go back to school at the end of August, the Cadillac still sat in front of their house, untouched since the Fourth.

O U R little house wasn't really safe. I learned that as the summers passed. My father would become ill, my brother and I would fight and never reclaim our past closeness, and my sister would be killed in a motorcycle accident on a mountain not far from here. All the winters of school and all the summers spent intimately in our snug house above the Everetts couldn't prevent those facts.

But the summer after Eddie's death we arrived in Telluride to see the house above ours finished. It was huge, modern, and ugly, made of glass cylinders and sharp white corners;

Gwen said it looked like a giant coffee-maker. Its front jutted out above our backyard and the first thing my mother said was that we'd have to hang curtains in the rear windows.

We always packed sweaters in the car for our first night back in Telluride, transported them through the sultry Midwest as an act of faith, not really believing how cold the mountains could be. Town was chilly and silent in the Sunday dusk. We could hear the river, full of runoff, carrying on.

The Everetts were usually the first to welcome us back and ask how our winter had been, but there didn't seem to be anyone home. Their yard was empty of cars, the house dark. We'd carried in several loads and lighted the hot water heater before Earl appeared on his concrete stoop.

We all stood in the side yard, arms full of backpacks and pillows. He called out hello and told us he and Lucy were fine. Then he pointed to the front of our house, out of our line of vision. He said, "Is that your dog on the roof?"

I thought I'd misheard him but he repeated the question: Was that our dog on the roof? I know we were all wondering if he had broken. Was that this winter's change, along with our new neighbor behind us? I was excited—and terrified— to believe he'd lost his mind; really, to believe so much could happen to one family, that they could be so luckless. Earl pointed to our roof, but for a moment, none of us would look. We didn't look at each other or at the roof; we looked at Earl.

And then we walked cautiously to the front of the house, to see. Our dog, twelve years old by then and both blind and deaf, was halfway out the bedroom window. For a second it was as if the need for him to be there had put him there. Then more reasonable explanations occurred to me. The dog turned a mournful confused face to us. Gwen said, "I guess I accidentally shut him in."

"He wants out," Earl called to us. "You keeping him locked up?" He smiled, just barely, and waved. "Welcome back."

My family laughed in relief, then hauled their luggage inside. I waited beside the car.

Oh terrible small town, I'd written in my Intro to Poetry Writing class that winter. I meant Telluride, but it wasn't such an awful place. It was just that I'd already passed the last summer in which I could feel simply exuberant in being here. On the periphery were unhappiness and bad luck.

I watched Earl go in his door, watched him pass through the kitchen. He stood at his window to look up at our house. I couldn't make out his features but I saw his shape. I raised my hand. He raised his.

BARE KNEES

LYNNIE LINK had so often in recent weeks opened the YWCA Saturday lap swim with a hangover that today, without one, she could not quite find her rhythm. Clean the filter before or after switching on the sauna? Was it the pool or hall door to the men's locker room that required a key? She was not hung over because she had attended a wake the night before. A boy from her high school had killed himself. His twin sister, an unpopular and notorious narc, had served a deep red wine in silver thimblelike cups to Lynnie and her three best friends, who sat on the couch in short dresses with their knees exposed, holding the cups with their pinkies out. None of them finished the drink. The parents padded from room to room in the sad little house, letting the daughter preside as if realizing the world no longer was one in which they could make rules. The father sat down for a moment on the piano bench opposite and looked without curiosity at them. Lynnie bumped her eyes over her own and the six other bare knees. This dead son, brother, had not really been their friend.

Years away, when she would have access to the names of things she merely experienced now, she would understand why sweet red wines always made her feel teary and inadequate. At the wake, she wanted to reach back into the week before and invite Kevin Pedigo on a date. They could have gone to the movies, to one of the discreet downtown bars that didn't card,

to the sun roof of her own house where Lynnie often sat after
a night out, hearing through the rustle of mulberry leaves the
sirens and cars, the more local aching rub of limbs against
plaster, glancing, as the wind opened holes in the thick shelter,
at the blinking lights from a distant radio tower. There were
a hundred things she could have said to him. It would have
been easy if she'd known he wanted to die.

But, then, it was February and there were no mulberry
leaves. At home, plastic insulation had been stretched over the
window to the porch. The Y was perhaps the only building in
town uncomfortably warm. Lynnie stripped in the employees
bathroom and stepped into her red-and-white suit. It smelled
of chlorine and mold. She found herself looking around the
small room for her soda before realizing she didn't have one.
Most Saturdays, hung over, she stopped at the machines upstairs and bought two Cokes and a package of cashews. Today
she'd eaten with her brother at home, Cheerios.

Her brother, John Gamble, was twenty-two. He'd graduated
college and come back. "I've commenced," he told Lynnie,
holding his hands open-palmed. "Can't you tell?" Their parents wanted to know what he would do next; their father kept
mentioning résumés and haircuts.

"Where'd you go last night?" John Gamble asked over cereal. Lynnie enjoyed telling him, holding up for his inspection
the life she'd looked forward to. It used to be her asking him.

"I went to a wake," she said. "That guy who hung himself."

"Ugh. Hanged."

"We had to sign a book when we came in, our name and
address. There was this sickening wine." But saying it felt
dishonest—and John Gamble was heat-seeking concerning dis-
honesty—so Lynnie quickly added, "His father got laid off a
couple weeks ago at Boeing. His mother sews. I found out
she's been making all the cheerleader outfits for South, maybe
since when you were there. Blue collar." She had recently
discovered what the two collar colors meant.

"How'd he do it?"

"In his closet, I think, with a belt."

John Gamble looked hard at Lynnie. He hadn't shaved his

chin whiskers—his only whiskers—since he'd come home in January. As was often the case these days, Lynnie felt she'd said something to offend him, though she didn't know what. Perhaps she had been too obvious in pandering to his interest in the working class. Lynnie could forget that he was not like other people, that he did not have around him the typical force field. He was right there, sometimes impolite. He accused her with a dripping spoon. "You don't think of trying that, do you?"

"No." But this wasn't strictly true, either. "Well, everybody does a little, don't they?"

"A little. They think, 'Won't everybody be sorry when,' and then they don't really do it. They leave nicks on their wrists. Don't do that, hear me?"

"Shut up. Yes."

"You do that, I'll kill you."

For the first three hours of Saturdays Lynnie was the only guard, as lap swimmers were all adults and self-sufficient. She propped open doors and flipped on fluorescent lights. Without a hangover she felt newly sensitized to the Y, as if she'd just been hired. It seemed older, grimier. Somewhere in the men's locker room water dripped patiently on tile. Lynnie followed the sound, stopping briefly at the sink. Where there were at least five mirrors in the women's room, there was only one in the men's, and it was cracked. Lynnie looked into her split reflection, thinking of Kevin Pedigo. As a sophomore he had been an alto in choir and had stood beside her on the third riser during the Christmas program. Last night when her friends had falteringly reminisced about his virtuous acts, Lynnie thought of his earnest voice beside her own, singing not "*hal*-lelujah," but "*aya*-tollah."

Cautious of athlete's foot fungus, she tiptoed into the shower stall with the leaking head and twisted it silent, waiting to make sure it was off. Now, in this close space, she could hear nothing but the faint murmur of her own inner turbulence. The brilliant cold tile made her imagine blood on it, red on white.

Though she usually broke the rules and swam a few laps by herself, today she abstained, leaving the men's room and taking her guard's seat. She flapped open her chemistry textbook and sent her eyes over the typeface. When she looked up, a model hydrogen molecule hung imprinted over the steamy high windows level with the parking lot. She had comprehended not one word of what she'd just read. A face appeared on the other side of the window, hand cupped against the fogged glass. This was Anne, Lynnie's idol.

Tom and Moira and Dennis and Leonard, most of the core group, appeared straight-up nine A.M., waving to Lynnie as she punched their file cards. Others came with damp orange tickets purchased upstairs. The three men regulars watched for Anne to arrive, bobbing in the water to warm up, slicking their hair back, greeting her and making room in the lanes. Lynnie had learned a lot from Anne's coolness, the plain black one-piece she wore and the simple smiles and comments she bestowed. There seemed to be no artificial elements to her, as if she had never in her thirty-some years had reason to tell a lie. She reminded Lynnie of an exotic animal, sleek and odd and mesmerizing, not one ounce superfluous weight. Furthermore, she had believed that if she brought her brother, John Gamble, to the Y lap swim he and Anne would fall in love. But then they'd gone and found each other without her help, like magic, like fate. In this city of cowboy hats and big-wheeled trucks and 1970s music, somehow Anne had discovered Lynnie's brother. They weren't in love yet, Lynnie told herself, they'd only met for coffee. But love was coming, and though she knew she ought to feel happy for her brother, she only felt excluded. And shaken, for if Gamble could find love here, who was to say she couldn't? She wanted to believe in the East Coast, in the school John Gamble had attended and where she would be, come fall. She wanted to believe she would inherit her suave adulthood when she left home and childhood foolishness and the anecdotes that had somehow come to embody her.

It upset her that Gamble did not feel failed. He'd returned

like Dorothy from Oz, set to proclaim Kansas his home forever and ever, ready to live his life in black and white after all that color.

Anne dropped each Saturday like an arrow straight into the water, surfacing teeth first, clean and sharp and white. She lived across the street from the Y and, following lap swim, taught the children's dance classes upstairs.

The other woman, Moira, was quite a bit older than the rest of them, probably seventy, yet swam until noon, staying until the first children arrived for family swim, her faded blue bathing cap coming up at one end and then the other, lap after diligent lap of the American crawl.

"Could you turn that down?" she asked Lynnie before getting in. Lynnie dropped her book on the table and grudgingly went into the office. Every week she turned down the music until Moira settled into her laps; then she slowly elevated it again.

Lynnie had thought she would meet men being a lifeguard. She thought she'd meet men going to bars, too. And she did meet them, but nothing came of it. She got drunk with them and made up stories. They were older and better-looking than the boys at school, and they had jobs and their own apartments and cars. In the end, however, those things didn't seem to make much difference. In the end, they simply wanted to go to bed with her. In the East, she told herself, there would be a man.

At noon the lap swimmers were reluctant to leave. They didn't have to, of course, but Lynnie started reeling in the lane ropes so that they would have had to swim around the families playing ring toss or beach ball, the little inner tubes sporting small children, the splashing thrash of arms and legs and the yells of Marco Polo. Dennis and Tom and Leonard swam the ropes in for her; actually, they swam them in for Anne, who paid no mind, toweling off her calves. Did she think of John Gamble? Moira refused to quit her crawl until it was utterly impossible to move in a straight line. Whole strips of orange tickets were dropped on Lynnie's lap and a

parade of children plopped one after another like puppies into
the shallow end.

The other guard, Dixie, had arrived a few minutes before
noon and now emerged from the changing room in the same
red-and-white outfit Lynnie wore, its vertical lines spread tight
and curved over her stout body. Dixie had been hired after
Lynnie so at first Lynnie had shown her around. They'd gotten
along fine. Now, four months later, Dixie was aquatic director
while Lynnie was still just a guard. Lynnie would be the first
to say she had no ambitions concerning the Y and planned to
quit her job in August; Dixie, she knew, worked harder and
had superior training. Still, a mild tension hung between them.

Dixie turned down the music before joining Lynnie at the
desk. "How's it going, honey?" she said brightly. She was
twenty-nine, a plump happy woman from Tribune, Kansas.
Tribune's one claim to fame was the fact that it sat on a time
line. Dixie's house had been in Mountain time while some of
her friends had been in Central. She was engaged to a man
who would be a minister soon. They had yet to have sex. Along
with her monogrammed whistle (for Christmas, she'd given
Lynnie one with her own name on it), Dixie wore a gold cross
around her neck. Her sisterly affection toward Lynnie shamed
Lynnie. Dixie shone so aggressively pure that Lynnie didn't
feel sophisticated around her—as she usually felt—but tar-
nished.

Dixie dropped a bag of Tootsie Rolls next to the card box
and pulled up another rollaway chair, facing the pool. She
loved sweets. Her front teeth had the thin silver frames around
them you usually saw in older mouths. She patted Lynnie's
knee. Moira had pulled her trim body from the pool and
was gathering her belongings together. She did not trust the
women's locker room and dressed in a bathroom stall, leaving
her things right by the pool. She checked her wallet before
drying off. The sides of her bathing cap were folded upward
so she looked like she had pig ears. Today Lynnie hated her.

Moira pointed at the suspended stereo speaker and said to
Dixie, "Do you believe that noise is necessary?" She removed

her bathing cap and fluffed her bobbed gray hair, walking off holding her back erect, not waiting for an answer. Last week she'd told them the ceiling was covered with asbestos, that little chips were falling in the water.

Dixie made sounds as if thinking about the necessity of music. Lynnie said, "Maybe we'll just give her a key and let her come in after hours. Maybe she'll drown, old cluck."

Dixie clicked her tongue. Then she asked Lynnie what she'd done last night. All day Saturdays the two of them would exchange anecdotes, a wearying conversational technique John Gamble called candy yak: empty calories.

"We went to a wake," Lynnie said.

"What?" Dixie's dark plucked brows lifted like question marks.

"This boy hanged himself with a belt."

"Oh no." Lynnie, seeing Dixie's expression, realized a deeper terror than she'd felt before, a small black sucking in her midsection. Dead. The feeling flashed and passed—she saw Kevin standing on a choir riser, then saw herself sitting on his parents' couch the night before, that scathing row of bare knees, Mr. Pedigo's face, which, in holding no expression, had seemed featureless. She laid her hands on her knees now. She only felt she'd been wrong in shocking Dixie. There were times she relished doing so; Dixie occasionally seemed not innocent so much as timid, not good so much as smug.

Tears came to Dixie's shiny eyes and Lynnie wished she'd softened the news. There were those less graphic, candy words.

Dixie's hand rested on Lynnie's knee. "Lynnie, was he a good friend?"

Lynnie blew her whistle and yelled at a child not to run. He jumped, startled, and began the fast and stiff soldierlike steps kids always used around a pool. She liked to yell at them; she liked the flat clichés of her profession, the prefacing emphatic NO. "Yes," she lied to Dixie. "We went out once on a date, over Christmas a couple of years ago, after our Christmas show at school. We went to a movie, then to my house. We sat on the roof and talked. It was freezing cold but we just kept talking and talking, like we could just say whatever came into our heads."

"Did you go out again?"

"Huh-uh. I guess we were too good of friends to go out on dates."

"You want to take the rest of the day off, honey? If you think you need to go home . . ."

"I'm okay. You know, I think he was going to ask me to the Valentine's Day dance, just as friends."

"Sugar, I'm so sorry."

Lynnie flushed. Dixie sighed, then began talking about a suicide in her own high school, years and years ago.

"I can't remember why I stopped being in choir," Lynnie said, interrupting. "I liked it."

"I didn't know you could sing, girl."

"Used to."

Dixie seemed to feel it was now appropriate to unwrap a Tootsie Roll and poke it in her mouth. She worked the lump from one cheek to the other as she carefully folded the wrapper into a small square. Afterward, she stood up and pulled in her stomach. "You want a soda pop?"

Lynnie made a gesture of patting her bathing suit and bare thighs for money.

"I'll get it," Dixie told her, smiling.

"Diet, please."

T H E R E were two ways to approach lifeguarding: singular or plural. In the beginning Lynnie had used the singular tack, in which she isolated swimmers and watched them perform their individual dramas: A boy waited for his mother to ferry him across, clapping when his sister arrived on the other side; a man spun a frisbee, submerged blowing bubbles, came back up ten feet to his left. The pool was not as frantic in its parts as in its whole. But the more efficient way was the plural, group tack, in which she scanned, making sure every body had a head and that every head continued to come up for air. This way made things seem more riotous, loud and busy and chaotic, skin and toys erupting randomly as from a consuming aquatic beast. She had learned to pick through the tangle automatically, focusing only where there might be trouble.

She'd told John Gamble she could do this job in her sleep, it was that easy. Frighteningly easy, really. Except when the boy of the deaf parents came. Then CPR tips trotted across her mind. Then it was a responsibility instead of the humid raucous place she spent Saturdays watching the clock.

At first Lynnie had thought he was retarded. He screeched and garbled words, racing up and down the pool's tile without heeding her whistle, her threats. People stayed out of his way. That first day she'd grabbed him by the arm and yelled into his face, "What do you think you're doing? Didn't you hear me? This is a whistle and I'm the lifeguard. There will be no running, no pushing, and no dunking, do you follow?" He'd gone limp, heavy and afraid in her grasp. He looked beyond her, his eyes swinging wildly to see above her, up to the observation balcony, where two old people, his mother and father, it turned out, stood leaning over the wrought iron railing, screaming desperately with their hands.

Since then, she'd had to save him twice, once when he jumped from the diving board and simply didn't come up, sinking like lead, and the second time when he'd burst from the dressing room and slid face-first on the slick indoor-outdoor carpet toward the water, hitting his chin and chest on the tiled lip before tumbling into the pool. A swirling bit of blood had dissipated as Lynnie tugged him out. Because he'd graduated the Y's own advanced swimmer class he was permitted to come without an adult. His deaf-mute mother and father sat nervously and ineffectually in the front row of the open balcony, clothed in the unfashionable layered heaviness of recent emigrants. They lived in the same building as Anne, across the street.

"Poor things," Dixie had said. "They don't have a notion about what's happening with this kid." Their son, André, was a bully as well as a drowner. He had to be watched constantly. There was no talking to him; he just didn't register what you said. He heard it and seemed to agree and then dashed right back to what he'd been doing. Lynnie saw in his eyes a wildness that she had never seen before. She hated him, she hated his clammy skin and his pathetic old-man drawers. When she'd dragged him out of the water, she'd told him so, her heart still frantic at the nearness of death. His body was loathsome to her and she'd gone immediately to wash after touching it, holding her hands under the hot water until they stopped trembling.

Later that afternoon, Dixie was at the other end of the pool fitting water wings under the arms of a little girl when André began going under. Lynnie looked to her, then back to André, who sputtered, flapping his oversized flat hands at the surface, sinking. His fingernails were without curve, growing from his digits like guitar picks. A woman with her baby treaded nearby, laughing obliviously, flicking water with her fingertips at the baby's inner tube. When she realized what Lynnie was staring at she grabbed André, reached him easily, hauled him effortlessly to the side while her daughter bobbed behind in the tube.

"Hey!" the woman yelled up at Lynnie. "Snap out of it! This boy's taken a mouthful."

Lynnie heard the keys just before they fell on her head, a slow tin slice in the air. She flinched, shielding herself automatically against more. The whole gallery might begin tossing things at her, her hatred of the boy now exposed. André's parents were making sounds, grunts, straining over the railing toward their son. The father opened his mouth and bleated. Lynnie could see the broken blood vessels in his face and neck, he was that close. His gray scarf slid from around his neck and fell at her feet.

Dixie had by now reached André, who all along had been no more than six feet from Lynnie—somehow an impossible distance to traverse.

What was peculiar was the way time had given Lynnie about twenty seconds more than the rest of the world. In the instant André had been drowning Lynnie had thought no fewer than a dozen simultaneous things. One of them was that André might just as well drown, that his life was destined to be nothing but heartache. Another was that Kevin Pedigo would actually have been thrilled to see her and her friends at his house, sitting in their good clothes on his couch, knees exposed despite the weather. Yet another thing was that she would never be someone like Anne, someone whom men like her brother would fall in love with. She would want them but they would want someone else. And she thought about John Gamble's words from that morning. What he'd meant, she understood, was that if she ever planned to kill herself she shouldn't straddle the line: Either do it or don't. No leaving pitiful scars.

In the face of these facts, she realized Kevin's death, the possibility of André's, made her glad, set off in her an excitement she enjoyed.

The boy threw up on the tile, first water, then bright sodden orange cheese curls. Children around him, observing, gagged reflexively. He choked on some last piece of food. His funny unfashionable swim trunks had worked themselves sideways on his hips so that his hairless genitals showed, no more shocking in this context than a naked heel or ear.

Dixie sat confidently behind him with her legs spread, André safe in her grip, her gold cross dancing on his wet hair. "Attaboy," she told him, pulsing his chest with her fists.

AT HOME one of John Gamble's friends was over, Lewis something, or something Lewis. They sat on separate couches in the living room reading magazines, each under his own cone of lamplight, like miners in a cave.

"You're early," John Gamble noted.

"I'm in shock." She dropped onto the couch next to him. "Move your big feet. Hey Lewis."

"Lynnie." Lewis was almost seven feet tall. All John Gamble's friends had freakish qualities. He seemed to collect rejects; still, this did not make him one himself. Like Anne, he was so powerful as to be immune to what might otherwise have rubbed off. Lewis held an *OMNI* about two inches from his face. It was not uncommon to find more than one friend visiting John Gamble, everybody reading magazines or sitting playing solitaire. Lynnie had quit telling him it was weird.

"What is it you guys like about the dark, anyway?" she asked them. Neither answered. She shut her eyes and could still see the shape of the Y's high windows, three rectangles of dreary white winter sky. She wasn't sure she had a job any longer.

"Anyone hungry?" John Gamble asked them.

Lewis considered it, lowering the magazine and putting his hand to his abdomen. Lynnie leaned back onto a cushion, tired. A lengthy black heaviness stretched at every side of her, the cold months until summer, the more immediate burden of phoning her friends and reporting on her day. She toyed with the titillating things she might ask them, like whether they thought Kevin's sister was cashing in on her sudden celebrity, or whether Mr. Pedigo had been staring at their knees the night before, if anyone else had noticed the way he looked at their knees. "I'm not hungry," she said, though she hadn't eaten anything since her breakfast of Cheerios except a couple of Tootsie Rolls.

"In shock over what?" John Gamble asked.

"Kevin Pedigo."

"I thought you didn't know him that well. Not that you shouldn't be in shock. It *is* shocking."

"What is?" Lewis asked.

"Guy hanged himself," John Gamble told him. "Guy Lynnie knew."

"He had a crush on me," Lynnie said. She held an embroidered cushion on her lap, pulling at loose threads until they broke. "I think he might have liked me, a couple years ago."

John Gamble turned on the couch and looked at her without saying anything, narrowing his eyes. His whiskers, Lynnie saw, were black rather than the brown of his hair. He wouldn't bother shaving when he went out with Anne. He wouldn't wear nice clothes.

"I mean it. I think he must have liked me, John Gamble."

"He leave a note?" Lewis asked from across the room.

"I don't know. Nobody said anything about a note. Stop looking at me like that, John Gamble."

"I know I'd leave one," Lewis said. "I wouldn't be able to resist. In fact, I walk around all the time composing the thing in my mind, getting it word perfect, revising. 'Dear Dad, you cocksucker.' " He picked up *OMNI* again. A pink shrimplike fetus was featured on the cover, surrounded by the turquoise liquid of the womb, its home. "And I'm not even thinking about doing it."

"Me, either," Lynnie said, hoping this would appease her brother. He was making her uneasy. She wondered when that had begun happening—because there had been a time when he hadn't, a time when what she said was not only unrehearsed but always just right, when *saying* and *thinking* occurred at once. He looked into her now and she looked right back, seeing suddenly, with real physical pain, the dark hole of how much she would miss him, how much she would lose. She was turning one way, and her brother was flying another. They were heading different places, had already gone.

THE FACTS OF AIR

S H E had left a pretty enough life behind her, and because she could not yet be certain she had taken the correct step, Regina probed each new day the way one might old fruit, only too ready to find rot. She had been in her new home two days when she lost one of her cats in a sandstorm. Regina had not lived in Tucson long enough to understand that the storm was unusual, troublesome not only to a newcomer but to old-timers as well, people who took for granted benign, happy weather. Nor did she know that, for the duration of her time there, she would not experience another like it. For the year that followed, Regina anticipated sandstorms the way she had used to blizzards or tornadoes in Ohio, battening down against the luminous sky and the facts of air.

The second cat, sister to the missing one and a homebody by nature, stuck close to Regina's heels, howling plaintively as if recounting her side of the story. It was a late afternoon in September and the sun burned, though barely, on the wavering line of the horizon. The door slammed behind Regina and sand stung her skin like bits of broken glass. She tried to shield her eyes, face a friendly direction, but the wind and grit were omnipresent, erupting from nonspecific sources.

Giving up the search, Regina sat defeated in her new dining room gathering her wits. Sand flicked at the aluminum-cased windows. Door frames rattled and wind sent the loose lawn furniture sailing from the front porch into the gravel driveway.

She had rented this home—"home" because its owners had not yet taken their belongings and so a family personality remained—from a divorcing couple. One of them was, apparently, a gynecologist; on the concrete porch, arranged as a kind of centerpiece among the transient plastic chairs and chaise longue, was an inert stainless-steel examination table, complete with stirrups. Though the house had once obviously been custom-designed for these absent people and all its parts were therefore desirable, half empty it spoke of carelessness and waste, mutinous betrayal. Looking around at the ornately carved dining room chairs, Regina believed the family had tried to purchase a solidity, a comfort, they could not summon from one another. She felt not sorry for them but superior.

The wind seized the house like a contraction. Above Regina on the roof, a clatter followed; soon a piece of grillwork covering the swamp cooler toppled down into the withered backyard, blown bowleggedly on its corners across the dead grass until it fell into the contaminated swimming pool and slowly sank. Regina clutched her arms as if they, too, were in danger of disengaging.

She could not imagine that her cat would survive—her mere nine pounds would be nothing in this wind—and decided to go ahead and cry about it. The cats had been the largest constant in her life for the last eight years. They pre-and postdated her marriage; they reminded her of the good parts of single life. Most recently, they'd allowed themselves to be contained like luggage and hauled across the country, unpacked on the other end in the land of galing debris and dirt. Regina was thirty-two years old and by choice alone; it was not too much, she told herself resolutely and with no small part self-pity, to need her pets. She watched this unfamiliar city become further obscured in the churning air and thought nostalgically of Ohio, where storms originated in clouds and fell toward the earth, adhering to the basic laws of gravity and weather; life on the desert, it seemed, would be upside-down.

OVERNIGHT the wind died and the dust re-arranged itself over the cactus land. Lux, the missing cat, came home, her coat heavy and dull with grit, her eyes weary and resentful. She was not the same animal she'd been. Regina offered her a guilty smorgasbord of foods, everything a cat could want, cream and lox and rank canned beef and quivering raw liver and diced canteloupe, Lux's old favorite, but the animal would not eat, turning her gray nose up at it all. She did not seem to recognize her sister, though she didn't attack her, as she might a truly strange cat, but snubbed her, as if her experience out in the storm had elevated her to a plane of suffering the uninitiated would not appreciate. Regina thought of her friends who'd given birth; Regina would understand, they claimed, when she had a child of her own.

Regina's husband ferreted out her phone number, and for a few weeks his were the only calls she received. She continued to answer the phone because the odds kept building that it would have to be somebody else on the other end.

"Lux has a fever," she told him. She'd been testing the black pads of the cat's feet every few hours. When her paws felt abnormally warm, the two of them would head for the emergency vet clinic a few miles down the road. Regina's rented house was on the high desert outside of Tucson; she had believed the open-aired sanctuary of a western city's outskirts would be just what she required after her separation. She and Lux became such frequent late-night visitors at the clinic that the vet quit charging her for anything more than the medication; still, the bills ran up. Regina would hold Lux's front end while the vet bunched the gray fur at the back of the cat's neck and gave her an injection. Then the two women, the vet and Regina, would dunk Lux in a stainless steel sink of cold water. Soaking wet and shivering, the animal had the slick, grotesque look of a newborn creature, and Regina felt a frightening aversion to her.

"They have this disease here," she told Tom over the telephone, "called Valley Fever. It's from fungus in the air. Everyone gets it, but only some people get it bad. This man walks up and down Speedway talking to himself and scratching his back until it's bloody. Valley Fever went to his brain."

"Speedway?"

Regina paused, vindicated all over again in having left her husband. "See, Tom? Is it possible for you to ever really get the point? I tell you stuff about this horrible disease, this poor bastard, you say 'Speedway.' "

"I'm just saying, Speedway? Like a racetrack?"

"Anyway, there's Valley Fever in the air, getting sucked down in everybody's lungs. Speedway's just a street."

"So what *is* the point, Reg? You chose to go there."

She sighed, not sure herself. "Why did you call me?"

"You don't know what you're doing," he said in exasperation. "You're like a sleepwalker, about to step off a cliff."

Regina pictured then his laborer's raccoon-eyed tan, the soft white skin his sunglasses protected, the way his brown hair seemed permanently indented by the cap he wore, the way he whistled through his widely spaced teeth when he enjoyed himself, the way his slim hips never quite held his pants. At a distance, these things endeared him to Regina; in person, she had found them insufferable, just the presence of him, his long arm not even on her, but near her in the mornings. He was messy, indulgent, forgetful. His breath smelled of aluminum cans, he liked to make love in the middle of the night when Regina could barely rouse herself. It was no better in the middle of the day when he was seized with an urge to grab and squeeze and knead and push at her until she could barely breathe. Though by the climb's end their sex satisfied her, the journey up was stifling and mechanically arduous; he was heavy, his thinness an illusion. She had imagined nothing more pleasing than waking, fully rested, floating among the linens of a large cloudlike bed by herself. The thought that she might not need anyone again—that weight—seemed clean and karmic.

"I want to keep you," Tom said. "I love you."

"That won't get us anywhere," Regina said. "You can't just love me, unqualified like that, it's ridiculous. I don't believe you."

"Well, I do."

"The news at this end is: Lux doesn't have Valley Fever."

"Neither do I," he said, gathering steam. "I don't have cancer or worms or leprosy, either. I own my own teeth. If you fly home right now, leave your stuff, fuck the pickup, I ask no questions. That's a good deal."

His anger, more than his affection, inspired conciliation in Regina. "I know it's a good deal," she said quietly.

"No, you don't," Tom said, and then hung up. He had, in the past, ripped the phone from their kitchen wall. Regina, model of restraint, had clapped dispassionately from the doorway, refusing to join in, to ignite. He was flammable; she was not.

She now looked out her window into the gaseous glare of Tucson and felt dishonest, still, despite having left behind the marriage she believed to be the crux of her unhappiness.

REGINA'S move to Tucson had not been entirely random; she'd been promised a job at her uncle's law office. Her family, who had not very much confidence in her, assumed it was Tom who'd initiated the breakup and Regina who needed solicitous consolation. Her uncle's wife, Nanette, made sure to include Regina in dinner parties and introduced her to every divorced man she knew. Nanette was an energetic twenty years younger than Regina's uncle and was his second wife. He was her third husband; the two of them believed in getting right back on that marriage horse.

It was Nanette who brought Matthew to Regina's partitioned cubicle one lunchtime and presented her as "our separated friend," winking broadly behind this stranger's back.

He did not smile and when Nanette had gone, he said to Regina, "This feels like a pity date to me."

"Oh?" she said, rankling.

"I mean, you don't know me, I don't know you. To be frank, I don't even like your aunt, no offense." He hadn't moved from standing at the doorway, hands balled in his suitpants pockets.

"Step-aunt. Half-aunt, by marriage."

"My name's Matthew Llewellyn. I'm only a clerk, anyway, down the hall. I'd be just as happy if we called this quits. Just say it was a pleasure meeting you."

"Certainly," Regina said. "Nanette can be—"

"Pushy," Matthew said. "I worked here when she was going after your uncle. Used to call a half-dozen times a day and accuse me of losing the messages. Aggressive, huh? Her per-serverance paid off, though, didn't it? Squeaky wheel gets the grease?"

Regina smiled politely; his tone might have been unkind, and his questions were surely rhetorical. His physique and attention span seemed poorly matched to office work and he kept shrugging as if to slip from the confines of his business suit. He reminded Regina of Tom.

"Let's just say hi in the halls, huh?"

Regina agreed.

LUX'S CASE confounded Dr. Dierst, the emer-gency clinic vet. She was a pretty and athletic-looking woman, suntanned and well muscled, a tawny-eyed blonde whose hair hung down her back in a weighty braid, hair so long it had passed attractive and moved on to freakish. A copper-colored mole like a little penny rested just above the left side of her upper lip, giving her face a quirky sunniness that had nothing to do with her personality, which, Regina came to understand, was without humor. Regina's jokes and asides drew only quiz-zical, analytical looks from Dr. Dierst, as if she were diagnos-ing not the cat's problem but the owner's.

Dr. Dierst had eleven cats of her own at home, none of which she allowed outside her trailer. They were all female, all spayed, she told Regina, all slightly overweight. In the looming night, Regina, frightened over Lux's lethargy and hot paws, drove toward the dark strip mall and its single light, the red neon word EMERGENCY, feeling that if she could just arrive there, simply unload her anguish onto the capable, unsmiling Dr. Dierst, everything would be okay, or at least off her own shoulders. In this black hour she appreciated Dr. Dierst's solemn professional concern, her lack of irony, that steady unmoved mole.

However, when Lux's temperature had been successfully lowered, when the cat sat complaining in her aerated traveling box, her gray coat dry and lovely once more, when the bugs could be heard hurling themselves stupidly against the glass of the waiting room window, Regina thought her own panic— speeding down the country road, fishtailing around corners— and the doctor's somber approach to Lux's (or any other animal's) health overdramatic. This emergency, after all, was not about people. It was in this sneering mood that she would think of Tom, the way they goaded each other to depths of cynicism and black humor.

"Here," Dr. Dierst said after the fifth late-night visit, hand- ing Regina a rectal thermometer and jar of petroleum jelly. Regina wanted to scoff in her embarrassment; such provocative equipment. "Normal is 101, 102. Bring her in when it tops 104. Otherwise, sponge her."

During the next few weeks, Lux's temperature pushed the mercury to the end of the thermometer. Regina would hold the cat's tail up and watch the silver edge past 104, 105. Lux slept next to Regina in bed, a curled ball of heat on the sheets that Regina reached for in her sleep. She woke several times a night to touch the animal's dry nose leather or paw pads, at least once a week driving to the clinic for a shot. Sometimes she lay in her dark bedroom listening for the cat's small breathing, terrified that she would wake one night to silence. She would jolt from dreams, read the time on her digital clock, and be ashamed she had not wakened sooner, had not verified Lux's living more recently. With no other human in the house, with- out Tom to tell her she was going overboard, her priorities had rearranged themselves and lost context, a state she could be aware of and still not remedy. Her hand covered the cat's rib cage, which rose and fell irregularly, as if Lux were sighing instead of breathing, and Regina felt she might not be able to bear the cat's dying.

The other cat, well but neglected, began misbehaving. She used her litterbox less and less, preferring to dig and deposit in the plants or sink or even, once, on top of a door. She knocked over the bathroom trash and shredded tissue, spread tampons and Q-tips and wadded Kleenex across the floors. Regina came home from work to find the trail, cursing the cat as she cleaned. She allowed neither animal to go outdoors, following Dr. Dierst's example, and though Lux didn't seem to resent being locked in, her sister rampaged through the house. When Regina located the bad cat, she smacked her and banished her to the basement, throwing her down the carpeted stairs in anger, as if punishing the animal's heartiness. The cat landed at the bottom hissing and spitting, her eyes, in the basement gloom, glowing up at Regina demonically.

Regina shut the door and found solace in the sick Lux, who was always where she'd been left, asleep on Regina's bed. Lux still purred, still met Regina's petting hand with the upward nudging of her head and back, *more, more*. She could be coaxed into eating now and then, drinking water, licking ice cubes. The animal seemed to have fallen into a dreamy trance, as if preoccupied or sedated.

This was Regina's new life, centered almost exclusively around the care of her cat. Tom continued calling to hear her voice. She'd surprised him when she quit their marriage; she'd done it before worse had actually become worst. Though he would begin their conversations amiably enough, he always came around to asking why she'd left, what in him had merited abandonment.

"Just for future reference," he would try to joke. "What was my big mistake?"

"It wasn't you," Regina insisted. "You deserve better."

"Please," Tom said. "Please spare me that kind of patronizing *bull*shit."

"We are exactly the kind of people who bring out the worst in each other," Regina said. "You turned me into a shrew, and I made you act like an asshole."

"Oh, fuck you, Regina."

"See what I mean?"

"How can you be so cold? I never knew anybody as cold as

you." Of all the insults ready at Tom's disposal, this one struck hardest.

To him, she began to underplay the severity or frequency of Lux's fevers. How good an idea could Regina's leaving seem if, as a result, one cat was dying and the other was defecating on the tops of doors? Also, he would be the first to tell her she was no longer behaving within the acceptable boundaries of concern for an animal. She'd spent over five hundred dollars, a month's rent. It was important that Tom think she could make it without him. Besides, he was a dog person; he liked an animal you could knock around. He'd always told Regina she spoiled the cats and she told him he was jealous. He kicked them off the bed and threw things at them when they walked on the counters or tables. Cats, he said, didn't know their names or places, unlike dogs, who actually cared what their owners thought of them. Regina told him he wanted a pet who could properly grovel. But he'd grown to tolerate the cats, teaching them to spar with him, little paws darting at his fists. He refused to call them in the falsetto "kitty-kitty" Regina used so he developed a whistle and, by means of positive reinforcement, trained them to respond to it. In the six years they'd all lived together, Regina thought he'd come to find their idiosyncrasies charming, one cat's love of expensive chocolate (she would not touch Hershey's), the other's habit of sleeping beneath the bathroom throw rug.

"Put her to sleep," he recommended concerning Lux. "You'll spend beaucoup bucks, otherwise. You never did know when to say enough."

"Oh really? And not so long ago I was cold."

"Cold to me, sister; a sucker for those cats."

Regina and Tom had no children, and she often thought that was their problem, that the ordinary transfer of affection from husband to offspring had not occurred. But the predictability of such a solution annoyed her. She had entered love as one enters a party, intoxicated by possibility. What magical thing might happen? What did the evening hold? But parties wore on too long and rarely proved to transcend the given boundaries—the ice cubes melted and the food grew crusty, inevitable victims of exposure. Dresses rumpled and neckties wilted. The revelers became sleepy and fussy and drunk. And then the evening would end, as had her marriage, with the anticlimactic knowledge of the tedious cogwork behind the magic, the effort of joviality, the dirty clothes and day-old newspapers jammed into closets. Their marriage counselor (Tom's desperate, uncharacteristic idea) based all her advice on the premise that marriage, like any fine and enduring art, required work. But that was exactly Regina's point: Who wants to work? She had persisted in believing that love should not be a job.

She lied and said she missed the seasons. Here, she told Tom, it was either hot or hotter. Instead of trees, great loopy saguaros ambled across the landscape like gunslingers. And then there were the prickly pear, cholla, organ-pipe: thick-hided, antagonistic vegetation. The competition for water was stiff. Every day, she told him, driving to and from work she crossed a bridge over what they called a river, a huge dry wash. This wash had provided acres of loose topsoil and sand for the storm that had left Lux ill. Tom launched into an enthusiastic account of a Midwest fall that was meant to make her nostalgic, things he could take pleasure in only by parading them for Regina's envy. The turning leaves, the clarified air, the noise of migrating birds.

"Sounds great," she said flatly. She could have told him she lived where the birds were migrating to. She could have said it was almost November and she was still wearing shorts, that her legs were still tan. A window was open to the warm night air, thick with the oily smells of creosote and mesquite. Owls and mourning doves vied like melancholy wind instruments. In the distance she could see the endless chain of taillights feeding into the city, she could see the gravel quarry, could make out the faint metronomic beep of dump trucks in reverse. True, there were few trees, but so much the better; in their absence, Regina had developed a fondness for the curmudgeonous silhouettes of the miserly cactus. She envied their self-containment, the skeptic distance between them and other life.

★ ★ ★

OVER LUNCH one day, in the middle of a conversation with the other office secretary, Regina panicked with intuition: The cat was no longer breathing, dead this very second because Regina had not been there to prevent it. She'd called her house earlier and spoken into her answering machine, reassuring words meant to calm Lux should the cat be listening. Ridiculous, Regina told herself as she drove the whole way home on her lunch hour. There would be no time to eat, just enough to feel foolish at discovering the cat to be neither better nor worse than this morning, to get in the car and return to work. Still, try as she might, Regina could not back her dread into the corner. She tried to delude herself into believing that the cat, as repository for so much of her attention, could not simply die. Regina realized she had never worried about Tom this way, had never, even when anxious to be with him, feared for his life.

At home the bed was empty. Regina, heart pounding, began searching in places the cat could not be, inside drawers, behind blinds, finally relenting and looking under the dresser. The cat lay panting in the shadows. When Regina dragged her out, encouraged by the animal's struggle, she saw that Lux's feet were swollen like tiny baseball mitts. Beneath the fur a smooth tautness, the skin shiny and heavily bloated like sated ticks. Her fever was high, but Regina was too alarmed to investigate the number. She raced off to the clinic, rocks popping loudly under the truck's oil pan.

Because she had only come to the clinic in the night, she was not accustomed to seeing other people waiting. Regina had begun to stake a certain claim to the office, the way one might to a particular restaurant booth or library nook, one's private public place. She resented other patients' occupying the scooped plastic seats, their pets on their laps or at their feet like sacrificial offerings. The receptionist smiled in a huge false manner. Her white medical jacket hung stained and unbuttoned, obviously of inadequate size to cover her.

"Did you have an appointment?"

Regina expected to say her own and Lux's names and be instantly ushered in: oh yes, *that* cat. But no recognition lit this woman's face. "Without an appointment," she said smugly, "you'll have to wait for at least an hour."

Regina, indignant, nearly told her it was this cat and her puzzling illness that'd paid the clinic's rent the last few weeks, waived fees notwithstanding. Instead, she sat in the last available scooped chair with the box at her feet. When the man across from her, older and holding a small terrier, leaned over to look inside the box, she took grim pleasure in his astonished expression.

"She was stung?" he asked. "It was wasps?"

Regina told him the whole story, elaborating as much as she had pared down for Tom, emphasizing now what she had wanted with her husband to make subordinate. The man, a lover of all animals, offered his appointment time to her. His dog, he said with relief, merely needed booster shots.

"Count your blessings," Regina advised him.

The daytime vet was a nocturnal-looking young man with small, twitching facial features. His favorite animals, he told her, were cows. There was a patient beast for you. Obviously, he lacked any bedside manner with cats. Lux scrambled and hissed and scratched him as he lifted and probed with his little long-nailed hands. But he diagnosed her disease in less than five minutes.

"Allergic to herself?" Regina repeated, trying to understand.

"It's the immune system," he said in his adenoidal voice, his eyebrows and nostrils flittering. "Lux's is defective, basically. Because she's weak, other stuff is gonna hit her hard. She doesn't have defenses, basically." He ran his tongue over his upper lip and sparse whiskers. "We'll put her on steroids. It's not so uncommon a disease in cats. People have it, too. I bet she's a runt."

Regina nodded, thinking of her other cat, the healthy firstborn, terrorizing the house in her undeserved incarceration. "If this is so common, why didn't Dr. Dierst find it?"

"Beats me," he said. "You realize we have to charge emergency rates on this, right?"

L U X was not contagious; her disease, built uniquely and inextricably in, endangered only herself. After her feet returned to normal size, her mouth became scabbed. Little bits flaked off from her gums, which bled, then healed. Regina had been told to expect this. Every day she had to fight to get a steroid down the animal's throat; every day she wished it were the other cat who had to take a pill because she was, as a rule, more passive, happy, though who knew, lately? Still, the steroids worked. Since Dr. Dierst had been unreliable concerning Lux's disease, Regina decided to forego other advice the woman had given and let the cats outside again.

"Autoimmune deficiency?" Tom said. "AIDS?"

"AIDS is *acquired*," Regina began, "Lux was born with this—"

But Tom wasn't listening. "Somebody been buttfucking your cat, Reg?"

It had been made clear to him in the past few months that Regina wasn't coming back. When she didn't respond, Tom began clicking the dial tone button, yelling, "Hello, hello? Anybody there?"

"I guess crassness is one of the new stages of grief," Regina said. "I guess I should have expected it." But Tom had already hung up on her.

She was glad the cat was healthy but in place of the all-consuming worry a restlessness settled in her. She missed the way caring for Lux had preempted the other tediums of living, the preening and mating, the looking for love. As a way of remedying this, she turned to the neglected house and yard.

The divorcing family had allowed realtors to handle the upkeep and renting of their old home, discarding it wholly, the way a hermit crab does a shell. The fruit trees in the backyard had nearly died; in Arizona a mere two weeks without water could be fatal. Regina chose one of the four bedrooms and began filling it with the family's forsaken belongings, games, clothing, wildlife books, medical degrees (it was the husband who had the M.D.). Once started, Regina moved the majority of the house into this room, opening the door and tossing inside a lampshade or set of drapes. It intrigued her how much was superfluous, ornamentation to the basics of living.

In the backyard was a small swimming pool, filled with dead leaves and muck, its water as viscous as a natural pond's. Textured slip-proof paper curled from the diving board. Before Regina fixed it, the pump did not work properly and sent a stream of muddy water into the pool instead of out. After simplifying the rooms of the house, Regina began spending her free hours skimming the swimming pool and soaking the sparse trees. She remembered the real estate agent naming them for her: minneola orange, lemon, grapefruit, some munificent hybrid called Fruit Basket Surprise, which was supposed to produce all the citrus, limes right next to tangerines. Regina would flip on the underwater pool lights at night and admire the gradually clearing depths. Without leaves and seeds and mud, it was a larger body of shining water. Though the weather would not permit swimming for months, the sight of shimmering blue water, the sound of it running from the house's pipes and into the ground, soothed Regina. She sat on the sun-warmed concrete steps outside her back door and listened to the saturation.

S I N C E she could claim to know only a handful of people in all of Tucson, Regina was delighted to see Dr. Dierst at the benefit auction. Local artists had donated their work to be sold; proceeds went to the homeless. Regina had gone because it was Christmas and because, when Nanette had called to invite her to the office holiday bash, Regina had felt the prideful necessity of having other plans. For the auction, she spent an inordinate amount of time selecting an outfit, standing before her closet trying to remember what fashion was all about.

The benefit was being held in a downtown hotel lobby

where, on other occasions, the homeless flopped. Regina, nervous, a stranger still to the city, wandered peripherally, drinking free wine as a way of occupying her hands. Dr. Dierst stood at the top of a stairway studying a painting of two men and a cat. The men, emaciated, purple and gaunt in heavy acrylic oils, held hands and looked at the cat, who sat on a windowsill in the absorbed posture of the hunter, eyeing a bird outside, oblivious to the two men. Regina had made her way up the stairs, jockeying around the plastic champagne glasses, until she stood beside Dr. Dierst, who also seemed to have come by herself. She looked at the painting and tried to see why it would captivate the humorless Dr. Dierst so thoroughly.

Regina said, "I didn't recognize you without your white jacket."

Dr. Dierst peered into her face as into a two-way mirror before finally saying, "How's Lux?"

Regina, fortified by champagne, made lame jokes about Lux's burgeoning steroid bulk, the way she terrorized the neighborhood cats and disqualified herself from the feline Olympics. Her antics, as always with Dr. Dierst, fell on deaf ears. The copper mole never shifted. At some point Regina realized she was assuming a friendship, a familiarity and concern where there were none. Dr. Dierst must have had hundreds of patients; the overfriendly type was probably an occupational hazard. She kept flicking her eyes toward the bottom of the stairs.

"So how are *your* cats?" Regina asked.

"Excuse me," Dr. Dierst said. "I see a friend I have to talk to."

"Oh. Sorry to have kept you. I just wanted to say hello." Regina watched her move down the stairs, looking for the alleged friend, but lost sight of the blond braid before seeing where it went. She turned her attention to the painting Dr. Dierst had been studying. She recognized in the men's absorption in the cat her own past, unhealthy obsession with Lux. Thankfully, that time was gone. She decided to have more to drink.

Later, after she'd bravely horned in on a few conversations

and not only committed to memory the art up for auction but grown to loathe it, she found herself standing next to Dr. Dierst again. Again, they were both alone.

"Did you find your *friend*?" Regina said, the word sodden with sarcasm. She didn't care. She didn't plan to see this woman after tonight. Her cat was well and she had begun to miss Tom and the city she knew, Columbus, its damp brick avenues and terrariumlike gardens and monstrous fecund homes seeming the safest, most desirable places in the world. Over the course of the evening Regina had come to view Tucson as sinister; she'd stepped outside for a moment to clear her head and witnessed a man's jump from a moving car. He'd fallen into the street, rolling, cursing without emotion at the departing vehicle, then simply sat on the curb and begun patting his pockets for cigarettes. The event, plus her drunkenness, had made her feel wrongly placed here, unsuited to the dry, ragged edges of the West.

"Want to come meet my cats?" Dr. Dierst repeated in her serious voice, brown eyes narrowed defensively. "I mean, you seem so interested in my cats. . . ."

Regina focused on the face before her and felt the world flipflop. Dr. Dierst, though beautiful, was shy! The ejected man on the curb was a sad case, his plight the very example of what this auction concerned. "Yes!" Regina said eagerly, her earlier aspersions concerning Tucson instantly renounced. "Yes, I could use some coffee maybe."

Regina tailgated Dr. Dierst (could she possibly call her Laura?) to her trailer. The woman's Bronco seemed too large for her, her head poking up over the driver's seat like a child's. The park was an older one and Regina realized there were more trees clustered here than she'd seen since she left Ohio. Tricycles, lawnmowers, hanging laundry. Why had she thought this city so unlike her native one? The two vehicles rolled over speed bumps. Until she saw the Christmas lights lining Dr. Dierst's trailer windows, Regina had not felt the holiday season upon her.

She followed Dr. Dierst up the aluminum stairs and through the front door, chattering about Christmas depression. The trailer smelled of litter box and wobbled like a docked boat as they entered. Regina had the feeling someone else was there, in a back room, some dark, napping sensibility just out of sight. The compact kitchen was illuminated by the multicolored Christmas-tree lights hung over the sink.

"Oh, don't turn on any others!" Regina exclaimed, as Dr. Dierst made a move toward a switch. "They're so festive."

Dr. Dierst whistled and cats came running.

"That's just how my husband used to call my cats!"

The sound of them thudding from chairbacks and windowsills could be felt in the floor; they were the presence Regina had sensed. She shut her eyes for a moment to test the depth of her inebriation and went into a spin; it was more serious than she'd expected. Around her feet swirled a luxurious sea of cats. She heard purring. Their odor was overpowering.

"The last time I was in a trailer," Regina said, opening her eyes and trying to collect herself, "the whole group of us were at one end, probably twelve people, Tom's family. The thing tipped like a teeter-totter."

"Huh," Dr. Dierst said drily. She was pouring food into a large saucepan on the floor, squatting to see it in the dark. Her long braid fell into the concentric attitude of a sleeping snake on the floor.

"It seems like more than eleven cats," Regina said cheerily, hearing her voice clatter in the room like a loose ball bearing. It was the last bright thing she could summon in herself; she grew more languid by the moment, drowning in the evening's liquor, in the warm feelings she suddenly had for Tucson.

Dr. Dierst put the cat food away and sat at the kitchen table on a bench, doing nothing further. One leg tucked compactly beneath the other, braid beside her. Where was the promised coffee? And why didn't she now turn on a light? Regina wondered for a second if the woman weren't sinister, too. Cats who couldn't get a place at the food pan walked on the plastic checkerboard tablecloth, on the back of the bench, around Regina's feet. Their animal presence, the way they passed through the room like velvet, made her think of a jungle, of humidity, or of having a dream of being a cat herself. Their vision was limited like this, was it not? Strictly nearsighted? She seemed to recall a photograph of blades of grass meant to resemble what cats might see. She could not tell whether she should trust them, whether she should want to rub against them, to be rid of her sociable clothing, to feel the wet and dry parts of their noses exploring her, inquisitive and discreet.

Dr. Dierst said, "Sit down."

Regina obeyed, grateful for instruction, falling gracelessly next to her on the bench.

"My husband always said I was a sloppy drunk," Regina confided, though what Tom had said was that she was a slutty drunk. "Were you ever married?"

"No."

"I'm separated," Regina said. "Like an earthworm."

Dr. Dierst gave her a minor gratifying smile. Her mole rose, fell.

Regina asked her if she'd ever lived with anybody.

"Just my father. He died a couple of years ago. This was his trailer."

"It's nice. I like it. Like a boat."

"We got along until I was twenty-five or so. Then he couldn't handle it when I discovered I was a lesbian."

"Oh." Regina felt a small flame of dreadful sobriety light in her suddenly.

Dr. Dierst was still talking. "I couldn't ever tell him to his face about being gay, he just wasn't that kind of person—and I wasn't either, really—so I sent him a letter, even though we lived together, and told him the truth as best I could. He never said a word about it. Not one word. I wondered if he even got it, but I knew he had. That kind of letter doesn't get lost in the mail. After he died, I found my letter in his things, in a sealed envelope that said 'For Laura Only' on the outside. He'd saved it, except he'd cut out every word that had to do with lesbianism, just literally cut them out."

Regina said, "That's terrible."

Dr. Dierst shrugged. "He loved me. I loved him."

Regina wanted to object: It was not love. But she felt unqualified to make such a proclamation. The trailer and its odd

lights and smells now depressed her. She thought she understood why Dr. Dierst surrounded herself with cats and their
satisfiable and simple needs—and their neediness. But it was
stiflingly hot; these animals had been intended to prowl outdoors, to hunt, to mate, things Dr. Dierst denied them and
then claimed to be in their own best interests.

Dr. Dierst, without looking at her, laid a hand on Regina's
knee, and though Regina realized when it happened she had
known it would, the moist palm still seemed surprisingly heavy
and far too human.

"Do you feel a little electric surge?" Dr. Dierst asked quietly.

Regina felt nothing, really, except a lack of energy and
thorough confusion. She laid her own hand over Dr. Dierst's
by way of cowardly answer.

"I'd like to love you," Dr. Dierst murmured, turning her
face toward Regina's.

Regina pulled back. "I'm drunk," she explained, though
she'd sobered considerably since coming into the trailer. She'd
been misunderstood. "I have to go," she said, or meant to say
but only managed to mumble as she fumbled for the small
door handle, turning a window knob by mistake. She stepped
on one of the cats, whose screech seemed to make physical the
anguish in the room. Regina didn't stop, despite having no
idea where she was going, none, directions gone from her
mind. All she knew was that she had to get out.

TOM waited for two months before calling Regina, a piece
of restraint she both appreciated and found nerve-racking. In
this time Regina had made the effort of getting the attention
of Matthew Llewellyn. She needed a point of reference; he
would have to do. The episode with Laura Dierst had upset
her more than it should have, more than a similar pass from a
man would have, she knew. She was disappointed in her nar-
row-minded reaction and kept playing the evening over, trying
to convince herself that if she could do it again she would make
love with the woman.

She and Matthew met at a pizza restaurant in the middle of town. For the first half of the evening they interrupted each other and for the last half said nothing. Pizza suddenly seemed to Regina the food of children, disturbingly messy. Matthew appeared to understand she had not invited him for himself and spent his time glaring at her.

"It's been real," he said sardonically when they parted.

When she came home she found Tom's voice on her answering machine. He rambled to the end of seven separate interludes of tape, by turns angry and hateful and tearful. Listening, Regina was only curious as to what he would say next. His feelings, like his body and home, were not accessible to her, a realization that disturbed her more than the actual words Tom spoke. But she came to attention during the eighth message, when he said, "By the time you get this, I'll be out of your hair forever and you'll be glad." The tape rolled, oceanic as sonar, then there was the single local beep that meant the end of messages received.

Regina's eyes widened. She tapped the phone buttons anxiously, trying to decide who to call, then just hit 0. The operator acted as if this kind of emergency had so much precedence there was a standard modus operandi.

Regina waited for an hour, staring at the phone, hugging her cats. As soon as she'd hung up from talking with the Columbus police, she'd gathered Lux and her sister to her, locking the doors and pulling the shades, taking shelter.

When someone finally called her back it was Special Officer Sharon Hoagland, a deep-voiced older woman who said Tom was fine, intoxicated, lonely, only interested in scaring Regina. It was apparent from her tone that Tom had told Officer Hoagland everything and that she, too, despite impartiality, held Regina responsible. There was the same distant, accusing noise of sonar on the line.

"What time is it out there?" Sharon Hoagland asked.

Regina, caught off guard by the question, blinked once before looking at her watch. "Midnight," she said. "A little after."

"Well, it's past two in the morning here. It's always later in this part of the country, know what I mean?"

"I guess," Regina said, though it felt plenty late to her in her own time zone.

By way of signing off, Sharon Hoagland suggested coolly that Regina need not worry, that Tom had promised her he would never call again.

Regina looked around her empty, clean house, and decided to drive for a while. She took the highway toward the mountains and into the Saguaro National Monument. She drove for hours, circling side roads and trying to lose herself, listening to the radio and smoking cigarettes, feeling the statuesque cacti all around her like accomplices. She got gas in Ajo. She circled Tucson as if to contain it. When she saw signs, she considered on-ramps to I-10 eastbound. In two days, she could be with Tom, she could drive up to their small house and surprise him, have sex with him, lie in his arms. Make him happy.

But she could not claim to love him. She sat at a railroad crossing near South Tucson, the only witness to a long, lumbering freight train. She could not claim to love anyone. The obligatory emotion she held toward her parents was tempered by the fact of life they'd given her. What good was it? What design? She felt the lack of something vital in herself, some code or human gene she missed. The coldness Tom had accused her of made her quiver; she felt now she had denied his accusation based solely on the temperature of her skin, as if he had been speaking literally.

Regina drove home by way of the vet clinic. It had become four in the morning. In Columbus, for Tom, the sun was rising and last night was washed away. Regina saw the glowing EMERGENCY sign and thought of Dr. Dierst inside. She pulled into the parking lot and glided to a halt. Without the cat, there could not even be the pretense of an emergency. She tried to be tough with herself, discern what it was she wanted, precisely. She was thirty-two years old and not sure she'd ever loved anyone. What would she have to learn in order to love Dr. Dierst? What steps did one take toward warmth?

The clinic was lighted but no one seemed about. Regina waited, rolling down a window. She watched the bugs and listened to the neon hum of the red EMERGENCY. After perhaps thirty minutes, Dr. Dierst came from the back room and stood at the front desk. She stared unblinking at Regina, her life a dead earnest endeavor. She was not wearing her white coat and Regina felt she was looking inside a dollhouse. Suddenly a cat jumped up on the counter next to Dr. Dierst and rubbed against her. A cat from home, Regina thought, for company.

Dr. Dierst simply held her hand up, tanned and cuticle-free, and the animal took her pleasure, rubbing, nudging, sliding. Regina thought painfully of Lux, shamed by the memory of throwing both cats out the back door before she drove off, hardening herself, willfully ignoring the threat of coyotes.

She and Dr. Dierst stared at one another through the glass. Regina thought this could not be happening, yet it was. Depending on how long they could do it, any outcome seemed possible. If one of them smiled they might be friends. If Dr. Dierst motioned Regina inside, Regina could go. If Regina drove away she could never come back. What did she want? She could not manufacture love where there was none, but the question was sapping her, pulling her inside-out, making her crazy; nothing had been solved by leaving Tom, nothing. There was no new life; you turned an hourglass upside-down and simply rearranged the sand.

Dr. Dierst looked down to follow the cat's departure off the desk, the fleeting black streak, and Regina saw the serious eyes, the vertebrae of braid, the mouth that had no laugh lines forming around it. The hand, held now in empty air, that could have stroked Regina. She remembered the image of the cut-up confessional letter and took this opportunity to start the engine. She pulled away, watching the hood of the small truck overtake the curb, the highway. She felt at one with the machinery as she flew into curves, accelerated without pause all the way.

Just before the turnoff to her dirt road, Regina noticed a glinting reflection in her headlights in the scrub at the side of the road. She was exhausted and drove another mile or two—

rocks again banging underneath—before feeling duty-bound to double back. She then had to drive slowly by the brush a few times before the glint caught her eye again. She parked and got out, leaving her headlights on.

Morning was filling the sky fast, a cold and clear sun rising behind the Santa Catalina Mountains. Hidden in the palo verde trees and scrub was the wreckage of a burned car, an old wreck, nothing left in it but springs and glass shards, small pieces of charred cushion, melted plastic dashboard and radio buttons that had once spelled Buick. Its skeleton showed a large sedan. The license plate was intact and had as a preface to its assortment of numbers the symbol of a wheelchair. She looked for signs of a person, bones or clothes, but there was nothing.

Regina sat on a nearby rock and tried to blame sleeplessness for her feelings. She believed she could drive her own car off the road and kill herself, though not for love, like Tom, but for its absence. She believed she might have reached the end—most certainly the bottom. In the past, hope had come to her in the form of a new home, a new landscape, but what was here? The sun rose, its light hitting her as it would have in Columbus, two hours earlier. She felt void of desirable qualities, charity or love or patience or tolerance. She enjoyed the disaster she'd found here. She felt sure she would come home to discover her cats eaten by coyotes. She would deserve it.

WHEN she tried to locate the accident a few days later, she couldn't. She drove back and forth until she grew impatient and decided she was succumbing to melodrama.

This would mark the end of looking for signs, good or bad, the end of testing each day like bath water.

NAKED in bed one night during the following summer, almost a year since her move to the desert, hot, Regina opened her legs in a dream, or not quite a dream, but the halfway point wherein one makes a request, selects the numbers, and waits for the song to play. It was so palpably hot—frustration made concrete by the weather. Earlier in the evening she'd seduced Matthew Llewellyn and brought him home, but found, after making love, that in this heat she could not bear his body in her bed; she had become so adept at throwing off human concern she was able to ask him to leave based entirely on that discomfort.

Later in the summer, during the monsoon season, there would be a flood in the dry wash; the reason for its empty width and depth would finally become clear. Regina and the cats would be isolated in the desert house and helicopters would come in the night to shine lights and broadcast instructions, as in a war. The road and bridges would wash out, and live frogs would suddenly appear in the swimming pool. One cat would eat a frog and throw it up for the next few days in sickeningly identifiable pieces, and Regina would not take her to the vet. The water and electricity and gas would all go off and Regina would have to eat peculiar, cold canned goods and talk on the (mercifully) functioning phone. The desert, she would come to realize, is not a place for either high winds or saturating rains, a place that tolerates no extreme other than heat, its element. She would want to call Tom and beg him to forgive her. Gone so long from him, and so far, she would have no memory of her own old phone number and would have to search it out.

But for now, six weeks before these facts, she lay feverish in bed, only beginning to fathom the desperation that would drive her to need, and then be denied, her husband, hoping tonight simply to dream of something erotic that might displace, however temporarily, loneliness. The rehabilitated cat slept on top of the sheet and, between her legs, through the thin cotton, Regina felt her own moisture absorbing toward the animal. Clean me, she thought, remembering a sea of cats. She wished to dream about that small rough tongue, its natural pinkness, the nubby raised texture of it, navigating whiskers, the flicking alert hunter's tail. She wanted release. She wanted to be clean. Lick me, she thought, very gently right there, right there.

FORT DESPAIR

I

NICOLE turned sixteen and did not get a car. The big package from her parents was not an elaborately disguised set of keys; Nicole had imagined for days the nested boxes, all beautifully wrapped—she would laugh, tearing her way through the ribbon and paper—revealing in the final, small, cotton-lined jewelry box a pair of keys (one for the ignition, one for the doors) which fit the silver sportscar hidden around the block. She'd been out there a few minutes before her party looking for it.

Instead she received a mustard yellow suitcase that matched the luggage her mother owned. Inside were elastic straps intended to keep her shampoo and mousse upright. Nicole snapped one hopefully, as if a pair of keys might slip from behind the satin lining. A mirror in the lid reflected the dining-room light fixture and made her blink.

"Not like we're trying to tell you anything," her father said, taking a Polaroid of her with her new suitcase.

"Hint hint," said her brother, who was thirteen. He had gotten her nothing for her birthday.

Her mother said, "I know *I* always appreciated having a nice set of luggage."

"Thanks a lot," Nicole told her parents sincerely, disappointment a nodule in her throat. "It's great."

A couple of weeks later they went as a family to southern

Illinois for Thanksgiving. Nicole's father's two older sisters lived in Cairo (pronounced not like the Egyptian city but like the corn syrup) and Nicole's family spent every Thanksgiving visiting there. Nicole packed her overnight case with all kinds of items she couldn't possibly need in the short time they were to stay. Still, she felt obliged to fill the thing.

The whole trip from Chicago, down the length of the state, her brother, Boyer, kept requesting stops. "Ready for some R and R?" he would say to whichever of their parents was driving. Nicole believed he was jacking off in the bathrooms, then smoking a cigarette, then washing his hands and brushing his teeth. He returned to the car each time with toothpaste on his breath. She scooted as far away from him as possible in the seat, her square overnight bag between them. Last year, on this same trip south, Boyer had unzipped his fly and shaken his penis at Nicole, right there in the car, right behind their parents' backs.

Nicole's immediate family, the symmetrical foursome that always seemed as faithfully delineated as a dollhouse clan, had begun shifting in her mind. The lines between grown-ups and children evaporated. She'd found her father in tears one afternoon and, over the summer, her mother had taken a vacation without them, leaving them an unbalanced set of three, the children a majority. Though her father offered to let Nicole drive on the way to Cairo, she refused. In her own car, that might have been fine, but in this one she preferred sitting in the back where she and Boyer belonged.

She cracked her window and tried to breathe the outdoors air; it made her carsick to think of inhaling the same used air a member of her family might just have exhaled. A lot of things made her carsick these days, things as simple as waving tree limbs or falling snow, things that never used to and never should cause queasiness.

"Hey," her father said good-naturedly into the rearview mirror, "you trying to heat the outdoors?"

In Cairo nearly all the houses were painted white. White sides, white trim, black roofs. Those that weren't white were brick or burned down. Most buildings were abandoned, holes for windows, scorched places from old fires. Dogs and children ran around in the streets and stared at Nicole's family's slow-moving car. It seemed always to be cloudy in Cairo. Nicole's father narrated a tour. A great-aunt's house, on the market for ten years now, offered complete with furniture. Best rib joint. Elementary school, half destroyed. Church where his father used to preach. The river bottoms, where teenagers went four-wheeling. Fort Defiance, where the Ohio and Mississippi rivers met, the place where Huck Finn and Nigger Jim went wrong. These days, according to her father, Cairo was suffering a minor decline.

"Minor?" Boyer scoffed. "There's more cars junked on the *side* of the road than driving around *on* the road."

"More gravestones than living inhabitants," Nicole's mother added.

"You know what?" Nicole said. "They ought to make those movies about bad history right here in Cairo, slavery and the Depression and all that. Hollywood spends a bunch of money to make sets look this terrible. It could help the economy."

Her mother laughed unkindly.

Their relatives were happy to see them and Nicole felt like a small child again in their arms. Aunt Dizzy, Aunt Velvet—twelve and fifteen years older than Nicole's father—Cousin Cammy Sue, Cousin Leroy, Second Cousins Louise and Cookie. Maybe Nicole's uncle Duke was not happy to see them; he sat watching TV in the back room of Dizzy's, oxygen tubes up his nose, and it was never clear how he felt. When she saw Duke, Nicole remembered how this house always gave her headaches. Back in Chicago she forgot Cairo completely, though once, staring at a United States map in school, she had suddenly begun thinking about how all of them in Cairo were going on with their lives at that very second, that little pinprick of a place half an inch away from Chicago, Duke and his oxygen tubes and tumor, Dizzy waiting on him, Cammy Sue and her little kids. It was one of those startling revelations, one of those moments when the universe seems to inhabit your head.

She wondered if any of them here thought of her or her family when they went away.

In Cairo, you watched TV. You ate too much and made runs down to the Quik-Mart for forgotten food items. Dizzy or Velvet would press a dollar as soft and worn as a handkerchief in your palm and send you for marshmallows or pimientos or canned cranberry. You played Old Maid with Louise and Cookie. You looked at Leroy's hunting pictures. Except this year Leroy was joining the air force, so instead of dead, inverted deer, he produced pictures of fighter jets and catalogs of military wear. Boyer, who would be a conscientious objector if the occasion arose, sat next to Leroy on the couch and said things like, "Join the army, visit exotic lands, meet interesting people, blow their brains out," while Leroy laughed.

Leroy's sister Cammy Sue was eight years older than Nicole. She already had three children and two ex-husbands. She wore an extension in her mousey hair and chain-smoked and had had a hysterectomy only a few weeks earlier. "Sixteen?" she said to Nicole. "I remember sixteen. I had Doby when I was sixteen." Doby was her son, who'd opted for living with his father in Monterey, California. "Who wouldn't?" Cammy Sue said defensively. "*I'd* rather live there, too." Cammy Sue had studied electrolysis but now sold real estate. Back when she was still planning to be a beauty operator, she'd rearranged Nicole's eyebrows with her electric pencil. Her two little daughters, Louise and Cookie, five and four, both had perms in their downy blond hair. They also had pierced ears, something Nicole's mother wasn't going to let Nicole do until she was eighteen and out of her mother's jurisdiction. Cammy Sue was the kind of mom you wanted when you were a kid.

"Who's your boyfriend?" Cammy Sue asked Nicole later. They were in a video-game bar called The Underground, drinking beer. Cairo didn't card.

Nicole always invented a boyfriend to tell Cammy Sue about. She would describe whoever she happened to be in love with. She had never had a real boyfriend. Now she talked about Hank Anthony, one of her driving partners in Driver's Ed. "His mother's black and his father's white," she told Cammy Sue. Nicole didn't know this for a fact, but Hank's skin color obviously came from a mixed source. She talked about him driving, since that was where her familiarity with him was best, failing to mention that also present in the car were two other students and Mr. Gross. It was Hank Anthony who had alerted Nicole to the dream of owning a car. One day he'd gotten carried away on highway driving—they learned to merge, to change lanes, to pay tolls—and speeded on toward Wisconsin, ignoring commands to exit, until finally Mr. Gross had had to use his passenger brake. "Was that too cool!" Hank said afterward, sitting next to Nicole in the backseat while someone else took a turn merging, changing lanes, and paying tolls. "I love to just *go*," he said. He slid one caramel-colored hand over the other, torpedolike. His fingernails reminded Nicole of buttermints.

Cammy Sue looked impressed. "Around here, black boys won't give me the time of day," she told Nicole. "I guess Chicago's different."

Nicole, happy to have discovered the secret to Cammy Sue's esteem, conjured up other mulatto and black friends. Her own life took on a more complex texture. After a pitcher of beer, she believed in them herself and felt saddened, as if by death, when she remembered she hadn't spoken three words to Hank Anthony all semester. Cammy Sue had excused herself and gone to the rest room, leaving Nicole alone at their table to face her real life again.

The cousins had gotten intimate over drinks, but when Cammy Sue came back she was all business, as if she'd peed away their fast friendship. "We gotta go," she announced without sitting down. "I'm a mother, you know."

Nicole walked back to Dizzy and Duke's in a sluggish stupor, listening to Cammy Sue quote asking prices on houses. Everything was shamefully cheap, according to her; Cairo could be bought for less than a song.

"A jingle," Nicole said.

"You drunk? What a lightweight."

Nicole tried to get serious. She made herself picture little vignettes of life in each home, tried to imagine how a banister would feel in her hand or the way the perpetual murky light might fall through a built-on kitchen window box. It was an effort. When they reached Dizzy's, she fell asleep as soon as she reclined on the couch, where she woke later in the night to find herself still dressed. Her mother hadn't bothered to leave her a pillow or blanket, so she shrugged herself under Leroy's simulated leather flight jacket, propped her head on the couch arm, and fell back asleep.

It was hard to be sixteen, her mother had wryly warned her. But her mother had said the same of fifteen and fourteen and thirteen and twelve. She'd said the same of being a girl, of being an oldest child, of being sensitive and a loner, of brightness, of beauty. Nicole objected; she was not beautiful. Ah, her mother would say, that's why it's so hard. You don't have a trendy beauty; your beauty is more eternal. Nicole looked down at her arms, which were pale and prone to moles, at her cushiony thighs and short feet. It did her no good, this eternal beauty. Her mother's looks had gone to Boyer, the thick wavy hair and clear olive skin, the long bones and fluid motion. Nicole shared her father's squat solidity; people, when they commented at all, told her she looked healthy.

When she woke up for real in Cairo on her aunt Dizzy's living room sofa, Nicole's mouth was tacky and dry. Yesterday's clothes felt oily. Aunt Velvet slept upright in a chintz-covered chair across from Nicole, snoring under an afghan. Nicole wondered if Aunt Velvet, who was a spinster, was happy. She wondered if she had ever been in love, though it was hard to connect the idea of romantic love with someone so ancient.

The kitchen cupboards offered nothing but old-people food: Rye Crisp and bran cereal and viscous homemade jellies. A Roach Motel sat on the counter beside the stove. Nicole could hear Duke's TV blaring from the back room; he claimed he never slept, never shut his eyes one time all night long. Nicole's mother, strictly a realist, used to tell him that was physically impossible, that brain cells had to regenerate, et cetera. Duke seemed to consider her newfangled and confounding, like a puzzling modern appliance.

Nicole peeked through the Dutch doors separating the

kitchen and Duke's room. He sat in his easy chair, one leg thrown over the arm, his pajama top unbuttoned so that his bare chest and stomach were the first things Nicole noted. Duke had a tumor the size and shape of a lantern in his stomach. Nicole could see its edges through his skin. Though he would undoubtedly deny it, he slept, the oxygen hose a clear plastic pretzel beneath his nostrils. Tubing ran from his chair past the bomblike spare oxygen vessels, over the sofa and through the door where Nicole stood. Behind her vibrated the machine, which looked like a tank vacuum cleaner. What had always frightened and fascinated Nicole was the simple switch—no more complicated than the one for the overhead light on the wall—that kept everything going. Nothing could have been easier than turning Duke off.

It thrilled her to consider it.

Outside, predictably, the fog looked impenetrable. Duke and Dizzy's blue tick hound, whose name was Dog, rose from his ratty bed next to the clothes dryer on the back porch to greet Nicole. Dog had one ear and no tail; he'd been caught in a combine some years ago. Also he had absolutely no control over his bladder and was constantly dripping urine. He, like Duke, had managed to live and deteriorate beyond anyone's wildest expectations.

"Dog Dog," Nicole said. "How are you, old Dog, you old dog." Seeing Dog reminded Nicole of the story Leroy told the cousins one year. He said Aunt Velvet had sex with Dog. Cammy Sue, the oldest, shrugged—it could be true. Leroy went on. Didn't they ever wonder why she never got married? Wasn't it strange how she'd go off walking with Dog every evening for an hour? What about all those treats she brought him? And Dog went straight for crotches, didn't he, just like he knew how. Nicole had sat squirming, unwillingly imagining Velvet and Dog.

She couldn't see Dog without the same image flashing once more before her eyes. These days, she couldn't look at her father without remembering him in tears, nor could she be with Boyer and not see his unzipped pants, exposed surprising flesh. This tarnish covered most everything and made Nicole feel as if her life had turned grim and polluted. Once in a while she was struck with an instant of déjà vu, a tenuous memory from her childhood of a swing or hammock, of looking up into a brilliant sky. It seemed now that that moment had been her last unencumbered one, the last one in which she was perfectly and wholly happy.

Nicole walked through Cairo with Dog. From the abandoned residential area where her aunts and uncle lived, she passed through the highway strip, barbecue joints and gas stations, and then beyond that toward the river. Ahead of her, just within her vision in the smoky fog, she could see the two bridges, which both extended into obscurity like roads in dreams. They were farther away than they looked, but Nicole kept on toward them, fixing her mind on them as simple, attainable goals. Finally she and Dog reached the turnoff for Fort Defiance.

The parking lot held RVs with their curtains drawn. It began raining. Or, more precisely, it began moisturizing, a cool mist descending weightlessly from the low clouds. Nicole stopped at the historical site placard and skimmed the information. Beyond the board was the renovated fort, from which you could watch barges navigate beneath the bridges. Nicole had yet to see another human being out this morning. Everything had a depressing mystical cast to it; it was as if anything might erupt from the gloom. She climbed the stairs and stood at the top of the fort, feeling as if even gravity had given out.

Dog had followed her laboriously up the steps but now trotted down, his nubby tail stump disappearing. Nicole realized he was going to the water and raced after him, yelling. So thick was the fog, she thought she could hear an echo. Dog paid no heed and soon was swallowed by the clouds. Nicole watched her feet move forward and listened to her own breathing. A splash sounded: Dog in the water. She walked daintily over rocks and broken liquor bottles. The barges oogahed at one another.

Suddenly a mound of human activity came into sight,

alarmingly close. She was so startled Nicole at first did not understand what they were doing. Then she began backing up, tripping as she went. The two fat people, bums, Nicole supposed, did not stop, though the woman of the pair had seen her. The man's pants were lowered and he bounced rhythmically onto his partner as if they were both inflated. The woman's big white face had smiled up at Nicole over the man's shoulder.

Two fucking bums, she said to herself, all the way back to the highway, stunned. Fortunately, Dog caught up with her. She'd forgotten completely about him.

"Where were you?" her mother demanded when Nicole came through the front door and into the foyer. Her mother had quickly slid the phone receiver onto its cradle and at first Nicole thought she had been calling the police, reporting her missing.

"Walking," Nicole answered, still shocked. Who could she tell about the bums? Her mother cleared her throat, then said nothing. Her hands were in her pockets and Nicole suddenly realized her mother had a secret. She and Nicole moved at the same awkward moment to go through the foyer door and wedged for an instant, shoulder to shoulder. Her mother laughed and waited, then followed into the kitchen. The place where her arm had touched Nicole's felt hot, as if lighted.

Dizzy stood at the stove, where she always stood, and stirred, alternately, scrambled eggs, giblet gravy, country ham and sausage. Flat biscuits sizzled on a blackened cookie sheet in the overhead oven. The air was thick with maple and pork. Nicole asked if there was something she could do. Dizzy, as expected, said no. If there had been a private place in that little white house, Nicole would have gone to it. The foyer with the telephone was as close as you could come. She stood at the clouded kitchen window and watched Dog resettle himself on his filthy pallet, licking his muddy feet. Did he lick Velvet?

Because the two events had happened one after the other, Nicole began associating the half-naked bums at Fort Defiance with her mother's interrupted phone call.

11

NICOLE'S mother, Bebe, sat with the children watching the Thanksgiving Day parades on TV. She still thought of all of them as children, even her niece, Cammy Sue, who had never been a child, who had, it seemed to Bebe, spent all her young years vigorously denying there ever was such a thing as childhood. Cammy Sue's daughters, Cookie and Louise, could not be budged from their places a yard from the TV screen. Bebe mentioned to Cammy Sue what she had read about the harmfulness of this habit, but Cammy Sue simply glared at her aunt. Bebe had always disliked Cammy Sue and Leroy. They were such perfect back-country stereotypes. It used to pain her to watch Boyer and Nicole, just enough younger than their cousins, idolize them.

Leroy now proclaimed that his girlfriend was coming to dinner.

"That gal who can't smoke?" Cammy Sue said. "Her?"

"She can smoke," Leroy said.

"She doesn't inhale," Cammy Sue said. "She gets it in her mouth and blows it right back, damn novice." She bloated her cheeks, then sputtered out smoke. Bebe tried not to seethe. Cammy Sue demonstrated the correct way to exhale, which was to expel a slow stream from her mouth while inhaling with her nose, causing two braids of smoke to flow.

Though she knew it was a mistake, Bebe could not stop herself. "How can you smoke those things when you can see what they do? Hasn't Duke's situation taught you anything?"

"What's her prob?" Leroy asked Boyer, as if Bebe weren't sitting right there, as if Boyer would know.

Boyer shrugged. He leaned over to whisper in his cousin's ear. "Menopause," Bebe heard, but pretended not to. Every year when they visited Cairo her children became infected with insolence, which, fortunately, they lost once they returned home.

"I'm on estrogen," Cammy Sue said. Obviously the whole room had heard Boyer's explanation. "It can make you weird, all right. I got more bust, I think."

"You wish," said Leroy.

"No more being on the rag, though, thank God. I should have had this hysterectomy years ago."

From the floor, beside Bebe, Cookie said, "Mama don't want any more children." She didn't look away from the TV.

"We're enough babies," Louise agreed, also keeping her eyes glued to the screen.

"You bet you are," Cammy Sue told them.

Bebe would have preferred leaving the room, but her pride prevented her from being driven away by this uncomfortable conversation. That's just what these simple hicks wanted. It pained her to consider the fact that Cammy Sue and Leroy and her own children shared a blood relationship. Her daughter looked miserable sitting at the piano bench. Nicole had been unhappy for a long time, it seemed, but Bebe remembered her own teenage years well enough to know that it was not possible for her, as the mother, to help. It was a terrible time, but the years just afterward, the college years, were good enough to make up for it. She wished she could assure Nicole of that next, large, part of life.

This reminded Bebe that back in Chicago her lover was spending Thanksgiving by himself. He and his wife had separated earlier in the month. He wanted Bebe to do the same with her marriage. "Come clean," he advised. He seemed to think his behavior exemplary and to hold her in the unique contempt reserved for those who hang on to bad habits you yourself have successfully abandoned. This morning on the phone he had threatened to drive down to Cairo and get her, Sir Galahad. Bebe imagined the scene with equal parts terror and pleasure.

Louise, five years old, turned to Bebe and said, "What does P-E-T-E spell?"

Bebe gasped, struggled for an instant trying to figure out how the child knew Pete's name.

"Pete," she said as calmly as she could.

Louise smiled guilelessly through her crooked little teeth. No one else had even noticed; it could not be a plot. Nobody knew.

"P-E-T-E," Louise sang, swaying her frizzy blond hair.
"P-E-T-E."

Bebe recalled with relief a joke about pete and repeat. She
then allowed herself to resume thinking of her own Pete. From
his Michigan Avenue office, where he now lived, he claimed
he would be able to see Cairo if there were any clear days.
Missing him was so physical Bebe found herself responding to
television commercials showing couples, to embracing or
hand-holding strangers. It was like pregnancy, when babies,
anybody's, had made her heart leap. Love was sappy, no two
ways about it.

This reminded Bebe that she had to make love with Daniel
soon. She was afraid she could be pregnant—at thirty-nine,
she wasn't really too old, either, nowhere near menopause,
uterus intact, facts that had uplifted her—yet she and her
husband had not made love for more than a month. It was
funny how appalling truths of marriage no longer shocked her.
Moreover, another month could pass; it had happened before.
She'd forgotten in some basic way what sex was all about
before she met Pete. But until she made up her mind to leave
Daniel—which was not, she insisted to herself, inevitable—
she needed to cover her tracks.

Her nephew Leroy's girlfriend entered the house without
knocking. "Hey y'all," she said. She was a large flat girl,
hunched like a top-heavy paper doll, and she kept ducking her
head at everyone. She dropped onto Leroy's lap. They began
kissing, mouths open and working furiously.

"Pardon us," Boyer said, speaking for the group. "We
aren't cramping your style or anything?"

Leroy came up grinning sheepishly. His hands rested famil-
iarly on the girl's thigh and just under her breast. She was
Nicole's age, which made Bebe feel bad for her daughter, who
had not yet found love. Bebe recalled her own youth with more
clarity than she had in a long time, the song lyrics and poems
and leafless trees that encompassed a dramatic and suffocating
angst which she alone suffered. It made her both sympathetic
and impatient to know she could not spare Nicole the same
tedious phase.

Her husband emerged from the kitchen, snorting with laughter. Returning to Cairo brought out the worst in Daniel, in Bebe's opinion. The place encouraged laziness. He began dropping the ends of his words and leaving his shirttails untucked. His sisters waited on him as they must have when he was a child, treating him like the prodigal princely son, fearful of his displeasure. Since they'd arrived, he and Duke had been engaged in an ongoing argument about the past election, Daniel stating inanities and Duke refuting them. When Daniel first brought Bebe here, eighteen years ago, he'd worried endlessly and endearingly about how she would take it. He didn't want to lose her, back then. Now he seemed to think she enjoyed these trips the way he did, a visit to the rustic past, though Bebe had always known his family did not like her. They took to the children, but continued to consider her an outsider. A good vessel, Bebe thought wryly, looking at Boyer and Nicole, but basically useless beyond that and lacking a sense of humor, to boot.

"Fuck 'em," Pete had said, dismissing the whole lot. He swore easily and frequently. Bebe had started to pick it up. She liked the glib edginess of his language. One night she'd used *fucking* as an adjective, as in, "Get your fucking feet off the table," and frightened poor Nicole. What must the girl think of her these days?

The first time she and Pete made love (*fucked*, he would insist) was not a plan. She was not wearing her diaphragm. When the question came up, he asked her if she'd ever heard of the withdrawal method. Bebe had to laugh.

"Why, yes, I believe I have."

He nodded thoughtfully. "Usually it works. Unless I'm nervous, which I am, or unless I'm really attracted to somebody, which I also am. It might not work." Without his glasses he looked even younger than his young twenty-eight. She was his supervisor; she oversaw his evaluations of clients. This could be the most foolish thing she'd ever done, and that included a number of very foolish things.

"We can take that chance," Bebe told him. She would have taken any chance. He could not, or would not, withdraw, as it turned out, and for two weeks afterward Bebe relived her college days, fretting and praying and bargaining until her period came. Since then, they'd made love a few other times without using contraception. Spontaneity and danger, things Bebe had quit associating with sex, heightened her enjoyment of it. Making love with Pete, Bebe felt initiated into a new club. She began to call it *fucking*, too, because it seemed the activity needed a different word than the ones she'd learned to call it with Daniel.

This year she had made Daniel agree to go home earlier than they usually did so that she could see Pete on Sunday.

Her husband stood over her now and said, "Do they still make floats out of flowers?"

"Where you been, Grandpa?" Boyer said to his father. "Get a grip."

"Why, I oughtta . . ." Daniel wound his arm up Jackie Gleason style. He got this from syndicated reruns. Bebe cringed. She didn't even meet her husband's eyes very often anymore. She loved him but she was not in love with him. Her love came from being related to him, from habit, from knowing him so well she could predict him, the way Nicole probably loved Boyer.

"What's the score?" Cammy Sue asked.

"Twenty-seven, six, Oklahoma," Daniel reported. "Why don't you join us?"

"Daddy gets pissed because I didn't vote," she said. "Maybe by the Superbowl he'll forget."

"Don't hold your breath. The Duke doesn't forget. You need anything?" he asked Bebe absently.

"Nada," she said. Bullwinkle bobbed by on screen. Leroy and his date made out as if no one else existed, the boy's hands desperately roving her torso. Bebe's heart leaped involuntarily as she felt Pete's hands.

Little Louise turned her attention from the parade to look up at Daniel. "What does P-E-T-E spell?" she asked him.

"Pete," he said. Bebe watched and enjoyed his mouth making the word. Then watched as he bent his smiling face over her and kissed the top of her head, happy as a clam. Bebe frowned, remembering then that in the pete and repeat joke there was no spelling of the name.

Cammy Sue said, "So how do you like that boyfriend of Nicole's, Aunt Bebe? Uncle Dan?" She cocked her head, swinging her crossed leg, confrontational.

Daniel said, "What boyfriend?" but Bebe turned to Nicole, whose face had gone red and who now visibly swallowed. Was there a boyfriend? Was Nicole withholding something, or had she lied to Cammy Sue, or was Cammy Sue inventing it all? There was, Bebe knew, some element of truth in any lie. She had never hated anyone as thoroughly as she did her niece at that moment. It scared her how homicidal the girl made her.

Boyer said, "Give me a break, the Nick-head with a boy?"

"Nicole knows how we feel," Bebe told Cammy Sue. "It isn't really anyone else's business, is it?"

Cammy Sue held her hands up, surrender style, saying, "Oh, excuse me. Excuse me for asking."

"Boyfriend?" Boyer said. "You mean, like a male of the masculine persuasion? Get real."

"Have we met this young man?" Daniel asked Nicole diplomatically. He was so completely insensitive, Bebe wanted to smack him. She had expected some signal of gratitude from Nicole on her own performance, but the girl simply stared at her mother without any emotion, least of all generosity. Her blush had faded and her thoughts seemed to be elsewhere, as if the conversation did not involve her. Bebe wished she knew what the truth was; Nicole was so unforthcoming these days that any glimmer seemed a fragile clue and should not be squandered. However, she was hurt to think that Nicole would choose Cammy Sue as the recipient of this revelation.

"Me and Dina are going for a drive," Leroy announced. He seemed to have missed the entire scene that had just unfolded before him. He stood up and punched his shirt into his tight jeans, lifting Dina behind him. She ran her long-nailed fingers along her lips, wiping away smeared lipstick. Girlish gestures mixed with womanly ones, so that her age was a fluctuating guess.

"Tell Mama and Velvet we'll be back in time for supper,"

Leroy said. "You hear that?" he yelled toward the kitchen door. Velvet and Dizzy had been cooking since they'd gotten up.

"I hear you, son," came Dizzy's high, kind, voice. The clatter of pans and spoons subsided. "Have a good time."

Leroy winked meaningfully at Boyer.

"Bye now," Dina said, smiling innocently at the miserable room.

From the back of the house, beyond the kitchen, Duke could be heard whooping at the football game. Daniel rose instinctively, then started to sit again, then turned to Bebe as if to get permission to leave.

"Go," she told him impatiently. Her family seemed to her an abandonable group at this moment, obsequious and ungrateful and loutish.

"Come watch the game with your dad and me, Cammy Sue," he begged her.

"You go ahead, Uncle Dan," she said, looking at Bebe. "I'm gonna talk to Aunt Bebe some more."

"Boyer?"

"No thanks, Dad. No male bonding today, thanks. I'm gonna stay for the girl fight."

"Get out of here," Bebe told her son. "Go with your father, right now."

Daniel nodded seriously at Boyer, as if encouraging him to humor Bebe.

"Rah, rah," Boyer said. They left.

"You all up in Chicago must think ho-hum about something like mixed marriages, huh?" Cammy Sue said. "Down here we think it's kinda odd." At this, Nicole calmly got off the piano bench and started for the front door. Bebe reached for her, but Nicole shook her off.

Bebe turned to Cammy Sue and mouthed words she hoped her niece would take to heart. "You. Fucking. Bitch."

Cammy Sue only laughed. "I know you are, Aunt Bebe."

Nicole shut the foyer door gently. From the kitchen came a great din of distracting noise, something dropped.

"P-E-T-E," sang Louise, patting Bebe's shaking hands.

Cookie took up the song whose only refrain was the spelling of Bebe's lover's name.

III

AFTER DINNER, Cammy Sue led Daniel on a tour of homes for sale in Cairo. There were places he'd walked by as a child, growing up, and wondered about. Now he could see the insides. His niece Cammy Sue had a lock-box key.

The prices were unthinkably low. Daniel stood at a sloping dormer window of a grand Victorian home looking over the neat rows of a beautifully maintained rose garden. "Sixty-five, asking," Cammy Sue informed him. "Including lawn furniture and window treatments. Adjustable rate's at nine and a quarter, three-point lifetime cap, too."

Daniel smiled at her expertise. "Know what this house would cost in Chicago?" he asked.

"What?"

"Half million, easy."

"What do you live in, Uncle Dan, a trailer?"

"We bought early."

"Sounds like time to sell, to me." Cammy Sue raised her arched eyebrows at him and Daniel wondered if she was talking about something else. Her expression hinted at hidden agendas. She was the first grandchild, the beginning of a new generation, and had been spoiled mercilessly as a baby. She still held a special place in Daniel's heart; he remembered with great tenderness the excitement he'd felt when his sister Dizzy phoned to tell him she was pregnant. His own children's births had not been as amazing to him as Cammy Sue's. It had thrown him entirely that he and his sisters could be so grown-up that they would have children of their own, that he could be somebody's uncle.

"If I lived here," Cammy Sue was saying, "I'd knock out that dining room wall and build a bar. Place needs track lighting and a deck."

"Oh, I like it just like this," Daniel objected. He walked

through the cold empty rooms imagining a study for himself, a music room for Nicole's violin practice, a basement corner for Boyer's t'ai-chi. Bebe could have a study, too, a room for herself alone. Daniel believed if they could have a larger home she might not ever have to go on vacation by herself again. He understood her need for being alone; she'd explained it very well.

Daniel said, "I could garden."

"Yeah?"

"I might be good at it. I might have a green thumb."

Cammy Sue took his hands in hers and inspected. "I don't see it, Uncle Dan, sorry. Stick to rubbing backs. You want to tour more houses?"

Daniel sat in a window seat on the stair landing. His view was of the highway strip; beyond that, the low Ohio River. He felt more at home in this stranger's house than he ever had in Chicago, in the town house he'd owned for fifteen years. Did other people suffer the kind of inescapable landscape that had imprinted itself behind his eyelids? When he left Cairo he'd intended never to return; coming back would have meant defeat. His birth had been an answer to his parents' and sisters' prayers, coming so late in all of their lives that he seemed a miracle, everyone's child. They expected great things, and those things could not happen in Cairo.

He tried now to invent a realistic scenario; how could he come back? What could he do for a living? Cairo could not support a chiropractor, he was fairly certain. Yet this home tempted him in a way other possible changes in his life did not. If he moved here, he thought, his hometown would not decline. His marriage would not die.

"I should have them turn on the heat in this mausoleum," Cammy Sue said. "They're gonna freeze pipes if they don't take care. Seriously, Uncle Dan, it's my duty as a relative to tell you the basement floods. You don't want this. I can show you a split level out in the hills only a few years old. Couple's divorcing and they want to sell real bad. That's how I got my place so fast—people had a crisis and didn't care what kind of money they made, just wanted out right now. The buyer can take advantage of inside information like that." Again, Cammy Sue seemed to be saying something else, but Daniel had no way of interpreting. He tried to take her at face value, but there was no denying her sly glances at him, teasing him with all she wasn't saying outright.

"You want to visit the house?" he asked his wife when he and Cammy Sue got back to Dizzy's.

"I bet she likes her town house just fine, don't you Aunt Bebe?" Cammy Sue smiled.

Bebe ignored her. "Oh, I don't think so," she told Daniel. "Touring houses depresses me. Besides, Duke's been demanding your presence."

Daniel looked down at his beautiful wife and felt jostled, unsteady. Who was she? Daniel had only lately begun to take seriously the unspoken busy hum that went on just below the surface of any conversation or relationship. Cammy Sue's oblique insinuations were an example. These were the subterranean regions, the underground rivers that continued to move, whatever may have seemed stable and inert above. To hide his panic, his frustrating sense of dislocation, he left the room, went once more to the worn place on the couch by Duke's chair. He took comfort in his brother-in-law's age and afflictions and stasis.

"Nobody wants to visit but you," Duke observed. "Your wife's avoiding me."

Daniel did not have the energy to deny it. Though Duke seemed to enjoy being a plague to most family members, it obviously bothered him that Bebe felt the same. He'd always considered her special, something Daniel had taken great pride in. Her opinion, because it was generally so critical, impressed Duke as discerning. Daniel wished he could still claim to have Bebe's fickle, busy heart.

"She don't want to see a dying man, I suppose," Duke said, shifting his pajama-clad body in his chair. He flipped through the channels with his remote control, looking for sports and game shows. They were all that interested him. It struck Daniel that his own pride in Bebe had an element of conquest in it that made him ashamed. He'd left the small town, left the small-town girls.

Lived in a big city with a big-city woman. His love for her, in this light, seemed to be a case of hopeless overreaching.

In bed that night Daniel recounted the floor plan of the Victorian house for Bebe, describing the space and grandeur desperately.

"I have this impulse to just go ahead and buy it," he said in a whisper, wanting to inspire collusion: They would do this impulsive, crazy thing together. He would pull her to the surface of their marriage and set her to work on a new home.

"This bed is absolutely awful," Bebe said. She kept throwing herself around, pushing Daniel's legs and arms off her. "How can Velvet stand it? I feel like I'm on a hill, sliding toward a pit."

"So slide," Daniel said. "I'll catch you."

"Ha." She turned over to face him. "You want to fool around?"

"Maybe." He reached for her breasts, giving up the house in a second. They had not made love for weeks. He'd grown embarrassed, all his attempts to seduce her failures. She took hold of his penis and rolled it perfunctorily between her hands. "Careful," he said, flinching.

"Aren't you hard yet?"

He laughed, though her tone had been only half joking.

She flopped on her back. "Shit."

"What?"

"I need to pee."

"Someone's in there."

"I know." The bathroom had been occupied for over an hour. Every time the creaky door opened and Bebe started out of bed, someone else beat her to it. Hushed voices exchanged good nights in the small hallway. Bebe said, "I can't make love with a full bladder." Daniel hugged her, enjoying the flat-spoken, frank intimacy of Bebe, assured somehow that she'd just proved she still loved him.

Daniel drifted while they waited. He came in and out of a dream, rubbing Bebe's back, manipulating her spinal column, thinking how beautiful her skin was and how well she'd weathered their eighteen years together, reassured that her actions revealed the truth and that undercurrent he'd felt so strongly all day was largely the figment of a former, weaker man's imagination. . . . Suddenly he was wide awake. Amplified breathing, frighteningly harsh and regular, filled the room.

"Daniel!" Bebe whispered, scratching at his face. "Is that you?"

"No," he said, touched that she should worry so.

"Then who? What?" They listened, their own breathing synchronized.

"Don't know."

"It sounds terrible." The breathing went steadily on, like death, and Daniel realized it was Duke, emerged from the back room, sitting in his wheelchair waiting for the ever-occupied bathroom to clear, right outside their bedroom door.

Bebe, having reached the same conclusion, said, "It's just Duke."

"He sounds like he's dying."

"He *is* dying."

Their illicit laughter they muffled under the covers. After laughing they began kissing, long and passionately, almost frantically. They had not kissed like this in a very sad, long time. Bebe used to love kissing. Daniel could remember kissing her for hours, though by the time they'd been married a few years, she had lost most of her interest in it. Still, there were occasions when she responded to Daniel's tongue in her mouth, and Daniel felt a tug at a pure and primal longing that he believed was the bedrock of their love for each other.

They made love under the covers, full bladder and all. Bebe curled into a ball, wrapping herself around Daniel as he drew himself in close. Her knees were at her ears, her arms enclosing his shoulders. Daniel imagined the shape of an egg. There didn't seem to be any spare or cumbersome parts to them tonight, no awkward retrievals of deadening limbs. Instead, everything fit. This is the design, Daniel thought, imagining their skeletal structures forming a complementary whole, this is where the universe distills.

Into his ear Bebe said, "No diaphragm."

Daniel said nothing, responded by pushing farther inside

her. The thought of a baby filled his mind. He'd been a late-life baby himself. He saw them with a new child in the Cairo house, a fine picture. He understood that they would go ahead without protection, that that was what Bebe wanted.

But in his wife's movements he also understood that she had been with someone else. Her breathing was impatient, the rhythm of her pelvis a half-pace ahead of his own. While he continued to move, some deep part of him took stock, acknowledged unequivocally the existence of an uncertain lethal other world, and counted Bebe's certain betrayal as an element of its environment. He should have been angry but his anger, at this moment, was channeled differently, into a cold passion for her. It was passion of a tough nature and he moved violently against her, wanting to hurt her, his breathing raspy and loud as Duke's. She paused, perhaps understanding what he was doing and why. Daniel believed they were communicating—this was, after all, the way this other world worked, wasn't it? Saying anything, he knew, would be wrong, would be spelling out that which unquestionably should not be spelled out and so he said nothing, hoping that Bebe would follow suit, hoping that she had pursued the same marshy tributaries he had taken to arrive here. Hoping, in a way that approximated the prayer of someone faithful, that she knew what they were doing.

I V

B O Y E R' S sister, Nicole, drove home. Their father was always trying to get her to drive, but today she suggested it herself. Boyer knew when his turn came to learn to drive, his father would find some reason not to let him. His father was always letting Nicole do things. Boyer studied the way she steered, thinking about his own hands on the wheel. His sister was a lousy driver, even though she took Driver's Ed. She didn't like to pass cars and, as a result, their car frequently got lodged behind slow-moving vehicles for miles on end. Boyer wanted to scream. Eventually their father would clear his throat and suggest, as if to a retard, that she might make a go of passing.

Boyer lay down on the expansive backseat. Nicole's new suitcase was on the floor by his head. While considering opening it, he remembered spying on his father the night before. Leroy's bedroom, where Boyer had slept, shared a wall with the kitchen, and its heat vent led right into the other room. Standing on his bed, Boyer could see through the slats into the kitchen. There, in the middle of the night, after everyone had been in bed for hours, sat his father and Dizzy, talking over coffee. They discussed Dizzy's husband, Duke. Dizzy cried. She said she got really scared. Boyer could imagine; the old guy gave him the creeps. A couple of years ago he'd flipped the oxygen tank switch off, just to see what would happen. Duke just yelled for Dizzy and she turned him back on. Big deal. Dizzy told Boyer's father she wished she'd married somebody else. She told him there was a fellow down the street whose wife was blind and she wished she'd married him, instead. "It's terrible, but I think those two invalids deserve each other. Isn't that terrible?"

Boyer thought it sounded all right to him. Illness and inadequacy disgusted him. He couldn't help thinking that people could overcome these kinds of things by willpower. His dad put his arm around Dizzy, who wept into his shoulder. When they separated, his father pointed at his chest and said, "It makes you hurt here, doesn't it? Bebe is . . . I hurt here all the time. Nothing is right anymore."

Boyer wanted to know what his father was going to say about his mother, but Dizzy seemed to know already, nodding her head and weeping, so his father didn't have to go on. Boyer wished Leroy were awake but didn't want to get him in case he'd miss something. Here were their parents, getting personal. Boyer needed a witness. Then his father began crying. At first, Boyer couldn't believe it; he was glad he hadn't wakened Leroy to see this. He watched his father convulse, as if he might be choking or have to throw up, and then just sob, his face hideously contorted. This made Dizzy cry even harder.

Boyer felt tears in his own eyes, the way watching someone else vomit made him gag.

Now, driving back to Chicago, Boyer wondered if his father broke down often, though his manner last night had seemed fairly amateurish. He apologized a hundred times to Dizzy, but couldn't stop once he'd gotten started, as if it'd been building up for a while. He said, "She's gone." But of course she hadn't gone until this morning.

Boyer opened Nicole's suitcase a crack. Makeup, bottles, brush and comb, tampons. He ran his finger along the crinkly paper of one, thinking of when he'd picked the lock on the bathroom door at home and seen Nicole in the shower. She stood dripping wet trying to cover herself, screaming at him. There hadn't been enough time to take everything in. After carefully closing the suitcase lid, Boyer rolled over and faced the seat back, hands between his legs for warmth.

That morning a skinny man with a runny nose showed up at Aunt Dizzy's front door asking for Boyer's mother. Aunt Velvet showed him through the house to the kitchen, where she left him with Leroy and Boyer, who were eating country ham.

"Howdy," Leroy said to him. "Get you some coffee?"

"Pass." His cheeks and nose were hilariously red and he reminded Boyer of some loser biology teacher. Because he'd ridden a motorcycle, his hair looked like a black fright wig. The three of them could hear Velvet explaining through Boyer's parents' closed bedroom door that there was a man visitor for Bebe. Velvet returned to the kitchen wearing a scowl. She really hated surprises.

"You all done stuffing yourselves?" she'd asked the boys angrily, gnarled hand already stealing the plate of ham away. When they nodded, she took it outside to feed to Dog.

Boyer felt the urge to make jokes during what followed.

"It's now or never," the skinny guy said to his mother when she came out in Velvet's bathrobe. Everyone seemed to be standing except Boyer at this point, though no one moved. Where was his father? The bedroom door was closed. A chival-

rous fight was not going to take place. Instead, everyone hung
on the guy's dumb words, waiting for Bebe to say hers.

"Now."

One word and the slow-motion fog that had filled the room
disappeared. The guy went outside to wait and Boyer's mother
got dressed. Boyer sat next to Nicole on the couch.

"What is happening?" he asked.

"Don't be stupid," she said venomously.

When Velvet finally came in, after Boyer's mother had
strapped her mustard yellow suitcase on the back of his bike
and ridden off with the skinny guy, she said, "I never." This
phrase made Boyer giggle, as he took all of Velvet's statements
as further proof of her legendary virginity, and somehow infected Nicole, who also laughed.

After that, Aunt Dizzy probably thought they were insensitive city-slick children and made Leroy take both of them to
the fort at the river. You always thought Dizzy got pushed
around, but Boyer could tell she was the real boss in the house.
When she gave orders the family jumped. The fact that their
father had not yet opened the bedroom door made Boyer perfectly willing to get out. Nicole agreed to go, though once they
stopped at the fort, she didn't want to leave the truck. Boyer
couldn't have cared less. Nicole was always in these tempera-
mental moods, laughing one minute, pissed off the next. She
used to be fun, but now she was a drag. Leroy, however,
thought it crucial she come with them.

"I already saw Fort Despair," she told him.

"Defiance."

"Whatever. Go ahead without me. I'll listen to the radio."

"It's busted."

"Then I'll just sit and watch the boats."

"Barges. You can see them better from the fort. . . ."

"Why do you need me to come?" she said to Leroy. "Go
without me. Take a hint, will you?"

"Your sister don't like me anymore," Leroy told Boyer
when they'd reached the top of the fort.

"So?" Boyer said. "She never liked you."

"I always thought she liked me."

"Nope."

"I thought she did."

"Sorry."

"Well, to hell with her, then."

"Fuckin' A," Boyer agreed. He was thinking that if he lived in Cairo he would be the smartest kid there. He'd probably skip grades. Girls would want him. When he got a car, he'd take girls in it to the bottoms.

But now they were going home without his mother. Inside Boyer a fight raged: the side that wanted things to stay the same and the side that loved an event. This was something to talk about Monday at school. "Oh yeah," he could say. "My mom took off this weekend." Very nonchalant. He'd shrug. He did it now in the car, practicing. Then the idea would streak through his head that she might never come back and he would be afraid. The war went on but he digressed, instead, and thought of his mother on her hands and knees with that guy behind her, sticking it in her, over and over. Of course that had something to do with her leaving, everybody but Velvet probably knew that. Her ass moving to meet him.

"Dad. Dad. Dad." His father turned. "Time for R and R, what do you say, Dad?"

"Nicole's driving. Ask her."

"I'm not stopping," she said.

Their father looked at her, perplexed, but didn't correct her.

"Come on, Dad, make her stop. I gotta pee. I had Cokes for breakfast. That stuff goes through you like battery acid."

"Nicole," their father began, his voice conciliatory, and Boyer knew he'd get his way. Now his mother was on a beach, in the sand on her knees. Nicole swerved into a rest-stop driveway without slowing, slamming the brakes and jolting them into Park.

"So fucking pee," she said through her teeth at Boyer.

He could barely manage to make it to the john. Nicole saying *fucking*, right in front of their dad! Boyer pulled a stall door shut and took out his cock, held it lovingly in both hands. He wished it were bigger or his hands smaller; he wanted to overwhelm his grip. He wanted to put it in a woman, a girl, a hot, moist place. He thought again of a woman on her hands and knees, on the tropical sandy beach. The woman was no longer his mother, and the man, on his knees behind her, no longer the skinny guy who'd picked her up this morning. The man, vaguely Boyer himself, was reaching around for her breasts, which she arched into his hands, breasts that belonged now to a younger woman, like Nicole, a woman he did not yet know, who pressed against him, and into whom he slid, then out, in and out, in and out, needing to cry her name, her name or simply a noise, a red noise, coming, coming, coming.

Afterward, cleaning up, he noticed there was no roof on the washroom. Snowflakes fell, had been falling all along, he supposed. They were getting near Chicago and the rain had turned to snow. Flakes fell on his blue Cubs jacket. He looked closely at the geometric pieces of snow that lay unmelted on his sleeve. Despite what he'd always heard, to him they all looked exactly the same.